The Time We All Went Marching

Other Books by Arley McNeney

Post (2007)

The Time We All Went Marching

Arley McNeney

Edited by Bethany Gibson.
Cover photograph by Dan Morgan.
Cover and page design by Jaye Haworth.
Printed in Canada.
10 9 8 7 6 5 4 3 2 1

Library and Archives Canada Cataloguing in Publication

McNeney, Arley, 1982-
The time we all went marching / Arley McNeney.

Issued also in electronic format.
ISBN 978-0-86492-658-6

I. Title.

PS8625.N54T56 2011   C813'.6   C2011-902906-5

Goose Lane Editions acknowledges the financial support of the Canada Council for the Arts, the government of Canada through the Canada Book Fund (CBF), and the government of New Brunswick through the Department of Wellness, Culture and Sport.

Goose Lane Editions
Suite 330, 500 Beaverbrook Court
Fredericton, New Brunswick
CANADA E3B 5X4
www.gooselane.com

This book is dedicated to
Elsie McNeney (1910–2010) and my parents.

EDIE

Nights, Slim would take her from the blindness of snow to the blindness of tunnels. Newly married and pent up in Zincton, she couldn't sleep without him. And he liked her company: the easy shadow she made perched on a ledge, listening as he translated the rock's cursive. His job was to read the long horizons of ore and determine where to timber the next path. Like a dowser, he followed seams black and snaking as rivers.

As he worked, he told her stories: his voice the one steady thing in the half-dark, in the sudden shocks of light when his headlamp veered toward her. The On to Ottawa Trek, mostly. The story of the dandelion wine in the work camps. Hobo jungles. How Arthur "Slim" Evans—a different Slim, the one jailed twice and shot in the leg at Ludlow—stood up to Prime Minister Bennett and said, "You ain't fit to be prime minister of a Hottentot village." Trains and marching: men pushing forward through towns Edie had never visited. "Saw a rally where there were so many people all crowded together they didn't even look like people anymore," he would say. "Saw weird little birds that sounded like babies crying and would eat anything from your hand. Saw a man who lost his leg under a train and he had a wooden one with all the names of the women he had been with carved into it."

Sometimes he stole her a headlamp and she would listen beneath the battery's hum, but mostly she had to stay within the range of Slim's own glow, straining her eyes through the Morse code of light and darkness. They drank whiskey from a Thermos for the heat and ate icebox cookies and sandwiches she packed in a lard pail. They sang call-and-response songs. Sometimes he was the call and she the response; sometimes they sang together and the mine threw their voices back at them.

Married only a few months, everything he said was funny—"Hilarious," she was fond of saying. "Oh darling, you're *hilarious!*"—and the mine was exciting both because it belonged to Slim's life and because she was dangerous down there. Illegal. No miner would have set foot in the elevator had he known a woman had been there before. By her very presence, Edie could inspire thousands of men to riot.

It didn't stop her, though; she loved it. She tossed food scraps into the corners to appease the Tommyknockers and murmured the Lord's Prayer as the elevator lurched her stomach. She loved hiding her shape in the baggy jumpsuit, slicking back her hair, loved the headlamp warm and heavy as an animal against her temples. She looked as if she inhabited a completely different body. When Slim needed to concentrate, she would prowl the tunnels with her headlamp stretching her shadow huge along the walls. She would press her body into the narrowest spaces to see where she would fit.

"Some men go crazy thinking about all the tons of earth that could come down on them," Slim would say. "Sometimes I think about that and it makes me crazy as a shithouse rat."

"That's because you're too tall," said Edie, thinking of how easy it was to wedge herself into crevices: her belly against the cool stone, breasts flattened and throbbing, the texture of the rocks outlined in moisture on her jumpsuit. "You're always reminded. I'm not bothered." Half drunk. Warm in the stomach, though her toes felt petrified.

She loved the mine with its lake odour, its shafts and caverns
crooked as a fuse, the rooms filled with immense cauldrons that still
reeked of fire: a scum of rock crusted on the rims. On days when
she was without a headlamp she would try to get lost and wander
blindly through the tunnels, guided only by her fingertips along the
chiselled grooves the miners left, loving the terror she could create
within herself when something dripped down the back of her neck
or when she tripped over a rock. Echoes made her voice big and
many-tongued.

"Tell me something," he would say when his voice went hoarse. "I
hate the quiet here. Tell me something."

"I once loved a prisoner and he gave me a piece of a spine as a sign
of affection." She was young enough to imagine that bold statements
gave her an air of mystery.

"Hah. That isn't true."

"I have it at home. You've seen it. You probably didn't know what
it was. One time the old cemetery flooded and all the bones floated
up." She wiggled her fingers to mime floating and the light from the
headlamp washed them out so they did look like bones. "You couldn't
imagine the stench, unbelievable, so they made the prisoners up at
the Pen load the skeletons into sacks and haul them to the cemetery
behind our house. This one fellow took a shine to me. Gave me a
bone as a gift and I didn't even know his name. I still have it. You've
seen it."

She did. She still does. A bone worn thin by water, its centre
honeycombed so it looked as if it once housed a colony of small
animals.

"You never knew his name and you loved him?"

"I was fifteen."

"Little tart. Hah. I don't believe you." He was too tall for the
mine: hunched at odd angles, his birdlike shadow huge on the walls.

His jumpsuit was too short and Edie could see a band of skin above his boots reddened with cold.

"Fine. Don't believe me. It's true. Why do you think my mother shackled me with Anne shortly after?"

Slim laughed. The noise turned choir with the echoes. "Oh, you didn't mind that kid. Don't be dramatic. You weren't *shackled*. Weren't anything more than what millions of big sisters are. Did you love him like you love me?"

"What do you think? I was fifteen. I only saw him a few times."

"So you admit it, then. Like I said. You couldn't have loved him because you were fifteen and didn't even know his name. Hah! My point exactly."

"I said I couldn't have loved him *more* than you. This isn't the Young Trotskyite Debating Society."

He chuckled, the headlamp's light shaking with his movement. "Trotsky*ist*. Marxist, Leninist, Trotsky*ist*. Damn. I've lost count here. Tell me something else." She could hear his pencil grinding against his notebook. "Better put that bone back where it came from, love. Bad luck. You're already below ground; only difference between you and that skeleton is you're not dead."

At dawn, they would walk home in silence, shielding their eyes from the snow's glare. In the moon-brightened living room, Slim would undress them both, his eyes watering as they adjusted. They would say nothing, hang their work gear on the hooks with the greatest care — if your clothes fell to the ground, you were destined to fall as well — and go to bed, safe above ground.

═|═|═|═|═

And now, nearly ten years later, the underground feeling is the same: the darkness of the tunnels, the odd strobes of light as the train emerges before plunging in again. Her son's face lighter then darker, shadowed then blotted out with light. Five years and three clapboard towns since she was allowed in a mine, four years since Belly's birth. They moved, then moved again. Slim went to his graveyard shift below ground and she stayed with her new graveyard shift above ground, walking in circles as she patted out the rhythm of love songs on the back of a sobbing baby.

Zincton, then Britannia, then Sandon, then Ymir. Two years in a tent in Ymir—minus a few months at Norah and Red's house during the coldest part of winter—six months in an apartment and now she is leaving. For two years she'd wanted out of that tent and now that she has a proper home, she's on a train headed away.

They emerge on the other side of the mountain and the landscape rolls by chilled and pale, horses the only darkness. Nothing about the view will calm her: not the white blurs of snow, not the grey sky, not the frost that spiderwebs the windows, making them appear cracked. All their belongings are piled on the bench beside them, and Belly often dozes against the carpetbag she's stuffed with his clothing. While he chatters or conducts military raids with his toy soldiers up the aisle of the train, Edie looks out the window at her reflection projected onto the frigid ponds and lone houses and trees limbs snapped under the weight of snow. Nothing she hasn't seen before. Again and again. Ten winters with Slim, four towns penned in by mountains.

Beside her, Belly names the horses he sees out the window. "Black one," he says. "There's another black one. Pal–o–mee–no. Uh huh. For sure. Chestnut. A chest and a nut. A chestnut mare." He is cheerful because he loves trains—their mechanics and brute force—and because she told him there might be neighbourhood boys in New Westminster with toy fire trucks and soldiers. He reads the Hudson's

Bay Company Christmas Toy catalogue well into August as if it was a fairy tale—rubbing the pages between his fingers, smearing inky fingerprints on all her linens—and knows that some goods don't come to the places he's from. Edie has promised him a tank. Her son will not stop talking: palominos, piebalds, Paints, the wrong names for half-dead farm horses anyhow.

She is gone from a man who for ten years was as straight and hard in her life as a spine. Now the track curving endlessly behind her is the only backbone, now she is filleted, now the snow falls down or it falls up or it falls horizontally or it hangs suspended in a haze. They are descending from a mountain whose guts were ripped open, its ore taken and taken. They are leaving the same way the coal does: by train, through mine-ruined mountains, past towns named after what men strip from them: Zincton, Silverton, Argenta, Silver Creek. Sometimes she turns to ask Slim a question—the time, how long until we get there, should we eat lunch—but he's gone and she remembers that she's left him passed out on the bed with the windows open on the coldest night of the year, snow in his hair, the mirrors blurry with ice. The idea of this is a strange fizz in her stomach.

The train's windows begin to bead with condensation and Belly rubs the moisture away, the horses appearing in the smeared arc his hand has left. The woman on the seat facing Edie's unbuttons her coat and helps her small daughter do the same. Belly's cheeks are red and Edie, too, feels slick between her breasts and shoulder blades. She has a few dozen sweat-dampened dollars pinned to her brassiere and a piece of spine in her pocket. Did he blame her? Because of the mining accident? Because she was bad luck? Stolen vertebrae were not the only things that could be cursed. But he was the one who ended up stuck down there, even as the war marched all the other men away overseas. Too knowledgeable to let go, too ruined in the lungs.

Still, Belly chatters away, nonsensical. "That one over there is a dog, and a dog is not a horse, but some dogs are big as horses and you can ride them and you can go anywhere." His singsong voice couples with the train's rocking and adds to her headache, but at least he is speaking English.

Slim would be at home on this train, Edie knows. He is a man at ease with them the way some people have a touch with horses. He speaks of trains as a thing to be broken in, that if you can tune yourself to the right rhythm and possess a musician's sense of timing you can mount one even at top speed. But then again, Slim could barely walk in a straight line on dry, flat land the last she saw him. Still, Edie suspects that just being here, on this train, might restore his dexterity.

Belly kneels on the seat with the side of his face against the headrest, absently stroking the fabric as if it were the hide of an animal. "And a white one. Another white one. I think that's the baby horse. A mom and a dad and a baby and — oh — a brown one that's got spots, so I think if he was my horse I would call him Spot, even though usually that's for dogs, right? Like Mr. Nielsen's dog. Can a horse be called Spot? And that one's called a Paint, but they don't really paint them; it's just a name; there's no paint at all."

"Hey," says Edie. "Do you want me to tell you a story? How about you lie down and close your eyes?"

Belly stops, eyeing her suspiciously. "About what?"

"About anything. I don't know. Did I tell you the story about the crows?" Sweat darkens the temples of Belly's red hair — Slim's hair, which looks wrong against the brown eyes he inherited from her — so Edie unbuttons his coat. Underneath his thin shirt, she can see his little ribs jutting out. Her son: skinny as Slim, the same devil's hair.

"What about the one about Mister Red Walsh and his cat named Trinket and how Trinket rode on the trains and stole the apple pie and lived in Mr. Red Walsh's shirt and that was a long time ago?"

"Belly, these people don't want to hear you chattering. You've got to hush." If she gave him a few drops of rum he would doze right off and she could have a moment to think for herself. She has done the wrong thing. There was no good reason to leave. No better reason to take Belly. She should go back; her mother won't take them in; she doesn't have enough money for the train ticket back; they'll be stuck homeless in the city; her mother might say, "You made your bed and you lie in it," shut the door and lock it; they'll end up in a bad way. All the plush seats and the people in them are pressed close together, spicing the car with the odours of hair cream, snacks in lard pails, cigarettes.

"Another horse!" Belly exclaims, but the woman and her daughter sitting across from them are caught in their own conversation and don't appear to notice. "A white one!"

"Belly."

"If I talk quietly like I'm just moving my mouth but hardly talking at all can I still tell about the horses?" His good dress shirt is damp with sweat and she's lucky he's too young for odour. He possesses only an oceany smell of salt, a hint of soap.

"Quietly," says Edie. "If I can hear you, you're being too loud."

Belly peers out the window and whispers to himself, his voice lilting with the sway of the car. When she gives him a Spam sandwich for supper, he complains about the lack of mustard. He leaves a fur of crumbs on his chest and lap, keeps talking, eats so quickly he gets hiccups, talks between the hiccups. Soon, he lulls himself into a stupor with the cadence of his own stories, or Slim's stories he's made into his own.

The snow turns red and orange as the sun sets. The flurries pick up, sanding away the silhouettes of houses and trees, and then it is dark. Edie smoothes her son's damp temples. He watches her, his mouth still moving, but either she can't hear or she's not listening carefully enough.

Edie reaches beyond him, then presses her palm to the glass hoping for a chill, leaving instead a smudge of her own sweat and oils. The train's movement thrums beneath her fingertips, and she cannot help but picture her husband the way she likes to remember him: the wind reddening his cheeks and fraying the cuffs of his jacket as he rides on top of the boxcar in 1935. The On to Ottawa Trek. The slogans painted with shoe polish on a boy's good sweater. The men snake-dancing from side to side down the road with arms linked so they would resemble a river when viewed from above. The story of the good fight. Of "Hold the Fort, for We Are Coming." She knows this Slim better than the one passed out grey-faced on their bed. The Slim who was there. The Slim who took part. She cannot help trying to reassemble him.

THE STORY OF THE ON TO OTTAWA TREK

The jostled men are singing through a chill no wool can keep away. On top of the boxcar: metal and what cold can turn it into. Who knew summer could be like this? Nightly cold snaps that leave morning frost as a reminder. Soon, there will be bodies of other men organized into three divisions — four abreast marching down the streets of Golden — but for now Slim's on a boxcar roof with maybe twenty others, a handkerchief over his nose and mouth, fingers stiffened around the catwalks. The men are singing that there is "'power in a factory, power in the land, power in the hands of the worker,'" the song a deep hum against the buckle and sway of the boxcar, the words blurred by wind and many voices.

Comrade Hold the Fort backs them up with a mouth harp, and the men on nearby boxcars sing along: all kinds of accents, tenors and baritones, churchy little voices from the fifteen- and sixteen-year-olds.

"'Money speaks for money, but never for its own,'" they are singing. "'Who's going to speak for the skin and the bone?'"

Who's going to speak for his fingers stiffened around metal? Slim thinks. Who's going to speak for the sore from where his hip has rested for the past six hours, rubbed crimson by the rhythm of the train. Another man also named Slim. There are so many lanky boys here that the Trek's leader, Arthur "Slim" Evans—jailed twice, shot in the leg at Ludlow—has become Arthur-Slim. Arthur-Slim will take them to Ottawa to make that bastard R.B. Bennett, Old Iron Heel, give them their due. Matt Shaw says that the fire of the working-class struggle constantly stoked inside him has burned off every ounce of fat. In contrast, Slim MacDonald (maybe they'll start calling him Mack on account of his last name, or Pop or Dad on account of his age; twenty-seven must seem ancient to these teenagers) feels scrawny, all frozen bones.

But this cold. Lord. And he's not some mama's boy warmed by parental love and central heating. He got up early to tend the wood-stove, started work at eleven, left home at fifteen. And, of course, he's been down to the mine: a different kind of freeze. Three years in work camps and you'll know what it is to be cold, what it is to be bored, what it is to go years without the sight of a woman's face. He knows he could use the padding: some meat to fill in the space between his ribs, soften his elbows, hips, even those fingers. Give me steak and eggs, he thinks. Give me apple pie with cheese, bread fried in bacon grease, glossy clots of blackberries so thick they snap the branch.

Even in the dark, Slim can see that Matt Shaw, one of the few Trekkers without a nickname, definitely the only one who gets his name said whole, is looking at him. He's the spokesman, that's why he gets his full name said. They write him up in the papers. Matt Shaw winks, waving one arm as if conducting a band. "'There is power in a union.'"

Oh, Comrade Hold the Fort is going strong now, boy, and the men launch into his signature song: "'Hold the fort, for we are coming! Union men, be strong!'" And damned if Slim doesn't want to sing along. It's too easy to get lost in the mundane details of getting your fingers working again. Best to think of all these voices and where they're headed. On to Ottawa to see that bastard Bennett, stopping in Golden for a bath, a piss, something to eat, on to Calgary, Swift Current, Medicine Hat, Moose Jaw. More than sixteen hundred men on three trains, and men from the relief camps in Alberta and Saskatchewan should be riding down to meet them in Calgary. Thousands of men still in their camp-issue khakis and sweaters so that they look like an army. Our Boys! On to Ottawa! "'Hold the fort, for we are coming!'"

Slim sings along, imagining his voice warming him like whiskey. He sings to Matt Shaw, Flash, Piper, Ace, Paddy, Red, to the sky lightening so he can make out the shapes of trees. He sings through the scent of pine and smoke, wet wool and body odour. In this land of mouth harps, it's too easy to feel like a lone guitar: thin as a string, a body of wood that warps in wind or cold. If not for these men, a fellow could go flat in this land. In the bars and pubs back in Vancouver, those who can afford it are dancing the lindy hop, the mad piano is going like stink, but here there's only the mouth harp, its high slide against the ears, moving as wind does. Just the mouth harp tuned to one key, reminding you what C is so you can find yourself in relation to it.

BELLY

The train is like a horse or like a Spitfire or a Lancaster or a Hurricane or a Hellcat; Belly can't decide. He's not supposed to say hell unless it has the word *cat* on the end of it. He's not supposed to say a lot of things. The train races the horses across the fields and sometimes a palomino or a piebald will stare through the window as it gallops, looking at Belly even as the wind whips its mane against its eyes, wishing him luck. Belly has been awake, then asleep, and now he is awake again, even though it's dark and he can't see the horses but knows they're there, looking back at him.

The train runs so fast for a thing with no feet—on wheels but not like car wheels, wheels that look too small for something so big—but anyways his dad has said that trains are nearly the same as flying, right, and a man who can hop a damn-bloody boxcar—he's not supposed to say damn or bloody and especially not both together—and live to tell about it can fly a fighter plane no problem. Problem is, says his dad, you can't put boxcar riding on your application. It's all about your g.d. bloody lungs and the name of your mom and pop, don't want no commies fighting for His Majesty no matter how high the body count gets.

So Belly gets up to use the lavatory car just so he can spread his arms out wide and sputter to himself up the hall, like he is made of metal, like the rose pattern on the carpet is really towns and bases viewed from far above. When he returns to his seat, his mom is still taking apart the sweater she's been knitting, which Belly thinks would be fun, to pull at the hem of his sleeve and have it fall into a ball of yarn. He would like to pretend that he is a cat playing with string and bat the yarn between his cat paws until it gets tangled. In the seat across from his mother, a lady reads a book and a girl has her head on her mom's lap but her eyes are open and she stares at Belly. She's a blonde girl and her face is spooky white.

When he tries to climb onto his mom's lap, she sets him beside her, telling him to sit like he's big. He doesn't want to. Sometimes he likes pretending he's much younger than he is, seeing if he can curl himself small enough to fit exactly on her lap so that not even his toes fall off. Belly pokes the muzzle of his soldier's gun into his finger. The soldier has a crazy look on his face like he'll stab you or he'll shoot you, he can't decide he's so mean and mad.

"When we get there you're going to have to be quiet," says his mom, even though he wasn't saying anything. "You can't go around — Nana will love you, of course she'll take to you, but she's a strange lady — not a bad lady, but odd, odd in a good way, eccentric — stranger since your grandpa up and left." His mom moves her hands in the place of actual words, and Belly wonders if he's supposed to know what her hands mean because he doesn't and she doesn't stop long enough for him to ask. "She'll tell you that crows take souls to heaven, tell you not to wash your hair when you're sick, wrap a sock around your neck to fight chills, all sorts of old wives' tales, make you throw bread and oatmeal up on the carport so those dirty birds can shit all over the place."

Belly doesn't like it when his mom cusses, same as how he hates it when she calls him William MacDonald Jr. or even William. *Poop* is a better word; he loves to say it. *Poop!* The word like a little bean shooting out. That makes him want to laugh, but his mom looks mean at him so he shuts his mouth.

"When my own grandpa passed, Lord, she thought every bloody crow was a sign." *Bloody* is another word no one should say unless they're talking about real blood; that's what his mom usually says. She rolls the kinked yarn around her hand, tighter and tighter, until her fingertips are white. Her lipstick has been chewed off, so her mouth is nearly the colour of her face; her face is red and her mouth is white and flaky and it's as if the colour of her mouth and the colour of her face have switched places and something is wrong, but he doesn't know quite what. "You'll be good. You'll be quiet. She'll just love you, but she's an odd duck, feeding those crows, taking flowers to the dead little ones in the graveyard. Busy household, but your nana runs a tight ship."

Belly thinks of ducks and ships and how the train is like a ship, rocking back and forth, and when she lets him go he will pretend to be a captain or maybe a pirate. His mom digs her fingers into his shoulder.

"William MacDonald," she says. "Do you want to go back to Ymir and maybe I'll just go and live with Nana on my own and buy myself that nice new tank?"

Belly is less scared by the idea of not getting a tank than he is that she's used his full name, the name she only uses when he won't speak right, keeps jabbering away like a kammer-cazzy-Jap and what would people think if they heard him?

"Sorry," says Belly.

"What did I just say? What was I talking about?"

Belly stares at her. They haven't even gotten to his nana's house and already he has been no good. "About the crows," he says.

His mom stares out the window like she didn't hear, then keeps up with the crows and the manners and the grandpa that ran off. Belly wonders where his grandpa ran to, but his mom's on a roll now all right and there's no stopping her, so he tries hard to listen, not to think of crows or ships or horses or airplanes or how if you had a gun with three muzzles no one could hurt you except maybe from the back, but you could probably have a gun in your back, though you'd have to have a special way to know who you're shooting at. His mom tells terrible stories, not like his dad, who can do all the voices and sings songs.

"So you've got to be polite. No yelling, no running and absolutely no talking that, you know, that language." She makes a fluttery gesture with her hand, as if Belly has been making bird noises. He wants to caw like a bird to see if he can make the sound and bets he could because he's good at making sounds. "One word of that and — Your nana would have a royal fit if she knew I'd let you run wild with little Jap children."

She continues with the list of *nos* and *don't*s until the train itself seems to be chugging *no no don't no no don't*. There are brown stains on the ceiling that look like bears with their mouths open.

When his mom used to teach at the Orchard school, Belly learned a secret language he suspects is the language of all boys everywhere, so that they can talk about things and their moms and dads won't have to know. *Tomodachi* means friend and *uma* means horse and *sensou* means war. He mouths the words to himself as his mom keeps up with the mind-your-manners and the crows who carry the souls of dead people up to heaven and the flowers on the graves of babies. *Tomodachi*, he says to himself, *uma, sensou*.

"It's late," says his mom in a soft voice like she's saying sorry. "I don't know what you're still doing up."

"You said before you would tell about Trinket the cat," Belly says. That crazy cat, riding on Mr. Red Walsh's shoulder like a parrot and sneaking away to get some mice for dinner. Stealing a pie! Right from a windowsill!

His mom sighs. "Lie down. Close your eyes." Belly does. He shuts them so tight his head hurts and he sees little red sparks, but his mom puts her coat over him and he relaxes, even though he was already hot and now is more hot. "Well. Now. You know this story." She sighs. "You could tell me this story." She taps her fingers on his shoulder as if his shoulder was a piano and she could make music come out of it. His dad can play a piano for real and sometimes he pretends that the kitchen table is a piano even if it's not. "Well. This one time when your father was on the On to Ottawa Trek, years and years before you were born, before I was even his wife, his friend Red Walsh found a tiny newborn kitten on the side of the road. He saved the poor thing's life by feeding it milk through a knotted handkerchief all day and night and he named it Trinket."

The story is nice because he knows it so well he doesn't have to listen. He can just wave his soldiers through the air so they can fan him and pretend they're marching, each with their own perfect cat and each cat having its own special pie. It's like being at home. They've lived in a tent and in an apartment and his dad has gone away and then come back and now they are going to see his nana whose magic pet crow takes dead people to heaven and he's seen more horses today than anyone can count. All these things have happened, but the cat story has been the same and is still the same, no matter who tells it, no matter what they say.

THE STORY OF THE MASCOT

Red Walsh travels with a cat named Trinket that he carries in his pocket, so tame she sleeps with her head on his palm. She's stunted somehow, Red doesn't know how, maybe because he found her on the roadside by Creston so young she was still blind and nursed her with a knotted handkerchief dipped in milk. She has grown to fit his pocket, into the exact proportions of the world around her. Thin, she passes through long grasses without rippling the stalks and emerges with mice, voles, once a squirrel, and no one complains because she feeds herself this way, by vanishing for a few hours and reappearing with her muzzle and paws stiff with blood and rests by the fire, licking clean, tasting and retasting the last of her meal. She is kitten-sized or maybe chooses to remain so, since after all can't cats collapse their skeletons to fit through the slats of a fence, under a window? Once, she emerged with her whiskers purple from the blueberry pie a woman cooled on her sill. If she were my cat, says Matt Shaw, I would hit her on the head with a shovel, bloody nuisance animal, can't hardly feed the men on this trip. If she was born at the farm, Red agrees, we would have drowned her in a sack. Cats are not work animals, but these days who the hell is working? On cold days, he wraps her in blankets like a baby and carries her in his mackinaw, so they can warm each other, so she can sleep to the rhythms of his heart and his footsteps, so she can collapse her bones into the exact proportions of his chest.

THE STORY EDIE DIDN'T TELL

The week Edie's father left for the first time, Edie inherited the crows. Katherine had to brush her mother's hair and bathe her; Tom had to make scrambled eggs and toast for every meal; and Edie took on the crows because they looked sad waiting on the carport for scraps that wouldn't come, their heads cocked to one side like pet dogs. She was ten, maybe. Her father was a policeman who rode a motorcycle, and every morning he would drape his uniform over the radiator to dry and his family would wake to the scent of diesel and sweat and know that he had come home safely. For a week now, the house had smelled only mildly unclean, like unwashed hair.

Edie stood on the porch in her bare feet. The porridge and crusts had a sweet, brown-sugar smell, and she wondered whether crows have noses on their beaks. Probably not, or they wouldn't poke around in the compost heap and the graveyard. The crows must have caught the scent of the food, though, because they began to sing in their scratchy old-lady voices.

The roof held a small pond from the recent snowmelt, and the crows bathed, ruffling their feathers as if they were prettier birds.

They live in the cemetery and take the souls of dead people up to heaven to be with Jesus—that's what her mother often said—and all that carrying is hard work, so the crows must be fed.

The sun was coming up over the muddy graveyard behind the house and made the little rooftop pond glow. All the neat rows of stones looked as if they were about to sink deep into the ground. Last week, a woman came from the church to sit with Edie's mother and tell her about how God gives us sadness to make us strong and how the death of the lady's own husband made her surrender her heart to the Lord and after all Edie's father isn't even dead and may still return after he gets all of this unpleasantness out of his system. Think, she said, what the Lord could do.

Edie's mother just sat there wearing Edie's father's old bathrobe. Katherine had plaited her hair into ridiculous French braids with ribbons woven in them so her mother looked like a young girl from the neck up and an old man from the neck down. Thin in the filthy robe. Edie was embarrassed, but the lady didn't seem to mind. She said that her own husband was buried in the cemetery, and Edie didn't want to tell her the truth that he's gone with the crows because that might make her feel sad. When the woman left, Edie fed her leftover cookies to the crows and told them to share with the husband.

Edie leaned over the porch railing. The trick was to toss the crusts from the porch to the carport, but when she tried, they fell to the driveway and the crows craned their smart eyes at her, as if to say, "Hey, little girl, we've been flying the whole night to get these here dead people up to the arms of our Lord Saviour, and you want us to fly down there in the middle of our lovely bath to get our breakfast?"

"Well, sorry," Edie told them. "I'm just ten and I don't play baseball."

Baseball, she imagined the crows saying. We fly a million, thousand miles into a secret trap door in the sun where Jesus lives and call out the secret passwords and last night I sure had a fat old soul to carry and now my back hurts. You want to talk to us about baseball? The crows turned back to their bathing.

Edie walked down the steps, regretting her bare feet. It was bright but cold, colder now with her wet feet. She held the bowl up to the crows with both hands above her head. They didn't move except to drink the puddle water, and Edie was amazed to see they had small tongues, black like snake's tongues, and their feathers were not actually black but blue when the light was on them the right way. If she were a younger girl, she would have thought the crows must have picked up some dust from the blue sky to get blue wings like that, but at ten, she knew better and told herself that it was probably a trick of the light. From the house, she could hear her mother making sad little sounds and it filled her with shame, so she held the bowl higher, stretching on her tiptoes.

Her feet hurt from the stones on the pavement and the wind ruffled through the sleeves of her nightgown. "Come get it!" she yelled. Her father had cows as a boy and that's what he said to bring them in: come and get it! She held the bowl high above her head. "Come on, fellows!"

They came in a flurry of wings flapping small breezes against her cheeks, tapping their beaks and claws on the china bowl as they pecked at the porridge. The bowl shifted as they squabbled for position and Edie's arms quickly went sore. The smell was not what she imagined the sky to smell like or the carrier of souls to smell like: a swampy, oily scent, like something half dead. They argued close to her ears.

Edie wondered if after they got done with the porridge, they might want her soul, even though she was still alive. Which would be fun, she thought, to fly in the claws of those crows, invisible, spying

on everyone with her newly dead eyes. Later, she would feel guilty
that she didn't think to have the crows fly her to find her father and
bring him home. Jesus wouldn't let anyone in the air without a noble
purpose, she suspected, and making her mother happy would surely
count, no matter what Jesus said about suffering. It didn't matter.
Her father would do that himself, a few months later, without anyone
dragging him back, without Edie's help at all.

EDIE

Beside her, Belly stares up at the ceiling, moving his toy soldiers back
and forth. She should never have brought him. Probably it would have
been better to leave him with Norah and Red, maybe send for him
when she gets back on her feet. She can picture it: a little apartment
with a girl from the office—what office, she doesn't know—and the
place would be frayed around the edges but clean, and she would
save for some of those collectible plates with the King's face or the
name of the province on them and display them on her sideboard,
and they would keep a pretty glass decanter of brandy on top of
the gramophone and every night after a long day's work they would
stretch out with their hair in rollers and sip just a fingerful in a tiny
glass and gab about office gossip.

She watches her son's breathing underneath his cotton shirt. Belly
snores, wheezes a little when he's running, and she's worried it's because of years of mould from living in that tent or the time they spent
in refinery towns and mining towns. He's not even five, but already
she's ruined him in some basic way.

Belly was born in a smelting town with streets named after the
owner's daughters. Between Elizabeth Street and Martha Street, there
was a clinic with one doctor and two nurses. At the time of Belly's

birth, the doctor was off celebrating his birthday and some minor Allied victory.

The nurse had given her something. Chloroform? The birth was a type of pain she was not meant to remember. Edie lazed huge in the bed, untethered, as he slipped out of her. There was not one clean thing in that town. Not the bedsheets with Cominco Refineries Ltd. burned into the corner. Not the windows or any of the buildings outside the windows.

She was twenty-three years old and all the others were teenaged farm girls newly married and naming their babies after their teenaged husbands, who were away overseas. After five years of marriage, she had assumed pregnancy simply wouldn't be possible for her. Her body was too boy-shaped maybe, or perhaps there was something wrong between her and Slim. She had not minded one way or the other; in fact, the only time she thought of children was when she would play bridge with the women's auxiliary and some toddler would run into the room to press his sticky face and hands into his mother's dress.

Edie peered out the window through the sick-sweet haze of whatever they'd given her, through the yellow fog that killed the apple trees every time the baffles were opened to let out the sulfur. Her son: a grey-blue thing. She'd dreamed about him in shades of white or pink, imagining she'd made him perfectly: his lungs, his pink toes. She'd dreamed of one pure cry, a red-faced child screaming. Instead, the nurse — her outfit rallying against the grey with its starched pleats and little cap — breathing into her son's lungs. There was afterbirth on her cheeks when she came up for air. The nurse slapped him. Her red lipstick on his grey face, brighter than blood.

And then her son became red again. It was not the cry she noticed, but his stomach, his belly's unrelenting moving and moving, working even in that air, filling him with colour. And so William MacDonald

Jr. became Billy, then Belly, within the first five minutes of his life. In the room with the greying sheets, the nurse stuffed the life back into him. His belly expanding and contracting: going and going. The child has not had a proper name since.

Nor a proper home. Nor a proper life. From the refineries to the mine, to a tent in Ymir, to an apartment, and now here. He has learned Japanese from the Jap children in the internment camp and his skin is always tarnished with the filth of some machine.

The train lurches. A porter hurries from room to room, calling out warnings, his voice low and soothing.

"Ladies and gentlemen," he says. "The Kettle Valley Railway is sorry to disturb you, but we're experiencing heavy snowfall that may interfere with the comfort and safety of your journey. Please secure your belongings and place young children in your lap. Refrain from moving from your seat. Our staff is trained in emergencies and will assist you if necessary."

He passes by their seat without making eye contact and Edie thinks for a moment he must be a miner whose face is streaked with soot, but no, he's a Negro. Swinging his flashlight around like a censer, he leaves a buzz of noise behind him as the passengers whisper to themselves. Edie's lower back aches from sitting: Lord, the thought of a night of this, Belly adding weight to her lap. She should not have taken him. She should not have left. There was no good reason. The bone she carries in her pocket presses a round bruise into her hip.

The woman in the seat across from hers stands to strap in her valise in the overhead compartment, her wax-smooth arms lifting the case easily, even as the train lurches. She has one snaggletooth that she tries to smile prettily around. The tooth glints with saliva.

"All this excitement. Makes you want to go to the observation car to see how high it's piling up," the woman whispers.

Edie nods, wanting nothing more than to take a clean breath that does not stink of other people's bodies or her own. Belly turns in his sleep as she hoists him on to her lap, still wheezing. Her son has spent much of his life running wild in darned pants and someone else's language. In homes that lacked four solid walls. What does he imagine as he clutches the toy soldier in his fist? Whose side is he possibly on?

THE STORY OF WHY THEY LEFT

The last night in Ymir the heat shut off and a pipe froze in the ceiling and burst, so she and Belly woke to a carpet of ice at least half a foot thick. Ice on the walls, icicles shining along the ceiling like chandeliers, following the path the water had taken. The apartment was bright and very cold. Edie bundled her son up in Slim's old coats and left him nested on their bed while she found Slim's rubber boots and the wood-chopping axe. The boots were so heavy and cold that walking was like wading through mud, and she started to cry but thought of herself looking like a child in Slim's clothing and stopped.

Only Belly's eyes peeked out and sometimes a toy soldier would emerge in his gloved hand and conquer a hill in the wedding quilt or the valley in the bearskin rug and then disappear back to home base. He knew enough not to trouble her.

She pushed the hair from her cheeks and the sweat from her eyes and was too mad to be properly cold. The ice had to come out before it melted and that was that, regardless of where Slim had gotten to. The rug and the bathroom tiles and the hardwood floor were all deep under ice, as if preserved in glass. Even the framed photographs had been knocked off the wall and had frozen face-up on the ground where they'd floated. Her own face stared up at her, serious in black and white, smeared by the ice's curved lens. She hadn't woken up because of the mine's eternal clanking and grinding: a sound that never stopped, not even at night, a sound that made it seem as if something in the distance was always being ruined.

With the wood-chopping axe, she chipped and hacked, heaving each shard out of the window with her cold-numbed fingers. As the ice shattered below, Edie began to imagine it was glass and took pleasure in smashing it. She was not cold. Sore but not cold. Who knew where Slim was?

"Pow," said Belly from beneath the blankets as two of his soldiers battled on the enemy territory of the bed. "You ain't standing a chance. Going to shoot you dead."

"You *don't* stand a chance," said Edie.

"You *don't* stand a chance," said Belly. "Oh yes I do. Oh no you don't. Going to shoot you dead. Not if I shoot you first. Wait until The Shadow gets here. Gonna swoop you from behind and take your gun. Ain't no Shadow in the War, stupid. Don't call me stupid, I'll shoot you dead."

She chipped away at the floor until she freed the picture frame. Slim's face grinned down at her, looking pleased, and her own too-young eyes were turned up at him. They were laughing at something. That was right before they left Vancouver and she was seventeen. A suitcase, a bone, a new husband, the promise of places she'd never seen. Anne screaming as their mother clutched her and said, "Your sister's made a choice and she didn't choose you." As she pried the ice away, the frame's glass fogged and her axe kept working until her face and Slim's face were cleaved. She threw the frame out the window with the ice and they shattered in the same manner.

"Mwa ha ha. 'Who knows what evil lurks in the hearts of men?'" said Belly, and his red hair was the one colour against the ice and frost.

"Nearly done," said Edie. "And then we can take The Shadow out for lunch."

"The Shadow doesn't eat lunch. He only comes out at night and there aren't any restaurants open, so he has to eat peanut butter sand-wiches. And apples. His mom tries to make him drink milk, but he only likes chocolate milkshakes so she puts an egg in them so he can have big muscles."

It was important to get the ice out before it melted. She worked for two hours without gloves and Slim was nowhere. All around her: trickles and fissures and the constant seep of the thaw. It was still cold and the window was open, so maybe her breath had melted it, or the heat from her anger, her burning arms.

Soon, Mrs. O'Connor from downstairs was pounding on the still-frozen door complaining of water damage and threatening to call the police.

"Door's frozen," Edie called. "Can't hear you."

"Can't hear you," chirped Belly.

Mrs. O'Connor pounded harder, but Edie couldn't understand what she was saying. Something about an old Victrola that was now beyond repair. A soggy couch puffed up to double its size. Edie yanked at the door with her reddened hands and it came loose with a crackling sound. She stood there still carrying the axe, red with sweat and cold, in her dressing gown and her husband's boots up to her knees.

"Yes?" she asked. "Do you want something?"

Mrs. O'Connor gaped at her and suddenly didn't, so Edie returned to her chopping. When she reached the wood floor underneath she couldn't help sinking her axe a little deeper just to feel the bite of some solid contact. Belly watched her from his blankets—only his eyes visible, the soldier still gripped in his hands—and dozed to the rhythm of his mother's splintering.

When the house was at last swept clean of ice, the floor was gashed in places. Just minor damage, though. Nothing a sanding wouldn't remedy. Everything smelled of springtime rot, though it was February, and the odour of her baby powder talc turned wrong with sweat. She dressed and took Belly and the last of Slim's dollars and they walked through the disappearing streets to Frankie's Café. Belly was delighted at the lack of demarcation between the sidewalks and the road and ran in every direction, diving into snowbanks, snow pilling his coat. She had a coffee and he had an apple pie and a hot chocolate. As their clothing dried and released the mothball odour of wet wool into the café, Belly picked out the apple pieces and sucked them between his fingers. He asked Mr. Frankie what he thought about horses, and Mr. Frankie said they're beautiful beasts, for sure, but get spooked easy as pie. Pie can't get scared, said Belly, and Mr. Frankie laughed and gave him an extra slice, which Edie mostly finished. Some kid you have there, he said.

When she returned, Slim was unconscious on the bed, wan and poisoned in the ruined apartment. The windows were still open and the heat appeared to be off. Something was wrapped around Slim's finger: the photograph now pulpy and greyed. The clean ice smell was replaced by an acrid scent.

"Dad's home," said Belly, pulling his toy soldier out from underneath Slim's leg.

"Don't step on a splinter," said Edie. She kicked at one of Slim's legs that dangled off the bed. Thought of the axe. Belly stood beside her, watching his father as if he were an afternoon matinee, completely at home in all of this. There were a million other women with the same booze-wrecked, mine-wrecked, life-wrecked husbands and all those women stayed. Some women ended up black and blue and they stayed.

"Belly!" she said. "Get on that rug right now! You want to die of a splinter?" She picked him up under the arms, set him on the rug and couldn't help but give him a little shake as she held him. "You understand me? Stay here." Which made Belly cry silently, only his shoulders shaking and mucus hanging in a bubble by his lip.

Edie went to the closet and took her church clothes from their garment bag: the fitted wool-cloth skirt, the mended blouse almost translucent after years of bleaching, the stiff wool-cloth jacket with its war-rationed three buttons and its starched lapels. Clothing that forced her into a straight-backed posture. It seemed important to look proper at a time like this. In the ice-warped bathroom mirror, she tried to arrange her curls into an appealing shape around her face. She kept looking back at the bed to see if Slim would wake up, but he never did. For what seemed like a very long time, she stood at the foot of the bed and watched him for a sign of movement, thinking, "Wake up wake up wake up," but he remained unconscious.

Finally, Edie went to pack her things and found herself packing Belly's in the process. Strange, she thought, the fierce and animal pull she has to her son. She tucked the dollar bills from the cookie jar away into her brassiere and lifted Belly up. His pocket bulged with his bag of toy soldiers. Slim's face was pale as she shut the door, snow in his hair from the open window, flecks of frost on his face like tiny scars.

ANOTHER STORY OF LEAVING

Matt Shaw left home at sixteen wearing the name of a dead boy, a lattice of scars his new skin. He slipped out of his old name—Matthew Surdia—when a black blizzard sanded him with the topsoil he had recently planted wheat in, the storm so fast and angry that dirt was the only horizon, the only atmosphere, the only sky, falling around him like rain though it was not rain, though nothing was rain, though rain had not come for months.

Soil stopped up his ears and rubbed his skin so raw that his whole body was a wound, wet as a tongue, the only moisture for miles. Like the prairie itself, he lay parched and useless. Water was acid when his mother bathed him, the wind burned when she fanned him with a

Sunday Post, all his little scabs fluttering. Matt Shaw had grown from a boy into a landscape, and no matter what he ate he could taste the soil's metals. The stink of manure in his nostrils for months to come.

As his mother sang hymns over his bedside, he could hear the soil grinding and beating against the house, untamped by water. The songs were in Hungarian and he knew only a few words: *man, God, hardship*. A lot of different words for hardship. The black blizzard scuffed the window's glass white until all he could see were the shadows of the soil piled in the corners of the sill. Three weeks later he stole the surname of a drowned boy he had known and headed for the mountains.

Matt Shaw had swallowed so much farmland that for months he worried his stomach would sprout the crops that should have fed his family, imagined all of his innards tangled with sheaves of Prairie Gold. There was an itch in him light as grain, and he blamed the prairie for its inability to shelter him, for its refusal to feed his family. All the seeds they could afford had flayed the skin clean off him, and he staggered toward the house monstrous and dark, his features hidden behind a mask of earth. During the Trek, when newspapers or women praised his smooth skin, he would say that the prairie stole his freckles, leaving his face pale and thin as watered-down milk.

The only time Edie met him, he snorted that God must certainly be on the side of the Allies, look at the bumper crop the year of conscription. After the young men left and their sun-freckled arms could no longer rip the carrots out of the ground or subdue the hay into the geometry of bushels, the rains finally came and the crops grew taller than all the little boys left behind. The old farmers stood on their porches watching the land turn green and gold of out spite as the only other male voice around came from the radio to announce twelve killed over Germany, thirty-one killed over Italy, their sons' bodies nourishing the grape fields of France for years and years.

EDIE

Her son sleeps tucked in on himself, his fists balled up. She strokes his head. Still damp with perspiration. Still wheezing. Could be that the steam that fuels the train also heats the passenger cars and there is no setting but red hot.

In the seat facing her, the woman sleeps upright holding her daughter. The girl is about Belly's age but so still and pale that the woman seems to be holding a doll. Edie cannot get comfortable. There's a halo of sweat on the lap of her skirt where Belly's head rests and her thigh prickles with pins and needles. Every time she moves, the stiff fabric resists.

Most likely, Edie's mother will turn her away. Edie was warned. She had her chance and chose to get married and run off with a man ten years her senior, up to godforsaken mining towns. Maybe, though, her mother would take Belly. Edie could send for him later. Have some time to herself, good Lord, straighten things out in her mind, rent a room maybe above a bakery, rise each day to the smell of yeast and sugar. Or maybe above a juke joint, the floorboards pulsing like a heartbeat, heated by the energy of men packed tight dancing, but, no, that's no place for a child to grow up. She's not thinking right. Her mother might slam the door. She might not even let them stay the night.

Squares of moonlight throb and morph on the carpet. The train passes through a stand of forest — the moon blinking through the snow-fattened trees — and the squares appear and reappear, prickling light over the toy soldiers Belly has strewn on the floor. Snow softens the window's edges. She imagines Slim's hands blue with cold and the snow's light, a photograph wrapped around his finger. It may or may not be possible for a man to die indoors, passed out on the coldest night. It may or may not be possible for a man to die even when there are others in the building and co-workers who might come looking for him when he misses a shift.

The porter calls up and down the aisles. "Please secure your belongings and hold young children in your lap —" Now and again, people pass down the aisle between the seats, sometimes brushing her shoulder as they stabilize themselves on the backs of the chairs, their bodies swaying as the train bucks. They look startled and sick and Edie feels the same. Lord, all she wants is to lean her head out the window. Each breath she takes is hot and gritty with dust.

And where is Slim? Maybe he will sober up and send for them. Maybe he will come down to New Westminster with his hair slicked back and shift from foot to foot in that ridiculous birdlike manner she loves, carrying flowers, unable to look her in the eyes when he tells her by God, Edie, am I ever sorry, no more drinking, no more shitty mining towns, I'll get my diamond-drilling certification and we'll go abroad, get some work in a better place. But by then she'd have the apartment, Belly with his grandmother, maybe a fellow who'd come around every so often and take her out to dinner. Maybe she'd be in another province altogether, her son nowhere in sight. She'd turn Slim out on his ear; just watch her. Missed the boat, she'd tell him. Should have thought about that before you figured the Salmo Hotel was the best investment for your paycheque. Maybe she'd be gone and he'd never find her.

Or maybe he is getting lucky in a baser sense, gone of her bad luck, seeking his fortune. Perhaps he blames her for the cave-in and what happened after: the smaller and smaller mining towns; the week-long benders; the war that wouldn't take him. But it's not her fault she liked to roam the caverns disguised in miner's gear, thrilled in the dark. Back when she was thin as an axe handle, able to hide herself in jumpsuits. And it was more than five years ago; and he invited her down; and he did like her company. He could not have carried her curse from the Lucky Jim to the Viola Mac to the Yankee Girl.

She sets Belly down on the seat beside her and instantly feels cooler. She has to stand. Lord, she thinks, could Slim ever play that piano the nights they went dancing and swing her in his arms so easy. Lord, could he be funny, and to watch him with Belly was a pleasure, the time he took explaining the smallest detail, the two of them following cougar prints along a riverbank pretending to hunt for monsters.

Edie stretches, feeling all of her vertebrae crackle into place. The urge is to keep moving, so she stumbles her way between the rows of motion-sick people. The train lurches forward and all the passengers give little gasps, as if taking a breath before going under water.

WHAT HE HAS TOLD HER ABOUT TRAINS

His memories of the train are a way to know flying. Slim knows how velocity can turn the air into a weapon against your face, how it chaps your cheeks rough as a hand callused by farm work. In his mind, he is always back there. Edie sees his face go slack mid-conversation and knows he is going On to Ottawa past trees blurred by smoke and trees blurred by speed and once, across the Crowsnest Pass, trees blurred by snow. The train is like flight with the piston-fuelled thrum of its *now now now now* — the rising of that sound — and his hair slapping his face as he speeds past abandoned houses and houses lit by families meeting together under the humming glow of the porch light, their profiles like cardboard cutouts in the windows, and he passes storefronts and train stations and the desiccated ruins of rabbits and gophers and even horses — their ribs like the hulls of shipwrecks — and boys heading east to find work passing boys heading west to find work. Soot cakes his nostrils, tinges every breath with the scent of ash, and he goes past brush fires and house fires and way stations with the mail sack hanging engorged as if something was about to be born from it as flames singe the bottom of the post. Slim knows that the train can confuse your body so much it thinks it's been airborne. He knows the way your legs reject solid ground when you've been moving so fast for so long.

MOVING SO FAST FOR SO LONG

Now, Slim ranges across the Slocan Valley, round the Slocan Lake and past New Denver like some kind of coyote. Roan-haired like a coyote, blond fuzz on his arms and legs. In bars, he looks down into his glass and tells a cluster of men the story of the dandelions; the story of Red Walsh and his cat, Trinket; how thousands of men hopped boxcars in the summer of '35 to give that bastard Bennett a piece of their minds, parading along main streets accompanied by marching bands, taking over museums and department stores until their demands were met. You should have seen us, he says. He longs for a microphone but blushes hard so prefers to tell his stories in darkness. Plays the piano but hates to sing.

For weeks, Slim hitchhikes loping arcs through towns, playing piano for tips to get him through, then slips back into his job and family. The other miners cover for him, since he's a savant with galena. His drunk-shaking fingers are still a good compass needle. Through territory hundreds of miles wide, Slim plays out his animal need to disappear. Edie turns away in bed.

He returns to her with pieces of stories to whisper to her at night, sometimes as they lie sweating with the sheet rope-twisted and mouldy at the foot of the bed, sometimes while clinging to each other in the winter when the only warmth was in the exact shape of their bodies. They were not stories, more like scraps, more like photographs, since he certainly couldn't tell her exactly what he'd been up to.

"Saw a church someone had turned into a house, and these people had their laundry stretched on a line they'd strung between the necks of a statue of a saint and statue of the Virgin Mary, a rope around their necks, and—this is the best part, wish I'd gotten a picture of it—the lady's unmentionables are drying in this poor saint's outstretched hand, like he was up to no good! Like he was a dirty old bugger!

"Saw this lady at a train station and she's got this great fur coat on, even in the heat, but I think, well, rich people don't properly know about the seasons, all these squirrel tails hanging like furry wings off her arms and she's walking with them outstretched, like this, and when I get close I realize they're squirrels all right, but they sure as hell ain't some fine woman's furs. They're fresh dead, just bleeding and mangled and tied there by rope and there are flies. And the smell. She's crazy of course, everyone in that town knows her. Story is that her babies were lost in a fire years back."

"Stop," Edie would say. "That's enough."

Lying there, Edie would pretend she could see out of his eyes, though she questioned how many of his stories could have actually happened. She wonders now if they ever had a conversation that was not about imaginary things. Still, she liked it, especially in winter with his big old arms wrapped around her, how his whole body would shake when he laughed, how he would speak into her hair so the top of her skull buzzed with all his little lies.

EDIE

She feels her way along the hallway from the third-class cabin to the Pullman sleeper where soldiers are bunked. When the door closes behind her, she's plunged into darkness and the reek of sweat and hair cream, the air thick with moisture from all the open, snoring mouths. Her vision adjusts to make out rows of bunk beds with pressed uniforms hanging off the posts that sway glowing in the moonlight. Pale arms dangle off bunks, floating in the dark as if detached. When Edie passes, the train lurches and a man's fingers brush her bare forearm. She feels a tang of contact. That little spark.

The man's fingers contract around her hand like a Venus flytrap, and she jerks back, remembering that once, when she was fifteen, she pressed her back into the metal embrace of a bronze angel mounted on a grave: the man's hot, milk-tasting mouth and its bristles in front of her, metal wings behind. The sun-warmed metal like body heat. She steadies herself on the opposing bunk and touches a leg or a knee, which moves in response. Nothing solid here. All flesh under blankets and the bleachy odour of semen.

They must be fresh back from some front. Edie forgets sometimes that when the war ended the soldiers didn't simply reappear in their homes beside their loved ones: the immense distance between the front line and the hometown; the machinery of war that needed to be dismantled. The dangling arms are so bloodless in the light, creamy as scars. When she pulls her finger back, the man opens his eyes. He stares at her, reaching his arm out. Pupils huge in the darkness, he watches her unseeing and she feels that spark again.

Her heart kicks like a jackrabbit. The train lurches. Her shoulder brushes someone's foot.

"Hey," someone whispers. "Don't be going now."

"Hey." A man sitting up.

She reaches for the door, almost pushed out into the hallway by another jolt of the train, wincing in the light. Her skirt allows her to take only small steps. Nobody follows her. All these moon-pale boys, years in these reeking bunks. The train jolts but continues forward, returning them home to their wives and mothers, to the good life they were promised.

THE DANDELION STORY

For the past seventeen days, they have been picking dandelions by hand and finally they stop. Matt Shaw stops first. Says if he has to pull one more goddamned weed from this godforsaken place, he's going to go crazy and end up in some bejesus lunatic asylum where the food is surely better and no one makes you pull up damned weeds in the middle of a forest where there's fifty million other kinds of pests of the plant, animal and human variety.

The others laugh, but Matt Shaw blushes and rubs the back of his neck so bits of yellow dandelion and dirt are streaked there. "Pardon my French, guys," he says. "But that's how I feel. That's just how I feel."

The dandelion is an oily damned thing, getting everywhere, a reminder of all the jokes the girls of their childhood used to say while twirling the petals under their chin, that you must like butter, must be soft like butter. The jokes have grown old without a girl around to say them, but still they tell them, especially Ricky, who is a little simple and doesn't quite know when polite conversation turns monotonous. Hey, look at your chin all yellow there, Slim, he'd say. You must like butter, eh? Bet you do like butter. Sure as hell would like some butter up here. Sure could use some.

Slim does feel like he could use some butter, though he's still on the right side of starving: just sharp in the jaw and the shoulder blades and the whip-thin spine bending down to pick the dandelions, pick the dandelions. Seventeen days and their hands are raw from a bloody weed.

Matt Shaw brushes his hands on his pants and heads for the picnic table, ranting. "Make the place nice for the tourists, eh? Because the good Lord knows people have enough money to go traipsing around the wilderness these days and are bound to flock to a place a thirty-hour drive away from anywhere for a spot of wilderness now liberated from the pestilent scourge of the dandelion. Bring your children! Bring Grandma! Come enjoy a spot blissfully free of those show-offy amenities like lakes or beaches or stores or running water. All the fresh air you can stand. Meat a fetching shade of green. All the wormy apples you can eat. Next thing you know, we'll be catching mosquitoes in butterfly nets. Goddamned make-work projects. Goddamned work camps. Goddamned Iron Heel Bennett and the bloody Fasco-conservative regime."

So Slim and Bobby (a.k.a. Shorty) and Stan (a.k.a. Red) and Fitzy (inexplicably known as Boo) wipe off their hands and soon enough the foreman can holler all he wants, no one's budging and there's nothing to do but sit at the picnic table and smoke dried versions of the weeds they've been picking since what feels like forever.

A few weeks before, Shorty had laid out the dandelion heads to dry on a flat rock and then rolled them into the newspapers that came two weeks late bearing the news that nothing was improving. The dandelion cigarettes are the worst they'd ever smoked. Slim suspects he's inhaled every manner of flora from here to Kamloops. He's smoked everything and none of it's any good. Someone's rum-runner brother had given them a recipe for dandelion wine and they'd buried their mixture to ferment behind the bunkhouse.

Matt Shaw is joyful at the small strike, keeps waving his arms and singing old union hymns. He was with the WUL before he left for the work camp to organize it under the RCWU. He likes to joke that he's in the acronym business. They've made a bonfire and it's a good, mild night. "This calls for a celebration," he says. "Think we should crack out some of that dandelion grog? Give it the first pull?"

They toast themselves, the other men in camps, the cook, the cook's wife, the ladies in the girlie magazines, even the dandelions themselves. Matt Shaw pours a snort into each man's shaving cup and it froths up from the residue of the lather.

The wine is pure spite. It sends them coughing and spitting into the fire, which flares up from the alcohol: the kind of bitter that clears your brain out along with your nasal cavities. Who knew such small, stupid weeds could be capable of that?

There's nothing to rid their mouths of the taste, not even a chaser to numb the throat. And no raiding mama's pantry out there either. The last time Slim had anything sweet was Christmas, since desserts are rumoured to make men go soft and this isn't the bloody Empress Hotel.

Out here, thinks Slim, the taste of one good apple could drive a man insane. Does, in fact, the first day of spring, since the apples are wilder up here; everything's wilder. Nothing is tame, not even the apple trees they've been climbing since their farm childhoods. At night, Slim recites a litany of the food to eat upon his return to civilization: blueberry pie, a lump of sugar meant for horses, ice cream that tastes of rock salt and the sweat his mother put into turning the crank. He copies recipes out of the newspaper in handwriting neat enough for a love letter. Still retching from the wine, Slim dreams of one pure taste of sweetness, enough to make him mute for days.

WHO'S GOING TO SPEAK FOR THE SKIN AND THE BONE?

"'There is power in the factory,'" Matt Shaw is singing and Slim is silent watching him. Just outside of Moose Jaw, more than a thousand miles from the godforsaken work camps. The melody is something like church, equal parts catchy and holy, the kind of song that makes a choir out of a lone voice. Matt Shaw sits against a tree carving, curling long, elegant rinds off a bar of soap until he's formed the image of a man or a horse or a dog. Sometimes he sculpts the other men, caricaturing their features. Though some complain that he should use the soap less for carving and more for bathing, there is no denying that Matt Shaw's penknife is blessed with the gift of minutiae.

"'There is power in the factory, power in the land,'" sings Matt Shaw. He is right because the power of the land is in the swampy scent of the river edged with campfire smoke, in the flat ground's ability to shelter them, in the miracle that this copse of willow exists even with the drought and the nearby city's constant need for something to burn. And there is power in Matt Shaw, who will voice their demands when they get to Ottawa so that they may have work they are not ashamed to write about in their letters home and enough wages to take a pretty girl out dancing. The soap shavings release their own ladylike odour into the campsite's stink of men. The city has allowed them to stay in a nearby livestock pavilion, but the smell is better out here and it's mild enough to sleep outside. Around Matt Shaw is a radius of the soap's blossomy scent, this hummed and guttural song, the river churning a few feet away.

"What are you going to say to Old Bill Bennett tomorrow?" Slim asks, eager. A committee of eight Trekkers is being sent by train to Ottawa to speak to the prime minister in the morning—an attempt to prevent several thousand men from reaching the capital—and he wants a scrap of history before it happens.

Matt Shaw shrugs. "Depends." He has a voice smooth and curled as a soap shaving.

"Depends on what?"

"Depends." He shrugs again.

"But you're going to give him hell, eh? Say, 'This is what we want and by God we're not going to leave until we get it.'"

Matt Shaw chuckles a little and flecks of soap fall away to reveal a man's face: a big nose, beady eyes. "There's no planning for these things, Slim," he says. "Just got to see how it goes."

He returns to humming, the sound right against the sonorous chatting and snoring of the men bedding down in the campsite. Slim lies back on his own bedroll near the fire and listens to Matt Shaw singing, carving soap into a man that might resemble Slim, might resemble Red, might resemble Arthur-Slim Evans, any of them. He imagines how much soap would be wasted to carve his own likeness, sees Matt Shaw's knife flicking in quick movements to craft his stuck-out ribs.

It doesn't matter, he thinks. Tomorrow Matt Shaw will bathe up for his big day and the river will smooth the figure's features away, will melt the scent into his hair, until the carving could be anyone, and then will be no one, an oily sheen on the river's current.

EDIE

Edie knows that she has no right to stray from what Slim has told her: Thunder Creek, Matt Shaw with his radio-friendly voice. She has no right to push her imagination into the story. But the observation car, with the blue light from the moon shining through the snow piled against all the long windows, makes her feel underwater. She has gone from the shock of heat to the shock of cold. When she stands in front of the rear window, she can see the track spooling out dark against the surrounding snow, bright in the radius of the lantern's light. She breathes. Feels her damp body drying. Her back releases its complaints, bone by bone.

A soldier stands with his hands pressed against the glass. She thinks of Belly smearing the windows, naming the horses. His body wavers with the rhythm of the train, his face blue and shining. A briny odour.

Up close, she sees that the soldier's eyes are closed. His uniform is perfect, but he stumbles, murmuring to himself. "It's a dog's breakfast," he says, dropping a hand to clench it in a fist by his side. (Once, she turned her face to the side and breathed in the green metal reek of the angel's palms, one finger broken off. Her pubic bones pressed against the man like stones in her pockets.) His thin chest is decorated with Lord-knows-what stripes or medals, his hands scar-silvered in the light. "A dog's breakfast."

She approaches him slowly, palms up. The soldier looks like a boy from a poster, except for his ruined hands. The fingers are cut off to the knuckle and on one hand the thumb and pinky are sanded clean away. The remaining fingers swish like fins. She wants to take his hand but does not know where to grip. Someone should be in charge of these boys. The heat rolls off him. Sweaty like her son, she cannot help but think.

The train rounds another bend. Even through the glass, she can see how slick the tracks are. The brakes throw up sparks as they try to hold on. She imagines Belly jostled off the bench, waking hurt without her. Selfish of her to want to wander the dark corridors. The young soldier's breath curls in wisps. A lovely boy, white as bone, white as Slim's pale face as she shut the door, snow furring the valleys of the quilt.

The soldier reaches out to her. "Throw me one. Don't hit me in the head," he says. He's so close. In front of her: the cold glass and the track. Behind: the cabin with boys' tattooed arms reaching like anemones. (The prisoner ahead and the angel behind her. There was a long chain between his handcuffs that swayed against her knees when he tried to hold her. She'd never seen a tattoo up close, one so near to her cheek. She cannot remember what it depicted. Prison-made, nearly illegible, a stain that might have been a heart with a name in it.)

In her pocket, the bone and the coins clink with the movement of the train. "Throw me one," he says. His faint blond stubble like salt crystals in the light.

"Hey," she murmurs. "Hey, hush now. You're okay." Like she'd soothe her son. Like she should be soothing her son.

She takes him by the good hand, which is cold from the condensation on the glass. Again, he jerks back and Edie nearly falls with the careening of the train. That pulse. A light in the ribcage.

"Fine," she says. "Get your own self to bed."

She wants to sprint blind through the Pullman car. To touch all the men as she runs, the way children rattle a stick along the slats of a fence. There's a padlock on the rear door of the observation car so she can't even open it and take some air. She imagines her blouse flattened against her body by the wind. The train jolts. Belly may have fallen off the seat, and might now be sobbing with a bloody nose. What time is it? The murky hours after midnight when her inner clock turns off.

The soldier faces her. For a moment they are very still. He is so much bigger than her, could lift her in the air like a child, could put his hands around her throat, could throw her over his shoulder. The train rocks again and he sways, steadying himself by touching Edie's shoulder. He looks as if he's going to pull her toward him. Moonlight jerks blue and white over his face. Her son has maybe woken up, terrified without her; right now, he may be crying.

She takes a step toward the door. When the train lurches again, the soldier reaches for her, finds nothing to stabilize himself; his hands scrabble at the air. The train lurches again and he touches the wall.

She shuts the door behind her as she enters the Pullman car, shocked at the darkness of the cabin after a few minutes of moonlight. There's no reason to put him back in bed. He's not her son. Her son is alone, maybe awake, hurt from the jostling of the train. Men murmur, some shift, all their little noises as sonorous as insects. All these countless boys, their arms tattooed with the names of their mothers, so if the dog tags were lost someone would know who to return them to.

OUR BOYS! A LOST GENERATION MARCHES!

A young woman clips down the sidewalk pushing a pram, following the pace of the parade, oblivious. She stops to stare at her infant, stunned by what she has created. Hers are the only eyes not looking back at Slim and the Trekkers as they march down the middle of the road.

Families line the parade route: a mother whose smoke-wispy hair won't hold the shape of a bun, a father squinting, teenaged girls, a boy of about ten. There is a hole in the lineup where another son used to be. The teenaged boys have gone missing like teeth, and the mother stands behind her remaining children with a hand on each of their shoulders, digging in. After every parade their ranks swell with boys who duck out of their family's line of sight.

At dusk, mothers hover around the Trekkers' campsite, peering at faces. They are sorry for the trouble, but has anyone possibly seen a boy of eighteen, skinny, dark hair, named Andy? Named Ralph? Named Max? Left home in '32? Because of the drought? They should not even be here; they know it's wrong to come; sons leaving their mothers is the way of the world, but if she could find him she'd invite him up to the house for supper—He wouldn't have to come back for good! Boys need their freedom!—but he could just come up to the house, sit at the table for a few hours.

At each face they pass, the mothers are more disappointed. The boys look like their sons but are not. The right shoulders but the wrong nose, the same colour eyes but without that cowlick. They wander the rows of boys and the Trekkers nod as they pass and the mothers nod back. It is impossible to guess what new name their son may have taken, impossible to know how they might possibly spot one another after all this distance, after all these years.

BELLY

Even the horses are gone from him and his dad too and now his mom. The train has taken her and outside are storms—a spray of snow patters on the glass—and maybe his mom was sucked out the window and is now running behind them trying to catch up, calling out his name crying, which makes Belly cry but just a little. His throat is like someone is squeezing it; sometimes he wakes up in the middle of the night thinking a snake is choking him, but there never is.

If he was bigger he would jump from the window, steal a horse and ride to her. He could call her name with a big-man voice and reach down to pull her up on the horse with one hand. Maybe his dad came in the night to take them back home but Belly was sleeping so they forgot him and now they're already back in the apartment; he will have to stay on the train forever, like his dad lived on a train, and look sweet so the nice ladies will give him food, but what if the ladies get off and then he's all by himself and the train men kick him off so he has to sleep in the snow and get dead?

What was she telling him? He didn't listen. Something about crows and something about a grandma and something about heaven and a grandpa leaving. He was bad not to listen and now she is gone because he was bad. The windows are smudgy with water and inside it's hot and the horses are dreaming in their horse beds. Their stables. Their horse stables. Something squeezes his chest. Sometimes he pretends he's got a bear in his chest, since if a bear catches you he will squeeze you until you're dead; that's where the word *bear hug* comes from; it's not a nice word. That's what the cook at his dad's mine said and is one thing he's not supposed to know.

Belly rubs his hand through the water on the window and licks it, but it's not enough and tastes like when he puts pennies in his mouth. He presses his tongue to the glass. The coolness feels good, but the taste is wrong and his throat is the same.

The lady across from him sleeps and her daughter sleeps nice on her lap, which is why the lady's still there, because the daughter is so pretty and good. His mom is so skinny that when he sits on her lap he always thinks he's sitting on a marble, but really it's her bones. He's only seen a few marbles and they were like beautiful eyes. His friend had some but wouldn't let anyone else touch them, just kept them in his pocket and would only show you if you asked in just the right way or gave him a penny, which Belly didn't have.

It's hot. Belly's hot. He wants some water, but his mom has the water and who knows if he will die of thirst. He feels sick thinking like that. He'll dry up and float away. The water is gone. So many leavings: horses, a town, his dad, water, his mom. His dad goes away sometimes for what seems like a very long time and his mom has to sleep with both hands around the flashlight so a bear doesn't come in. There are secret words for all these goings, words his mom doesn't know. There are two different ways to say everything and sometimes he gets mixed up which is which and his mom looks at him like he has fangs.

Belly stands. The two seats facing each other and the bags piled on top make a little cave home. The red—it's not a good colour, kind of an old, dirty red—furry seats look soft, but when you rub your cheek against them they feel like you're rubbing against a dad's cheek, which makes him think of his dad, who is probably with his mom at the apartment right this minute saying, "Where's Belly? Did we forget him? What if we never find him again?"

When he tries to walk, the train knocks him over. He holds the backs of the seats and passes sleeping people and the people who are awake look mean at him like he's going to hurt them by coming so close. Between where the two cars meet there's a gap and the air coming up feels like being hit with cold water. Belly crouches down and waves his hand over the spot, then puts the hand to his face. It feels like washing.

A dark man with white gloves on bends down to his level. "What you up to there, son?"

Belly stares at him. You're not supposed to talk to people with strange skin, even if they look nice, and you're not supposed to speak like them, and you're not supposed to know any words except the ones your own mom and dad teach you. The train bucks again and the man almost loses his balance and falls into Belly and when Belly tries to move back he nearly falls too.

"You're not supposed to be out of your seat," the man says and Belly stares at him. "Storm like this. How come a boy like you isn't sleeping?"

Belly doesn't know. He doesn't know. This one time a bad man came and took a boy away. There was this other time when a boy drowned in a river.

He hears his mom's feet before he sees her and starts to cry because he knows she's coming and he's mad at her leaving and letting his throat get scratchy because she took the water for her own self.

"William!" she says. "You can't go wandering off. You have to wait for me!"

He lets her lift him up away from the cold air. The man stands up. "He's fine."

"I was just hot. It's so hot here," his mom says.

The man doesn't say anything.

"What did I just say about being good and not wandering off?" She moves him from one hip to the other. "I'm sorry for the trouble." Her nice voice has meanness underneath it. The nice part is for the man and the mean part's for him. Belly clings with his arms around her neck, his nose against that strange long bone by her throat. Her jacket smells of starch and perfume and the bow on the neck of her blouse swishes against his cheek. She was gone and now she is not gone and he is both safe and mad. "How are you going to be a good boy at your nana's house if you can't be good on the train?"

"You went first," he says. "You weren't good. You weren't good and I could have got drowned or fallen out the train." He yells right in her face. Doesn't care if she slaps him; he's mad. "I could have died and—and—and I could have got drowned."

She doesn't say anything. He wants to hit her face. He is dumb for crying and he wants to hit her for making him feel like a baby when really he is so big that the older boys let him play war and spit cherry pits from his mouth that leave red marks on other boys because of how hard he can spit them.

Back in the seat, she sets him on her lap and holds him. Her skirt and jacket are as scratchy as the seats, but he likes the softness of her hair against his cheek. The bone by her throat is like a little handle and he wants to grab it and not let go until they're home, even if it hurts her. He doesn't care. He hates her. The snow is made of water—another thing the cook told him—and you can drown in water and what if he fell out of the train and no one knew and they left him there?

"I'm sorry you felt scared," she says finally. His cheek presses against her throat and it feels like mosquitoes when she speaks. "But you've got to stay put."

Belly is too hiccupy to talk. He would like some water and his soldiers and his books and some horses. Where his cheek presses against her is sticky, but he's not going to move.

"Do you want some water?" she asks because she knows him so well he doesn't have to talk.

Belly nods and she raises the Thermos to his lips. The water tastes like bad breath but makes a coolness in his throat so he doesn't care. She rubs his back and he tries to remember why he wanted to hit her face. She will not leave him. He has her tight. There are many puzzling things, but she is not one of them. She is with him forever. He says the words that sound nice in his mind, imagining all the *uma* he has seen today, imagining how he will show the boys in Vancouver to spit cherry pits and make their mouths into guns too. The trick is to suck the fruit from the pits so they're smooth, hold them between your teeth, then fire them with more air than spit. Which is another thing his mom can't understand—spitting cherry pits—like how sometimes she can't understand why he needs to put dry riverbank pebbles in his mouth because they look better when they're wet or why sometimes he has to yell at her with special words she doesn't understand but knows he's mad at her, mad at something, even if he doesn't know exactly what, exactly why.

EDIE

So few passengers sleep, though it must be at least 3:00 a.m. In the opposite row, a woman reads to her husband, the book open primly on her lap as if it's the Bible as her church-choir voice describes a cowboy finding his friend scalped. Her tone does not change as she narrates the bleeding pulp of the skull. The husband nods. He pats her knee: stares unseeing at mountains through the darkened windows.

Facing the couple are two newlyweds, the boy with a straight back and a brush cut growing out over his misshapen skull. The girl is slumped so her head can rest on his shoulder. (Edie thinks of the photo soggy with snow, her too-young eyes turned up at him, mashing into pulp as she broke through the glass.) She keeps staring up at him and biting her lip and he gazes at her, then they look elsewhere. One small valise rests between his legs, and perhaps the girl is thinking of her underthings and his rolled together and blushes at the thought. His face is flushed and haughty; he touches the girl's knee; they smile at each other and look away.

Edie is amazed at these small acts of love, shamed to have witnessed them, having left her own husband growing frostbitten in their bed with the windows open and the heat off on the coldest night of the year. Having left her own son and found him terrified in the corridor, being comforted by somebody else. Having left, having thought of more leaving, having considered how far her money would take her if she dropped Belly at his grandma's and took the train to Calgary to Toronto to Montreal. Her son holds on tight as she imagines being able to leave the house without buttoning up someone else's coat and lacing someone else's boots and explaining where we're going and why and tugging his small arm so he will walk faster and not have to stop so he can pick up every stick they pass and poke it in the mud.

Now her son is so hot he feels liquid and the mucus from his crying has tightened into a shiny scab on her throat. She lets the train rock him to sleep. It's not good for a boy to be packed around from place to place, left behind, especially in big cities where he could get hit by a tram car or stolen. Where would he go when she worked? What if she had to work nights? She imagines him alone in an apartment, terrified.

"Ladies and gentlemen," the porter whispers to those who are still awake. "The Kettle Valley Railway is sorry to disturb you, but we are experiencing heavy snowfall that may interfere with the comfort and safety of your journey." He walks lazily through the rows delivering his warning. "Cute little fellow," he says when he passes their seat. "When he wakes up, come find me and I'll show you the locomotive. We're going to stop and put the snowplow on pretty soon here and boys get a real kick out of watching the train scoop all that snow away. Looks like there's no track with all the snow, but the old train keeps on going."

"Thanks," says Edie. She nods. "Thank you."

The porter chuckles to himself. "'This train is bound for glory,'" he sings as he wanders down the corridor. "'If you want to ride you must be holy.'"

She feels sick with the heat from her son—a furnace, that kid, throwing off heat by the fistfuls—and the motion. Outside, the snow blankets its haze over everything. Everything is gone. She thinks of the snowplow forcing its way through the white. The sky and the mountains and the track the same colour. As if they are going no-where. As if there is nothing in front.

THE STORY OF THE NOWHERE ROAD

One day the wheat shrivels up and bankers dive flailing from their high-rises. It starts in the States but soon filters up to Canada the way music does: a year or so later, through the radio that croons of hard times, low times, mean times, though no one believes at first. Soon the topsoil blows clean away and women add water to the milk and flour to the stew and children grow up with their legs bowed out far enough that their knees will never touch in their lives. Some lucky rich bastards, though, still find the money to buy natty linen suits with buttons so shiny that magpies dive-bomb them, so dizzy with hunger that they confuse their love of bright objects with their need to eat.

People wait and then become angry while they wait, and the young men are the angriest. So the government drives them far away into the empty, dried-out middles of the provinces to work camps and tells them that for twenty cents a day plus room and board they can wait out the worst of it. Really, though, it is so that the heat of their anger will not boil the cities and towns and farms and inflame more young men.

But even without the young men, the cities and towns and farms find their own reasons to be angry. People write letters to Prime Minister Bennett begging for money, and for a while he sends a dollar or two, then stops making speeches in public and fashions his cars with tinted windows. Mothers seethe, boys leave home and for the first time people are angry on your behalf if you are poor. It's hard luck, not bad blood. It's everywhere. But this is a common story, one everyone knows, one Edie has lived herself. She didn't need Slim to tell her about hardship.

In the work camps, then: the place newspaper reporters never came, the place Edie can only imagine through Slim's eyes. In the camp, they build a road so smooth that if a car had happened along it, the passengers would have thought they were floating. For a year they hew rocks with chisels and sledgehammers as Matt Shaw tells stories of the slaves in Egypt building the pyramids. They fit the stones side by side, pack them in with the useless soil and in their minds there's a crew from some other work camp far away (Hope or Creston, maybe; beyond Hope, Matt Shaw liked to joke) whose road will join theirs.

This crew will have the same stained khakis and undershirts worn thin as gauze. They will have the same scars from bar fights or childhood accidents healed so you can only see them when the sun strikes at the right angle. They will be sunburnt, freckled as farm boys, with the same stuck-out ribs. Sometimes, in the middle of a workday, a man straightens and waits, as if feeling the reverberations of the other crew's hammers through the soles of his feet. The other men watch him standing there, his posture erect as a wolf that has caught a scent, and wonder if isolation sharpens a man's senses back to animal.

As the road lengthens, the men walk for miles in the dawn swinging their lard pails filled with sandwiches and bottles of milk against their thighs. They speak of the day when they will first see the other crew's outlines in the distance, still miles away: a shape that isn't trees or brush or mounds of earth but a moving mass hammering and chiselling its way toward them. The days will pass and the shadow will take the shape of men heaving dirt, packing, pressing, joking, tussling, levelling, and each day the camp will grow more excited. Someone will find a bottle of rum in preparation for a party. Maybe one of the fellows from the other camp will have a concertina or a guitar and will have been close enough to a radio's range to pick up a few new songs. What do people these days dance to? the men wonder.

One day, the new men will be only a few hundred feet away. They'll be shy at first—so long without new faces—and will be so busy stealing glances at the newcomers that some fellow will drop a load of bricks or bring a two-by-four down on his toe and everyone will laugh. The laughter will be an introduction and soon they'll be sharing nicknames and spending their lunch breaks around a common fire because by then it will be winter and the road will be brilliant with frost and ice, so smooth you could slide right to Vancouver on your stomach.

The two crews will sit around this fire and stare at the nearly joined road stretching out in front of them farther than can be seen in either direction. They might even have parties out in the middle of nowhere, everyone sharing tales of the shitty foreman, the shittier food, the twenty goddamned cents a day and how long it's been since they'd last had a woman.

One day, the work will be complete and the two roads will join. On this spot, the crews will link arm in arm and someone will take a photo of them all grinning, looking like a hockey team that has just won that Lord Stanley Cup.

They work for a year to make three miles. Why was the road made out of stone and not concrete? Why did surveyors never come? Somehow, though work on the road is never called off, the men are assigned to craft picnic tables for vacationers who will arrive when the highway is finished.

By that summer, the road is lovely with moss, the only greenery during August when the grass falls to powder. The road draws its own moisture from some underground source: a self-sustaining ecosystem in the middle of brush fires and dirt so dry it's white. In the spring, the spaces between the paving stones house a creek and Slim watches insects wending their own paths across the rocks that should have been flattened down by cars and delivery trucks. The road is as smooth as a river and the men hope that one day it will be busy as one, Fords huffing like freighters along it. When the winter comes, the ice on the rocks makes the road vanish against the snow. The weather is so cold that the only thing to do is to stand on the porch and stare at the horizon looking for a curve in the land where another highway might be coming through to meet it at any minute, any day now.

THE TIME THEY FINALLY LEFT THOSE GODFORSAKEN WORK CAMPS; HOW THE TREK BEGAN

All across the country, houses are not houses anymore. Hitchhiking down to Vancouver, they camp in the shadows of these ruined homes, bedding down on porches where men once played banjos and women rocked babies as they watched the laundry fill and empty with wind. But now, the houses have been long untouched except for animals and weather. Despite the drought, the dirt in the yards is pitted with the indents of rain as if the occupants had left town right before the storm that would have fed their crops and let them stay one more year.

In some houses the walls slope in or the timbers are charred. There are walls green with moss and carpets that are lush with weeds, the down of dandelions. The roofs have moved past tin, past rust until there are patches where the sky shows through and the carpet below has been faded in the exact shape of the hole, as if the damage was not caused by sun but is merely a stain from a party or family mealtime. Even the timbers creak with dryness, and the men wonder what sustains the moss on the carpets and the vines up the front of the house, if such vegetation can hold the memory of rain in their green bodies for years and years.

They expect to find dolls or furniture or cups or tinned food or photographs but such mementos have been either taken by the occupants or else scavenged. People these days are too poor to leave ghosts. Only the weather can afford a legacy.

And though the men know that the rest of the country prays for storms, they feel blessed that this dryness has held. If they cannot be warm, at least they are dry. Keep us this way until we are beyond these half-houses, they think as they bed down under part tin, part stars, as squirrels and mice bustle through the walls near their bedrolls. Let the storm wait until we have a true roof. So the storm waits. So the dryness holds. So they move ruined home to ruined home, all the way to Vancouver.

EDIE

Outside, pebbles tick against the window. Wayward snow. Clods of ice and earth. Outside, gusts of wind, something tapping like hail or stone, a noise in the background she cannot place. Something wrong and shifting, something loosening and picking up speed. There are little sounds the earth makes to alert you to danger — the *whoomp* before an avalanche, the creaking of a mine's timbered bones — but it's hard to tell in the foreign territory of the train, its unceasing movement, the nausea in the back of her throat, all these many stories she has inherited from her husband and cannot stop imagining, her child a suffocating weight against her chest.

She's so dreamy with story, so ill with heat and motion, that she recognizes the sound only an instant before the crash, so that the event and the premonition of the event arrive at nearly the same time, so that when the glass sprays over her she feels as if she's been doused with cold water and thinks, Thank God, and takes a breath, and feels briefly grateful until someone begins to scream.

FIRST BREAK

The sirens really did sound like screaming, like the scream of a rabbit in the talons of a hawk, and the women ran in packs toward the mine, driven half crazy by the sound. Edie ran, her pregnant belly churning in its own rhythm as she ran. But it wasn't Slim. Two other miners were crushed to death: Red Mackie and a new guy named Ralph, both of whom blessedly had no family. The war was heating up and there were so many fallen soldiers to mourn that the death of two miners did not even make the front page of the local paper.

It wasn't Slim, but it was. Slim's job was to know when things went too far: to track the ore, to shape timber into the mine's long bones, to know when the weight of the earth against the width of the ceiling was the wrong equation. Mines, said Slim, are not like rooms. With houses, you can build until you reach your property line. The size of your house is dictated by what you own. But no one owns the caverns the men hollow out underneath the ground. You can only take what you can, lay down the timbers, fortify the structure until the whole mess comes crushing in and is filled with sand. And then you run like hell.

He came out of the mine office at dusk, soil in his hair, his finger-nails black from when he dug his way through the suffocating earth trying to find survivors. He'd heard the creaking, sounded the alarm and was running from room to room checking for people when the crash came and he spent hours digging, praying that no one was missing, then praying for a pocket of air, then digging in silence. Slim, whose job it was to know what the earth could take, to honour the weight of the earth. You rent a mine, he always said, and one day the contract will be up.

When she saw him she hugged him, but the gesture was to calm herself because he stiffened. All the women had gone home and she was the last one. Her stomach kept her from holding him close. Underneath her skin, the child moved oblivious. She could hear Slim breathing and she realized it was because the processor was quiet for once.

He didn't reach for her. The front of her dress was scuffed with the earth from his soiled hair and hands. He was so tall: sometimes it was difficult to see his face. That night he sat on their bed with the thin-paged manifestos spread across his lap, the edges translucent with his finger's oils. Edie looked in the Bible for a relevant passage, but Slim said, no, he'd rather believe in the worker, not some hierarchy of heaven and earth and hell, not some Jesus flitting around in the heavens.

Then he didn't say anything, just sat slouched over with his long finger marking a word he wasn't paying attention to any longer, his fingernails still black. Edie held her stomach and swayed a little on the bed, as if the child was already born and needed to be soothed.

Finally, Slim stood. "Going to pay my respects," he said, which meant the Salmo Hotel and for the first time he wasn't home for three days.

EDIE

One moment there is nothing but the shards of a five-year-old story and the next, this overarching present glittering with glass, Belly too stunned to wail. A boulder made larger by the mountain's force has punched through the window in a burst of shattering, twisting the window's metal frame to its shape. Now, the rock sits on the seat next to her as if it had a ticket. Belly is heavy in her arms. He doesn't move, doesn't cry, and she can't look at him.

Pebbles of broken glass sluice in a tide with the rhythm of the train. The cold air blasts through the window with as much force as the rock had, keeps blasting, brings the smell of soot and winter. In the seat facing her, a woman freezes in the same pose as Edie. For a moment, Edie thinks it might be a mirror, but it's not, it's another woman holding a daughter. Same dark hair and thinness, but different eyes, a snaggletooth. Blue eyes.

Her son is the one still thing amid the rolling glass, the porters hurrying in all directions, the passengers hopping out of their seats and crowding to take a look. She presses him close to her and finally can feel a heartbeat knocking against hers, faster. Still, he doesn't cry. (She thinks of him grey and smeared with lipstick, clownish, as the nurse came up for air with blood on her cheeks.)

"Are you okay?" Edie asks, breaking the aureole of silence that followed the crash. Belly raises his head and stares up at her. A sliver of glass nearly three inches long the shape of a lightning bolt is embedded in his cheek, sending a red tear trail down toward his neck. Little gashes on his cheek, neck and arm from smaller shards. His luck is a matter of inches: his eyes appear unharmed.

"You're okay," she murmurs and Belly begins to cry, as if to prove her wrong. His little heartbeat kicks against her chest as if it was her own: as if she had an extra heart the way planets have hidden moons.

The woman's daughter joins in the crying and Edie stands, rocking her son. She is lucky and not lucky. The boulder picked her compartment, but not her son's life. Her son is alive but wounded and the glass must be removed and the child could take a fever from the filthy glass driven into his blood and who knows what veins are in the face.

If he hadn't been sitting on her lap. If he'd been in his own seat, the seat that now holds the rock. If he'd been leaning backwards to stare at the horses out the window. If it hadn't been night. If she hadn't found him wandering the corridors, crying and looking for her, and taken him in her arms out of guilt. If she'd told him to act like a big boy and sit in his own seat. If her arms hadn't remembered to hold him even while she was half asleep, her mind flung back years ago to a place she hasn't even been, to a story that isn't even hers.

Belly's wail turns into a scream and the brakes make a similar noise as the train jolts to a halt. Edie lurches forward, nearly dropping Belly, who is arching his back with the intensity of his screaming.

"You're okay," says Edie. "Shh, shh, baby. Shh, it's okay." Would removing the glass increase the bleeding? Who knows where the veins of the face are? Slim would know: all that first aid training, the tidy language of the manuals. If she leaves the glass, he will surely panic at the sight of himself. But how long can you leave an unclean thing in the bloodstream? But don't many people live their lives with shards of metal silted over underneath their skin? She needs warm water, a towel, some alcohol to clean the wound. Edie looks up at the woman and the woman stares back. They nod together over the sound of their children's hysteria.

Belly tries to grab at his face and she holds his hands together with one hand. "Don't touch," she says. "You're fine." He's not fine. The blood gels around the wounds, rolls thicker than tears down his cheeks, and he keeps screaming and he keeps screaming.

Four soldiers part the crowd that has gathered around their seats. Maybe the same soldier she saw before; she cannot settle on their faces: cannot settle on what she needs to fix this. Warm water, a towel, some alcohol, bandages. She has none of these things, only a canteen of rusty water, only her own clothes soured by sweat.

The soldiers are not even flushed. Someone escorts her away from the glass—a hand between her shoulder blades guiding her—and Edie cannot stop staring behind her at the soldiers as they squat and begin to sweep up the glass using newspapers like housewives, all these minor disasters so mundane for them. Where did they get the news-papers? she wonders. How did they decide what needs to be done?

A soldier removes his handkerchief and wraps it around the shard in Belly's face without asking Edie.

"Just hold it there," he tells her and leaves before she has a chance to ask for further instructions, so she obeys, though Belly is twisting and screaming and she worries she's doing more harm than good. Someone makes an official announcement over the train's loudspeaker, but she can only discern the words *stopping* and *emergency*.

When the porter puts his hand on her shoulder, she follows with-out knowing where she's going, through the crush of people hungry to see a bit of blood.

"Tilt your head back," she tells Belly. "Look up at the ceiling." He's screaming, unable to listen. "Hey. Hey. There's no need to cry. Look up at the ceiling. Hey." She has to force sweetness into her voice. "We're on an adventure, right? Like your father, right? Like your daddy."

She follows the porter out of the train into a night so cold it's like plunging into a fast-moving river. The tightness of her skirt allows her only small, quick steps and she tries hard to keep up. Her stockings provide sleekness but no warmth. "We're just on an adventure. Come on." Her voice is bright and smooth as plastic and Belly must sense the fakeness in it because he looks up at her, blinking, straining against her grip to try to touch his face. Someone—the porter?—covers her and Belly with a blanket. The shard of glass reflects the blood on his cheek, pink in the light.

"Like your daddy," Edie says. "What do you think your daddy would do at a time like this?" Such a long child—his legs dangling to her calves—but he feels weightless. She is strong with fear. Strong with the act of leaving. Belly stares at her. "Come on. Hey, come on. What do you think your father would do at a time like this?"

"Kill. The. Bad. Guys," says Belly matter-of-factly between his sobs. Maybe he is shocked calm by the cold. His red hair is dusty with snow.

"Because do you know where your father is right now? He's gone to the war." Edie looks up, away from her son's bleeding face, but the snowflakes float dizzily above and she must look back down again.

The porter leads them through the station: a clapboard structure, a deck of ice-slicked planks, the name of the depot obscured by night and snow. Across the street, a few other buildings huddle at the edge of the tracks as if for warmth, their shapes muffled by the blizzard.

"He's gone to the war and that's where he is. In the war. Being brave. He wouldn't want you to be crying. He would be proud that a boy like you got out of the way of that big rock." Surprising how quickly the lie comes to her, as if Slim's gift for storytelling is now her own. Saw a rock bust through a window, she thinks. Saw our own son clawing at a shard of glass embedded in his cheek.

Belly considers this. "Flying the airplanes?"

"Exactly. Because the war—see, the Russians. No one trusts them. And your father's a communist like the Russians are communists, so they like him. He flies planes. So we have to be brave. We can't cry. Because your daddy is very brave and now we're on an adventure to see your nana, right? Isn't that right?"

Belly nods and droplets of blood drip off his chin onto her arm. Snow on the blanket caped around him, snow on his lovely red hair. The porter touches her shoulder. She's never been touched by a black man before: had expected a different smell. Something different. He leads them toward the stairs, murmuring warnings of ice.

"My son," she tries to tell him. She gestures him toward Belly's half-ruined face. His lungs are ruined and his face is ruined and even his English is ruined because Edie did not keep him away from the internment camp, packed him along so that she could teach school. Like she is packing him along now. The porter nods.

He pats Belly's shoulder. "When we get you right again, we'll take you to see the locomotive and maybe you can even meet the conductor and try on his hat. Would you like that? To try on his hat?" Though his voice is calm, Edie sees fear and pity in the man's eyes.

Belly nods solemnly. "My dad's in the war," he says. "He's flying a plane."

The porter looks away for a moment. "I'm sure he is," he says. "I'm sure he's really brave too."

Edie glances back toward the train, but they're too far away from the station to see it. She imagines that their compartment looks the same: the luggage on the seats, the half-eaten can of Spam, the toy soldiers. Only the rock and the shattered window it left are new, the glass still rolling with the rhythm of the passengers are likely disembarking, bright in the moon's strange light. Her husband is gone from her life in much the same way. Against her, Belly's sobs have died down to hiccupy snuffles. She is blessed and she is not blessed. She is blessed and she is not.

ANNE

Anne knew something was wrong and cried like a stuck pig before Edie had even left the house. She arched out of their mother's arms, reaching for Edie with each small finger straining. Their mother looked at the ground. Kate gone married, Tom gone to police training, her father gone, now Edie taking off on the next train. A three-year-old and six-year-old twin boys: gifts from each time her father had returned.

"Come along," her mother kept saying to Anne. "Come along now. Your sister's made her choice and she didn't pick you."

Anne cried so hard she started to retch, and Edie wondered how her sister could possibly know. Her vocabulary was limited to a few words, though she had an owl-eyed stare that Edie often interpreted as wisdom. Edie's mother considered children to be psychic because they were not fully moored in their bodies and could slip in and out to other places and times.

"Come along," said their mother. She kept turning as if to leave but didn't. Edie stood at the door prickling in her good hat. In her suitcase: bottles of scent wrapped in old dresses, her few good outfits, the chocolate box of small gifts her father had given her, a vertebra. In those times, no one was expected to have a hope chest.

Anne's screams intensified as Edie closed the door. She must have known. Anne looked like her but wasn't her child. The same dark hair and eyes but wasn't her child. Now, she cannot remember the scene in its entirety. She cannot recall what was said, but she remembers leaving.

BELLY

Something tried to hurt him and did and now his face feels wrong. He was asleep and woke to this and now he hears a big noise and his mom says, "Shh, hush, baby, hush," and the noise is him. Rooms are brighter with broken glass in them. His face. Someone has his hands so he cannot touch the place he hurts. Where are his soldiers in their special bag? He can't see them. He can't see right: the mess of people and bags and the little bits of light all around the room even though it's night. His soldiers like to sleep warm and jumbly together in the soft bag like mice and maybe they were hurt by the glass. By whoever brought the glass and the hurt.

He's up adult-high and his mom whispers in his ear and her one hand around his wrists, and he cannot get down, cannot touch his cheek, cannot ask her what's bad with his face or where the soldiers are because, he doesn't know why, because there is a great noise and it's coming from him, so his throat is full up. He arches his back to dive away from the pain. He cannot hear over his own screaming. There are no words to say what's happening to his face.

EDIE

Standing on the platform with her son heavy and bleeding in her arms, Edie can only stare at the mountains. The early dawn renders them blue shadows that swim in the distance like the afterimages of shapes left on your vision after you've stared at the sun. Already, she feels cupped between these mountains, trapped, imagines herself suffocated by the snow filling up the valley, silting away the houses first, the spires of the church last. If she left now, she wouldn't be responsible for what needs to be done. Someone would mend Belly's ruined face and take him to his grandmother, who would raise him as her own. Edie raised Anne, after all. It's only fair. It's only a type of balance. When you leave one thing, the urge is to keep on leaving.

But this is wrong. A terrible way to think. She should not stare at her son's bleeding face and think of how, if she left now, he would forever associate the scar beneath his eye with her. Perhaps he would think that she cut his face herself to mark him so she'd know how to find him again.

There is nowhere to go anyways, since the snowstorm has reduced her options down to just one: to follow the porter as he parts the snow to make a road for them. She could not put her son down even if she wanted to, since her muscles are frozen in the position of holding him. It's so cold she feels brittle, even with the blanket around her, the kind of cold that gets through whatever you throw in its path. The woollen fabric of her clothing feels stiff as metal against her skin.

All the small wounds on his cheeks and arm are drying brown, but the wedge of glass lodged below his eye still oozes fresh blood against her neck and chest. How much blood can a child lose? How much more will he lose when the shard is removed? He's already pale. Maybe it's just the station's anemic light. The porter leads her down the wooden steps, forcing a path on to the sheaf of snow spread out before them. Belly shakes a little.

"Are we going to a doctor?" she asks.

"Only comes once a month," he says. Or at least she thinks he says. He's speaking over his shoulder into the wind.

Even Ymir had a doctor, though drunk and trembly, though he eventually drowned and no one took his place. "Is there a nurse? Or at least a veterinarian? Or at least some bandages? He needs——" She doesn't know what he needs. She keeps walking.

The porter looks back at her. "Tough boy like this..." His voice is made ragged by the wind and the exertion of pushing the weight of snow out of their path with his legs. The snow is calf high and he walks in sweeping motions, as if he's ice-skating. "You can have him seen when you reach your destination. Courtesy of the Kettle Valley, of course." As if the whole valley was at fault and would pitch in to mend him.

Edie can feel the leather of her shoes becoming soggy and warped in the snow; her stockings, too, are ruined. "Why would you stop here then? What good is this place going to be? Might as well have kept going. At least it's warm on the train." Her voice grows shrill and she feels Belly's shoulders tighten in response.

"Not my decision, ma'am," he says.

Edie is balanced finely on the points of her high-heeled shoes, her feet made stupid by cold. Her arms made stupid by cold. Her brain. (In Slim's ridiculous boots, her bare hands numb around the axe.) She could drop her son at any time. Belly stares over her shoulder, still for now. "Darling?" she asks, suddenly shy at saying his strange name in public. "Are you awake?"

"Yeah." His soft, cracking voice: she wants to hug him closer. Lord knows what the child is thinking. Lord knows how she's managed to calm him. "What do these people do without a doctor?"

"Don't get sick." He stares back at her, his mouth lopsided with a weird half-grin. "Naw, end of the month the doctor does his rounds. Emergencies get driven up to Princeton. Or the train, if there's time. Train comes twice a day. With this snow, though—"

They wade past what must be the main street. A few buildings, their signs hazy with snow. The porter leads them into a hotel: The Coalmont Hotel, it says. A hotel made for the mine, now serving a railroad. Twice a day the train slices clean through the town, takes people, brings food and booze and tractors, disappears. The town waits for it to arrive again. Lord, she is always thinking of trains. She is always thinking of him.

HOW SLIM GOT THAT LIMP OF HIS

A train is like the sea in how it makes a man earn his legs. Like a horse in how it bucks and snorts up mountains. Already, their thighs are bowed and they can thank the deprivation of their stew-and-porridge childhoods for this gift of stability. They are solid as arches, their stomachs brown keystones. A train does not just move forward but side to side, and their bodies have learned not to expect a straight line or an easy course. Watch a man who has walked on the hot, sloped metal of boxcars and you know he will be graceful on roofs, spires, scaffolds, tightropes. If you live long enough atop a moving train, you could waltz through an earthquake.

It's on land that they falter. The rock and sway of wind, the cars coupling and uncoupling against each other lent them grace. The wind and sun passed around them and they remained unsettled. On solid ground, though, they are close to tripping, always bracing for a fall even when they know the sidewalk will stay true. Even when they know that they are not aloft and no flight, no descent can possibly come.

HOW SHE MET HIM

Edie watched with Anne on her hip. A group of men marched down Columbia Street—half a parade, half an army platoon—followed by people with signs. Edie had no idea what they were doing, these men (boys, some of them) marching in rows of four, their bodies thin and long, their shadows thinner, longer. They were no kind of army with ears and necks filthy as that. They grinned with chapped faces: the glow of youth, maybe, or just too much wind, rain, night, cold.

The men nodded to her as they passed, maybe thinking her too young to have a baby, especially since Anne was nearly three and could hardly be called a baby anyhow. Especially since Edie was seventeen. One of the men broke rank and reached out to tickle Anne under her chin, making her giggle and buck. The man—boy, really—looked at Edie with an expression between pity and shyness, then jolted back into the rhythm of the men and their marching.

Some Trekkers had words painted on the backs of their sweaters: *On To OtTaWa! We Want Work and Wages!* Edie thought of the skin underneath the letters. She was seventeen years old and stuck in the house with someone else's baby. All those men, she thought. All those chances with all those men.

Which was the reason she had been saddled with Anne anyhow: her sister had caught her with one of the convicts who tended their garden on the grounds of the cemetery behind their house. As the midwife coaxed the afterbirth out, Edie's mother stared up at the little angels carved on the headboard and said, "You might as well get used to it, Edith." The angels were shining and wax-scented from her mother's nesting impulses a week before, and Edie wondered if the back of her mother's head smelled of polish from where her skull had pushed against the headboard. The baby, too, was slick with something that looked like wax.

When Edie protested that she wasn't even the eldest, why not put the baby in Kate's care since she's already out of school, her mother sighed. "Because Katherine is not a girl like you," she said. "Katherine doesn't need to be reminded."

Anne reached toward the men and Edie shifted the child's weight to a more comfortable muscle. Wherever she went, she balanced that baby on her pelvis that had never cupped another life, on her shoulders and back that had only been caressed on five, maybe six occasions. Sometimes, Anne's feet would kick out in laughter and bruise Edie, reminding her that she is the kind of girl who, if she is not careful, will feel the small, constant pummelling from inside out. It feels like fishes at first, her mother told her, and then like a punch.

The men paraded by: marching, hamming it up for the crowd. Some of them carried cats wrapped in their shirts, some had dogs trotting along beside them, but mostly they were alone. The New Westminster high-school marching band was even out to usher these boys to the park where they camped out. People handed out leaflets advertising a dance and Anne grabbed one, sucking on the paper until Edie took it from her.

Edie knew just by looking at these men that she was that kind of girl. Already, she was thinking dress, talc, that tortoiseshell comb from Kate's drawer, a red mouth and cheeks pinched to the verge of bruising. Already, she was picturing how the conversation might go. "You know, I think," he would stammer, "I think you're really something else." After nights of lullabies, her sister falling heavy to sleep in her arms, Edie wanted to be whispered to. She wanted to be something else.

EDIE

She enters the hotel room and is caught in the gazes of dozens of dead women who stare dreamily out of half-ruined frames. The portraits are crammed so closely together that when the snowy light strikes the right angle, the wall seems made of a blinding sheen of glass.

"The Gallery of Judgment," the hotelkeeper says, grinning at some joke Edie does not understand. "Got them from a burned-down house. A little damaged, but they're still good." Her voice is whiskey-scarred and sharp.

Edie stands at the threshold, soaked through and unable to move, as if her muscles were made stronger by cold and have now slackened. Her arms tremble with the effort needed to carry her son, who has gone still and quiet for the first time this whole trip. The room smells of char and mould. On the wall above the bed, a woman whose eyes are almost translucent stares up at the ceiling, her body dissolving in a patina of smoke damage. The woman's gaze is strange and calm. She seems to be politely looking away from a sight that offends her sensibilities.

Edie takes a step. She takes another. She attempts to lay Belly down on the bed, but he lets out a sudden shriek and clings to her.

"No," he says matter-of-factly. Her legs burn as sensation prickles back into them. (She has seen miners lose toes. She has seen the smooth places where limbs used to be. At picnics, men would pull their feet out of the river to scare the children. Lookit! A fishy took my big toe! Lordy, he's a big fellow! Swallow you whole if he could!) Everything below her waist is ruined: her stockings, her shoes. Maybe the hem of her skirt can be saved, though she imagines it puckered with water damage. Her last pair of stockings, mended with varnish. Another thing the war needed but has now given back; she can buy another pair.

"No, Mommy," says Belly in a soft infant voice. A simple instruction and she obliges. She sits on the bed, which sags to her weight, and pulls him on her lap, unsure of what to do.

The hotelkeeper bustles in and out of the room with an odd, scuttling gait. She has a face that looks like someone carved it out of wood with a pocketknife but wears a dress so low-cut that Edie can see her puckered aureoles, dark as burns. She stares at the choir of framed women who seem to be trying to avoid her gaze. The smoke-ruined glass blots out their full profiles and Edie thinks of the mirror in the tent, how the patina of coal dust would darken your reflection, a different part of your face blotted out with each shift of the wind.

Squirrel-like, the hotelkeeper assembles a heap of supplies on the bedside table. A bottle of whiskey and some glasses ("Something to clean the wound and a little to steady the old hand, eh?" she says). A pot of boiling water ("the chef's specialty"), a needle with royal blue thread, some rags torn into strips, towels, a candle in a pewter holder, glasses of water.

"Ever pierced your ears as a girl?" she asks, resting a hand on Edie's shoulder. She smells of ruined fruit, nail polish. She moves her hand over Belly's head as if healing him.

"Have you done this before?" Edie asks. There should be someone more qualified to heal her son. All she's ever given him is wheezing lungs and a father unconscious on the bed.

The woman smirks. "Poor bairn," she says, stroking Belly's hair. "Such a good little boy too. Quiet as a mouse." She pats Edie again. "You're the mother, love. It's not hard. Like piercing an ear." She wanders toward the door, touching the portraits of the women again, as if smoothing away their disapproving looks. "Poor bairn," she mutters. "Poor little fellow."

"I'm not sharing a room," says the woman standing at the doorway. The blonde girl and her mother from the train, the porter holding their valises.

"Passengers in other cars are sleeping on the train," he says. He sets the bags down. "It's only this car we're bringing in."

"It won't do," says the woman but without conviction. She sounds out each word perfectly, as if forming smoke rings with each syllable. "It won't do," she repeats.

"I'm sure we could find a place on the train for you to sleep if that would be more to your preference," says the porter.

The woman walks in and surveys the room. The skirt of her dress is full, not weighted down by water damage as it swishes against her knees. Her daughter trots along beside her, clutching a wooden airplane and a pillow sewn out of a man's shirt. "I'm Vivian," the woman says to Edie. "And this is my Sadie."

"It's only for the night," says the porter. "Usually we just board up the window and get on our way, but the cold, you know, and the incident." He gestures at Belly.

Like Edie, Vivian is thin, but it's a slimness that looks practised: the result of coffee for breakfast, cigarettes for lunch. Her arms are free of muscle, smooth as wax, and Edie wonders if this woman could mould herself into anything she wanted. (Once, Slim built a steam box and smoked planks he found rotting behind the mine, trying to bend them to the right shape for a house, leaving a campfire scent on their warped bodies. These will be our walls, he'd proclaimed, and Edie wondered if she could ever sleep soundly in a house that smelled of fire.)

"I'm Edie," she says. "And this is Belly."

"Belly? As in the stomach?" She enunciates each vowel as if she's on a stage. "You named your child after a part of the digestive system?"

"William. Billy," Edie says. Vivian bends down to examine Belly, who remains perfectly silent. Blood continues to seep from his wound. "I don't have time for you to mock me right now." She gestures to the shard of glass in her son's face.

"Oh," says Vivian and her mouth makes a perfect *O* around the sound.

Sadie stands beside her mother, her frizzy curls forming a smoky aura around her face. She resembles the women in the photographs with the haze around their cheeks. Sadie stares at Belly.

"You're hurt," she announces. Up close, her dress is stained—grease spots that no one bothered to pre-soak, grass stains from another season—and the knees of her tights have a filigree of small holes.

"My dad's in an airplane," says Belly softly. "He's going to bring me a horse. He's going to drop it from a plane with balloons on its back so it doesn't get hurt when it falls." Edie is amazed at the way he has created a lie to soothe himself. She reaches around him to uncork the whiskey and pour a little on the cloth. "He's flying an airplane and no one can even see him because he's up so high and he goes through clouds and makes holes in them." His voice is thin with pain.

"That's right, and your daddy will be very impressed at how brave you're being," Vivian coos.

Belly is still. With Slim's red hair and her brown eyes, he is such a strange monster made out of the both of them. He's too stubborn to cry. Or maybe there's only so long someone can cry before realizing it's not doing any good. Edie can't figure out what to do. The glass must come out and he'll probably need stitches and the wound must be staunched and cleaned, maybe cauterized, and she must hold him and soothe him, though she lacks enough hands to do all these many things.

"Are you a W-I-D-O-W?" Vivian asks. "Your husband army or navy?"

"My daddy's flying planes right now," says Belly. "And no one can see him."

Vivian leans over to stroke Belly's head and Edie pushes the hand aside. Up close, the woman has a strange scent of talc and roses and sweat. "Oh is he now?" She looks up at Edie. "Is he D-E-A-D?" she asks cheerfully.

Edie nods, lying without saying a word. The shard of glass is not too deep, held in mostly by the handkerchief, but the wound is wide and long.

"Ah, well then. My husband too." Vivian kneels down to Belly's height. "Darling, Sadie's daddy is off flying planes right now too. Far away on a secret mission."

"He flies for RCAF," explains Sadie. "He's been on many dangerous missions and he's won the Germany star and the Air Crew Europe star and the King's Badge for War Service and the Memorial Cross and I have them up in my room at home on a special piece of cloth that's furry."

"Velvet," says Vivian.

Sadie nods and rubs her fingers together. "Velvet. It's lovely to feel."

"My daddy was in a war in Ottawa too before I was even born," says Belly. "And now—and now—and now he's flying a plane."

Edie reaches into her jacket pocket. The bone is there, worn smooth by her fingers. "It wasn't a war. It was a protest march. During the Depression. They took boxcars and—" She gestures. All of the stories she has are fragments. They're nothing anyone would print in a newspaper, just a few fragments, a thread of an anecdote, forgotten punchlines; all of them depend on Slim.

"Mommy's going to have to fix your face," Edie tells her son. "So your job is to hold Mommy's good-luck charm—"

"Can my job be to cut with a knife?" asks Sadie. She leans over Belly, studying the piece of glass as if she's had years of medical training. "Or I could bring the morphine. You have to put a rubber band around the person's arm and that's because you want to veins to get fat so you can get the blood out."

"Don't be dark, kitten," says Vivian. "My sister's a nurse."

Edie offers Belly the vertebra from her pocket. It's soft, a depression smoothed by the indent of her thumb. It has no scent but her scent. No warmth but her warmth. It looks more like a piece of ocean-worn porcelain than something that came out of a human body. Belly holds it.

"For good luck," she tells him.

THE ONLY GOOD-LUCK CHARM WE EVER NEEDED, BY GOD

Arthur-Slim Evans keeps the bullet tucked in his femur like a thimble in a hope chest. His limp reminds everyone that he was at Ludlow and the men tell and retell the story. Took a hit shielding a lady and her baby, eh? Shot five cops—at least five—and they needed twenty more to restrain him. Carried little children to safety, even with his leg torn up, even with the National Guard opening fire, even through the smoke as the coal mines burned, singing "The Internationale" the whole bloody way, that's the way I heard it from Johnny from Division Two and he doesn't deal in tall tales much.

By the campfire, Red Walsh worries his fingers over the shrapnel his flesh kept after the Battle of the Somme, the metal's edges dulled smooth by the rush of blood. He imagines, maybe, that if someone cut him open the shard might stink of diesel, mud, burning horses.

Edie's husband boasts only a few tips of pencil lead in his knee and shoulder, schoolyard bullets as minor as freckles.

One of Matt Shaw's ribs broke in childhood and never healed and there is a spur so hard you could mistake it for metal. The scar where the bone once came free from the skin is round and puckered like a mouth and even when he hasn't showered for weeks it gleams. Slim wonders whether it causes him pain. He can imagine that one day when they are back to normal, some woman might polish it with her tongue.

After the Regina Riot, more of these talismans will be lodged in their muscles, and they will carry them like a lucky coin in a pocket. Grapeshot, billy-club splinter, glass, bullet. Treasures that will ache and predict the rain for years to come.

BELLY

His mom gives him a real shark's tooth to hold for good luck while she is fixing him. It's smooth but has two fangs. Two fangs in one tooth; that's because you need lots of big teeth to be a shark. He holds the tooth in his palm and is surprised when he is not cut by it, but maybe a tooth needs a strong mouth to make it sharp or maybe he has had enough hurt today like how you can have enough food and not want to eat anymore. When he is better he will put the tooth in his own mouth and see what hurt he can do.

Horses have teeth that look like people's teeth, he knows, but if a horse bites you you'll be sore for days; a horse can turn an apple into mush in a second flat; he's seen it up close. Not like people. Belly once bit himself to see what would happen and it didn't even make any blood. Maybe his mouth is not good at hurting because he's too young. When you have a horse you must feed it hay and apples and water and carrots and you cannot feed it bread because that makes horses sick. When his father comes back with the horse, it will be named Mr. Stink but his mom won't like that so he'll call him something plain like Blacky or Joe but will whisper in his big, soft ear, Mr. Stink, Mr. Stink, Mr. Stink, over and over, so only he and the horse would know.

EDIE

They hear music and laughter from the heating vent and it's a strange accompaniment to the work they're about to perform. For a moment Edie thinks that the dreamy women in the photographs are laughing at them, but no, there must be a bar downstairs. Edie stands at the bedside stroking her son's forehead, over and over, as if he was a cat. She's finally gotten him to lie down alone and she wants him to look at her hands and not at Vivian burning the needle clean and ripping a sheet into bandages. She doesn't want him to imagine.

Outside, the light is frozen in a hazy blue: a shade that could be found at any hour. Fear has burned away her hunger and even Belly does not ask for food. Their bodies have no clocks, since the blizzard has silted the sun away and they cannot follow its movements.

Vivian twists the needle into the blue of the flame and removes it glowing, candlelight brightening the film of sweat on her forehead. She pulls the thread from the glass of whiskey it has been soaking in. Booze and candle flames are the only ways to clean in a place like this, Edie thinks. A salve of liquor, antiseptic of fire.

"This nice lady and I are going to fix your face," she tells him. "So Mommy's going to sit on you so she can see right." This seems reasonable to Belly; he nods. Edie straddles her son, holding his arms down and wishing she had an extra arm so she could still stroke him. All the war-rationed stitches on her skirt strain against the movement. He holds the bone tight in his fist and she holds his wrist and they are still. Sadie appears beside the bed and Vivian pushes her away with one arm.

"There's blood," the girl notes. She stands with her feet turned in.

"Go on," says Vivian. Sadie stares. She reaches her finger forward, wanting to press it into Belly's wound. "Kitten," Vivian warns.

"I could wash the blood. I could get the knife. I cut a chicken one time right after it was dead and got to pull its feathers and it didn't have a head but it could still run around."

"Sadie," says Vivian. Sadie looks at her mother, crestfallen, but disappears out of Edie's line of sight. "Okay. You want to pull the G-L-A-S-S and I S-E-W or what?" She brings a chair up to the bed and sits down beside Belly. Edie can't remember asking her to help. Vivian has simply rolled up her sleeves. A war effort of two.

Belly's eyes dart between the two of them, but he doesn't strain against her hands. Edie should be the one to give him all this pain. He's her son. The hurt should come from her touch and then she will soothe him. "I'll S-E-W. Do you think we need to — " She cannot remember how to spell cauterize. "You know, B-U-R-N the edges?"

Vivian looks momentarily uncertain. "I've never — " she begins to confess but instead pushes her curls off her face. "See what it's like when we get in there. Shouldn't need much."

Edie nods. "Close your eyes, Belly love. What will your father say when he finds out how brave you're being?"

"He's flying an airplane," says Belly. "He's bringing a horse." His eyes flick between her hands and Vivian's hands, unsure of who will attack him first.

"That's right. He's a million feet up in the sky."

Edie looks at Vivian; she's so close Edie can smell her sleep-curdled breath. They nod.

THE POULTICE

Her fingertips throbbed with mustard powder. She added water and patted it into a poultice for Slim and Belly's chests. They both lay on the bed with their shirts off, Belly imitating Slim's pose, their chests pale and tender.

She slathered on the mixture with her salve-heated palms, feeling their small bones, their quick hearts.

"It's making a fire on me," cried Belly, squirming. "Mom, it's making a fire!"

"Don't you want to improve your constitution?" Slim asked and Belly nodded, going still.

("Improve my con-sit-itution," he would later beg her during an attack of the wheeze.)

Her husband and son quiet on the bed, a vinegary reek in the air, their chests stained yellow as if with old bruises. When she touched her fingertips to her eyes and teared up, Belly patted her arm, thinking she was crying but not puzzled as to why. The poultice hardened, then cracked with the rhythm of their breathing.

Edie doesn't know why you put a poultice on the skin when the problem is deeper inside. She doesn't know a lot of things, though, but trusted someone when they told her it would help.

I ONCE LOVED A PRISONER AND HE GAVE ME A VERTEBRA AS A SIGN OF AFFECTION

They laid the flooded bones in rows and topped each grave with a small white cross. It was nearly impossible, the prisoner told her, to determine which bones belonged together, since the flooding had jumbled everything up. Like pick-up sticks, he said and smiled crookedly at her. But they tried to lay them out neatly, in equally spaced graves. Toward the end, the prisoners became tired and it seemed meaningless to pretend to be burying whole people when they were really sticking this man's head on that woman's body, creating whole new creatures.

The children's bones were the saddest, said the prisoner. Thin as fish bones. He wanted to do a good job with those and would often cross their little arms over their little chests and put a dandelion or something bright between their fingers. He had a kind, craggy face and looked more like someone's doctor than a real convict.

Each grave was topped with a white cross and none of the crosses had names. None of them had names before in the old graveyard. The prisoner was doing his best, he said. He wanted to do a good job, especially for the babies. Most of them were Chinamen who built the railroad, he said, but some were just dead people no one claimed.

As a child, walking with her mother in the graveyard to feed the crows and offer flowers to the dead, Edie had always searched for the graves of babies, or else stones that contained hints of a love story. She especially loved the old couples who had died within weeks of each other, though her mother maintained that was not the work of love but of the Spanish Influenza. As they walked, Edie would eat raspberries and leave red fingerprints on the whitest stones, imagining that her prints looked like small roses. Time had sanded away some of the names and many stones were hunched inwards, buckled by tree roots. Only the soldiers' graves were decorated with the circumstances of their deaths.

Edie, however, would only leave her flowers by the babies' graves, which were adorned with lambs and tiny cherubs. Some of them were too young to have their own names, so they were buried as "infant son" or "beloved infant daughter." Edie knelt and sang the babies lullabies. A few rows down, her mother was kneeling by a grave, kissing the letters, coming up with moss on her cheeks. Her mother stood, moved to another stone, knelt again. Her face was streaked with mud. Edie ran in looping circles through the headstones, trying not to step on the crusting roses someone else has planted, leaving her fingerprints over other people's names.

EDIE

The handkerchief is clotted with blood and sticks to the shard as Vivian eases it away so that she can remove the glass. "Close your eyes," Edie says. She raises a hand off Belly's wrist to stroke his forehead and he doesn't move. She doesn't need to restrain him. He's looking beyond her, up at the ceiling. He trusts her so much he won't flinch, unable to imagine that she would cause him harm. She's about to put a needle through his face. "We'll be done in a minute and then we can get a treat. You're being a very good boy."

Edie can feel Belly's heartbeat through his wrists. The bone in his hand is white and his knuckles are white around it. When Vivian lifts the shard — the glass giving way with a little sucking noise — Edie raises one hand to hold the towel against the wound and presses firm, thinking of bread dough rising, about how you must beat it down and it swells up against your touch.

Belly gives a single scream. He jerks upwards underneath her but then falls silent, breathing heavily, shaking a little as he looks beyond her. He whimpers again when they pour whiskey on the wound, the blood running in thin streaks amid the liquor and pooling in his ears, and then he is still, his breathing quick and shallow. She looks away from the ragged white edges of the gash and the blood welling up to see his eyes moving back and forth staring at the ceiling. He's crying silently, still shaking, though the rest of his body is so still the tears looks as if they're merely sweat.

Edie can hardly believe her fingers are the ones pressing the needle into his cheek. She must forget that the face she's sewing belongs to her son. She's done this before: for Slim, for his friends after bar fights or the thousand small ways someone could get wounded underground. The doctor was often away on a drunk and the money for doctor's bills was better spent elsewhere. She must imagine her son's skin is wax or cloth. Her hands begin to shake.

The sharp odour of whiskey, the mineral odour of blood. Once, she pressed a whiskey-soaked cloth to Slim's cut shoulder after he fought with Old Jim. He was drunk—so was she—and it was all either of them could think to do. The next morning, dried blood had adhered the cloth to the wound and it bled worse to pull it off. An infection, a week of fever and eight stitches. Hold still, Edie told her husband. One stitch. Hold still, Edie said. Two stitches. And so on. The work was ragged but held fast. I hope you mend dresses better, Slim said. Dresses don't complain, said Edie.

Vivian, this woman she has met only today, holds her hand over Edie's and guides the needle through Belly's wound. An odour of talc, sweet against the smell of whiskey. Vivian's hair is damp with sweat. They are darning her son as if he is a housedress and he lies still as one. Braver than his father. It's the longest she's seen him go without talking in at least a year. He doesn't move, hardly flinches, but when she looks up his eyes are open, staring beyond her in a kind of wonder.

She follows his line of sight. There's a mirror on the ceiling and she can see her skirt bunched around his small body, his stricken face staring intently upwards. He is watching them stitch his cheek. He stares transfixed as the needle dips in and out of his skin. She cannot imagine what he must be thinking.

BELLY

A boy floats on the ceiling. He has the same devil's hair as Belly and cries red tears. Maybe it's a dead little boy, an angel who's come to fix him, and this makes Belly feel calm. The angel boy stares. He is maybe the little boy of the women on the walls. They are dead too. His mom's face floats by the boy's body.

It's only a mirror. It's only his own face. His own devil hair. His own red tears. He can see everything they are doing to him.

EDIE

Edie has her son's blood on her fingertips. He lies immobile beneath her, eyes flicking back and forth, chest rising and falling. Sadie twirls in the corner of the room by the window with her arms extended, making sputtering noises to herself. She flies in tightening circles, careening her arms like wings, then falls to the ground.

"Plane crash!" she explains, lying red-cheeked on the carpet before standing up to do it again.

More music and laughter, the sound of glass being broken. The shard they pulled from Belly rests innocuous on the bedside table, streaked pink with blood and whiskey. Together, they put in the final stitch. Her hand guides the needle, and Vivian's hand guides her hand. Vivian's hair sways against Edie's cheek. They breathe together, many-armed: arms to mend and arms to soothe.

Edie ties off the thread, douses a cloth in whiskey, and presses it to Belly's cheek. She still holds his wrist with one hand and wonders if he can feel her trembling. "That's it, darling. We're done."

Though his eyes look beyond her, he nods a little, tears pooling in his ears. Those tiny seashell ears, the downy hair on them. With her long red nails, Vivian picks smaller shards out of Belly's face and neck. Someone plays a song Edie knows she has danced to.

"I think," says Vivian, "that this is a flophouse."

"What's a flophouse?" asks Belly, the first time he's spoken.

"A naughty place," says Vivian before Edie can answer. "But how else you going to make money in a town like this? Now that the mine's closed up." She gestures to the mirror on the ceiling and Edie looks up. The sight of Belly's pale face with the blue thread garish against his skin almost brings her to tears.

"We'll get you a treat," she says. "You've been such a good boy. Won't your father be just amazed when he sees you?"

He stares warily at her, waiting for the horse he imagines his father will bring. The chunk of spine is still clenched in his fist, a gift he'll have to return to her. What sort of treat could make up for something like this? For all the harm she has done to him?

EASTER SUNDAY

Once, her father came home from work on Easter morning with a scrap of blood-red rabbit fur.

"Bad news," he said. "I ran over the Easter Bunny on the way home from work." Her father had a handlebar moustache that was both ridiculous and scary, like a cartoon villain. Edie and her siblings all started crying and her father laughed for a very long time, then brought out four chocolate bunnies. He lifted the children one by one and tossed them up in the air in their Sunday best.

"Don't worry," he said consolingly. "That old critter was only maimed. Hopped away leaving a trail of pixie dust. Maybe I'll get him next year." He pointed his fingers in the shape of a gun, pretended to fire, winked. "Work on my aim."

Then he laughed again and pressed the chocolate rabbit into Edie's hands.

"Eat up," he said.

THE DAY THEIR EYELIDS FROZE SHUT IT WAS SO BLOODY COLD

Coming through the Crowsnest Pass, their eyelids crust over with soot and ice from the mountain wind forced through the walls of the tunnels. They tie handkerchiefs over their noses and mouths to strain the air, but grit still accumulates on their tongues, an edge of bitterness in whatever they taste for days.

You'd think it'd be warmer because we're closer to the sun being so high up, says one Trekker; it's bloody well supposed to be summer. Matt Shaw tries to explain the principles of elevation and atmosphere, but no one can properly hear him over the wind. He makes an Icarus joke that Edie will later explain to Slim and feel smug for doing so.

Darkness and cold and smoke and darkness and then the train blasts into so much light they must close their eyes against the glare and their tears freeze on impact. Jerry Winters (his brother took the name Bill Summers) panics and forces his eyes open with his fingers and the tender skin tears. All day his gaze is sticky with blood, vision rose-tinted. His eyelashes are gone and pink tears weep down the sides of his nose. Who expects such freezing in June?

Trinket licks Red Walsh's face until his eyes open as if he was a blind newborn kitten. Funny beast, he says. She thinks I'm her kitten, the darned fool.

Matt Shaw is the smartest one, though. He makes Red blow hot air on his eyes until the ice melts into sooty tear trails, then he cups his mouth around Slim's eye. All that hot air comes to good use, Slim says. Sod off, Matt Shaw says. Wanna keep your eyelashes?

One by one, their breath frees each other's eyes, though it is hard to sit still as a man presses his mouth to your face. Still, they work this way down the line of blinded men. One by one, their lips are darkened with a film of ash and oil as they hold each other's faces in their palms, freeing each other with the only heat they can offer.

EDIE

This woman she's just met today has her son's blood on her hands. Vivian leaves fingerprints sticky with Belly's blood on the bedside table and the decanter and Edie watches the prints as if at a crime scene. This, she thinks, is proof of something. Her inadequacy, maybe. Her countless mistakes.

She has the urge to give Belly a bath, but she's disoriented. It could be midnight or it could be noon. And he should eat something, but he should also sleep, seems to want to sleep, dizzy with blood loss. One thing she knows about mothering is to not let the child go to bed with wet hair, especially in winter. Hair keeps in the body's warmth, a nurse once told her, and sleep is like a little death in how it lowers the core temperature. These are the phrases she knows about mothering: *catch your death of cold*; *feed a cold, starve a fever*; *Cleanliness is next to Godliness*. She's swabbed the blood from his face with a cloth and the wound looks small and neat all stitched up, no bigger than a birthmark. Four stitches. Only his shirt is still stained with blood at the collar. He still smells faintly of whiskey.

"Do you want some water?" she asks.

"No." He doesn't look at her, as if he's angry.

"Have some water. You need to drink." Belly glowers at her. She raises the glass to his lips and holds his head up; he resists her touch. "Come on."

"No," says Belly.

"I bet your father would like some water out there in the middle of Russia."

Belly forces his head back down on the pillow. "You don't have to drink water when you go to Russia," he says as if this fact is obvious.

"Fine," she says, trying to keep some gentleness in her voice. "It's here if you want it."

Vivian pours two whiskies for them, both adorned with the sticky whorls of Vivian's fingerprints and Belly's blood. It's an odd coupling, strangely intimate. She wants to bathe her son: has always loved the moment when he emerges new-skinned from the water, his tiny hip-bones glowing wet and the filth sloughed off. She is always amazed by what accumulates on him through the day.

Sadie has fallen asleep by the window with her arms extended, her dress crumpled and metallic-looking in the light. Her clock, too, is off. It's only noon — probably noon — but she's spent too long on trains and in winter's perpetual dark. There are dozens of dead women on the walls, but no clocks. Sadie has fallen asleep in the shape of an airplane, dreaming of flight.

Vivian walks over to the pile of baggage and fishes out Belly's Crown Royal bag filled with soldiers, seeming to anticipate Belly's needs in a way Edie has never thought of. She places them in Edie's lap, then steps over her daughter and peers out the window. Vivian's curls have gone wild during the night on the train and crackle with frizz like her daughter's hair. She sips the whiskey, sets the glass on the sill, then bends to pick up Sadie. Her fingers are newly wet with the condensation on the glass and she leaves a bloody fingerprint on Sadie's arm.

Edie looks back and Belly has the bone in his mouth, the points jutting out between his parted lips. He gags a little but tries to keep it there. Gags and spits it out.

"I'm a shark," he murmurs. "I'll bite you and then you'll be dead."

She has carried that bone everywhere but has never thought to taste it and for a moment she's curious. She imagines, somehow, it tastes of metal and salt. Isn't that what the body's made of? At a company picnic of Slim's once, some boss said the human skeleton is made up of this much iron, this much zinc, this much calcium. You're lucky it's not in greater quantities, he joked, or we'd have you mining yer own arms and legs.

"Bedtime," she says, too cheerfully, and takes the saliva-wet bone he spits into her palm. She peels back the covers and helps him into bed, smoothing his hair as if this was any other night, as if the bedside table is not covered in rags stiffening with blood and whiskey, as if she had not just passed a sewing needle through the skin of her own child. "Bedtime," she says again, and he plays along. She is blessed to have him. She is blessed and she is not.

Beside her, Vivian tucks Sadie into bed and folds the child's arms across her chest as if she was dead. She arranges her daughter's hair, curling a strand around her fingers to smooth its shape. She hums something.

Belly stares bravely up at Edie, the blue thread of the stitches like an insect on his face.

"It tickles," he says. Still, she cannot believe his calm. Take a toy away from him and he twists himself into a spine-arching fit. Didn't he whine just last supper when there was no mustard for his Spam sandwich? But now, faced with real pain, he stares straight ahead and lets her stitch his face with nothing to numb the skin. She cannot remember being four years old. She cannot imagine how his brain works.

Edie offers him his soldiers and he's happy to trade her good-luck charm for his own. Lying on his back, he twirls the soldiers around in his hands as if they're falling from a great height in slow motion. Quickly, he's far away in the planet of his own make-believe, murmuring in words she knows are not English. With one soldier in each hand, he knocks his fists together as if trying to draw sparks. Some of his soldiers are metal and some are wood. Even at the height of the war effort she never made him give up the metal ones, figuring that their family's lack of a proper home was contribution enough. What kind of solid plane, she wondered, could be made out of a boy's tin soldiers?

"I'm not sad when the soldiers die," he says, looking up at her. "It's mean to make them die, but I'm not sad." She can't read his expression.

"It's just pretend. You can make them alive again."

He stares upwards, as if looking half at her and half at his own reflection on the mirror above the bed. "I'm sad when I pretend horses die. Even when I know it's just pretend."

"Maybe you should pretend happier things."

His scornful gaze looks as if he's copied the expression from the women on the walls. The wind's picked up and the room seems to sway a little, as if they're still on the train. "Sometimes I pretend you die," he says.

She has no idea how to answer him. "Want to know what your daddy is doing right now?" she asks and tells him before he has a chance to speak.

THE STORY OF THE SECRET WAR

Well. They took him away to a special place in Alaska that's up so far north that there isn't any sun in the wintertime. They took him there to train him and all morning every day he had to learn how to fly. His legs were so long they had to make him a special plane, but no one minded because he was just the right man for a special mission. A long plane for your daddy, so he could fit, with a special seat and a special helmet and special long black boots. Shiny new boots. The plane was so thin and light it was almost magic and hardly even left a shadow when it flew across the snow. It was painted grey and white like a horse because in Russia the sky is always cloudy. Living in Russia is like being in a cloud because of the sky and the snow. So flying takes up the morning. Your daddy flies and flies: right ways up and upside down. They can hardly get him down out of the plane, he loves to fly so much.

In the evenings, an old man comes to teach him Russian. It's a strange language, sounds like someone coughing, which is perfect for your father, you know, with his cough, with the way his lungs are. And he's a Communist and the Russians are Communist, so he knew a lot of the words already. Communism is like another language. *Bourgeois, proletariat, manifesto, feudalism.* He knows all the songs. They don't have to teach him those. You know those songs too.

And pretty soon, any day now, they're going to send him into Russia. He's going to fly away in his skinny plane and touch down in the middle of the snow. Your father has a special talent for withstanding cold because he's spent so much time down in the mine. He can get himself out of all sorts of messes.

ANOTHER SPECIES

The children's eyes are too big for their skulls. Their dresses were not made for them: pulling or sagging, their colours weakened into a dishwater hue, paisley faint as grease stains. Impossible, think the Trekkers, that we might one day father one of these creatures. They feel like creatures themselves, bedding down on straw and concrete, barns where the necks of cattle have been slit. They awaken with the pattern of a drain bruised into their backs, marked by the places where blood and shit once flowed.

Endless card games. Matt Shaw and Slim talk into the early morning. Slim talks, Matt Shaw sips tea with pilfered honey because he is the face of the Trek and also its throat. He sings their story into microphones that have faces big as drain covers. On the spot where cows have been slit, the men wrap themselves in their many sweaters and talk about the children they see lining the parade routes. Babies with their limbs jerky as silent film reels. Children with their fat, staring eyes. Go too long without the sight of something and it will look alien. Women, too, are from another planet.

BELLY

Once when he was little, Belly carried a cat under his shirt for a very long time. The cat was warm and had no claws and felt nice there. His name was Mike. Mike the cat. It was a good name for a cat, and Mike cuddled against him and told him that cats like to eat mice and also pie. Then one day he went to school and was running at lunch break and Mike fell out from under his shirt on to the ground.

"What's that you got up your shirt?" one of the boys asked, getting ready to laugh at him. Belly looked down at the flour sack stuffed with socks and said he didn't know. It was a mistake, he told them. He looked down and saw how wrong he was. Mike didn't even have eyes. No whiskers or ears or paws or pink scratchy tongue.

The boys all nodded. They didn't laugh and Belly ran off with them, sad to leave Mike there, even though Mike wasn't a real cat. His mom took the socks out of Mike and was sore because she had to wash them. Often, Belly hears yowling when he's trying to sleep, which his dad says comes from real cats, wild cats, tearing each other's fur out at all hours of the night.

Now, his dad is far away and cannot explain the noises Belly hears. His dad flies a plane named after a horse, painted up like a horse, and is so skinny that people can't see him when he's far away until he opens the stomach of his plane and the bombs come out like poops—*poop!* He loves to say it—and all the Russians are dead forever.

EDIE

"Might as well wash up," whispers Edie, thinking less of water and more of music. The muffled lyrics are maddening now that the room is silent. She knows that song.

The wind has picked up and gusts of snow slap against the window. Through the vents: a keening sound that may be part of the music or may be the wind over the hotel's gaps and crannies. Outside, the snow has slowed and the landscape burns in strange whites and greys, reminding Edie of her hunger. She wants some white bread with a tang of mustard, some Spam in between. Vivian nods.

Belly is asleep, having dozed off to her lies. He has his arms folded across his chest, the head of a toy soldier poking out of each fist. Such a long day. He'll sleep until morning, whenever morning is. That's all the medicine children need, she thinks. Just to sleep.

As they open the door, music fills the hall so suddenly it's as if they've lifted the lid to a music box.

"'I've got my love to keep me warm,'" says Edie.

"From that movie," Vivian says.

Saw a whorehouse decorated with prissy dead ladies, Edie thinks.

Saw a rock the size of a dog nearly crush our son's head.

Saw a needle coming up through our son's face and him not even screaming and bright blue thread against his pale cheeks, braver than you were.

═╪═╪═╪═╪═

The bathroom wallpaper is paisleyed with mould and reeks in a way that allows only mouth breathing. On a rust-stained sink, a pretty little cake of soap shaped like a shell dissolves into grey sludge. The water runs brown, then yellow, and Edie and Vivian submerge their hands together under the spout. Silent, they dry their hands on the fronts of their skirts, since the towels the hotelkeeper gave them have been used to mend Belly. Some of Belly's blood has dried on the front of Edie's jacket, but it is hardly visible on the black fabric. She wipes the blood from her collarbone and neck. The bloodstain on the collar of her blouse can be hidden by her hair.

The water that fills the white basin with a yellowish hue reeks of metal and Edie wonders if it must be boiled before drinking. The tap sputters, the jaundiced water falling down. It smells of moss and metal and stone. A mine scent: ruined water. Nothing is clean in this place. She sniffs her wet hands: copper, rust. They are clean, but still they stink of blood.

ZINCTON, BRITANNIA, SANDON, YMIR

Men leave their scent on the river, tarnishing the water with mine runoff. All mills—lumber, ore, paper—squat over water. The mines are named after women, but no women are allowed inside. It is bad luck. Many things—dropping your clothes, not leaving your sandwich crusts in the mine's corners—are bad luck. It's been years since Edie's sat on a ledge of rock eating a sandwich as if in a boy's secret tree house, since she fit her fingers into the drill-mark grooves raked along the walls.

The processor jawed on day and night, so she couldn't even hear her apartment being ruined by the force of water from the frozen pipe burst in the walls. Of course the ore had to come out—she knows that—but she wishes they didn't need to be so loud.

During the school Christmas play, the processor clanked.

"Hark! I hear the sound of wise men coming," the child actor called, his bath-towel turban slipping down over his eyes. The processor's stamping filled the silence. "They sure have loud feet!" said the child, saving the moment.

SAW

"Saw a man with gold teeth who slept with his mouth bound up with rope so no one would steal them in the night," Slim would tell her.

"Saw folks getting baptized in a river, coming up with pond scum on their white clothes, and then everyone started singing."

"Saw a fellow who'd lost part of his jaw who was running a store that sold peppermint drops and taffies and the like and he made out like a bandit because people would come in just to see his face. It made them hungry, how he couldn't properly eat."

And then what? And then? Edie has spent ten years trying to fill in the blanks in everything Slim has ever told her, trying to force him back into the story.

EDIE

Neither of them says drink or food or music. Neither of them says, "But the children…" or "What if he takes a fever?' or "Did we lock the door?" They simply follow the music, charmed, down the hallway. As they pass a half-open door, Edie sees two people pressed against each other in the threshold. A woman kissing with her eyes open watches them as they pass before the man reaches out to close the door.

Edie wonders if all the rooms feature the same portrait gallery that now watches over the children. Eyes meant to stare at you, to reflect the moon's spotlight on your naked body. Someone plays "You Won't Be Satisfied." The sound of broken glass, a cheer, laughter.

When you leave one room, the urge is to wander down further halls. The urge is to keep leaving.

HOMECOMING

Once, she paced hallways with her newborn sister screaming. The formula was warming on the stove and the kitchen filled with its rotten-sweet stink. She was about to test the milk on the tender part of her wrist — baby thrown over her shoulder like a rag, bottle in one hand — when the door opened. Her father.

Edie froze in the slice of light the door carved. Anne stopped crying.

"How are my girls?" he whispered.

"I don't know," said Edie, suddenly angry. "How are they?"

It was too dark to see if her father flushed. Though he was not in uniform, he laid his coat on the radiator and a dusty, mothball scent rose up. Anne stared in her father's direction with her eyes that could not focus at that distance yet. She looked stunned by the sound of his voice.

In his sock feet, her father passed them down the hall. He touched Anne's forehead as if in blessing, then patted Edie's shoulder.

"Goodnight, Bessie," he said. "Be good." He had nicknamed her after the cow he loved as a child. She warmed the milk against the mesh of veins on her wrist. He plunged into the darkness of their mother's bedroom.

HER MOTHER

Enough of her father and all the times he returned and left and returned and left. She can hardly keep track of his many absences: the two major ones, but many smaller wanderings. Like Slim, she supposes, though her father had no trauma to drive him from home. There was no good reason for him to go — many men carried out affairs during the day and returned to carve the roast at the family dinner table in time for supper—but he left and her mother allowed him to return and he left again.

She knows she should think instead of her mother but can't. Her mother is not even an anecdote because she was always there, steady to the point of inertia. The only life story she had was "he went away and went away and I waited for him."

Bread dough swelled under the damp cloth and she pounded it down and it rose again and she pounded it down and it rose.

Her mother staked out the garden like a homestead, plucking the twine to make a long, howling music. The roots feed from the graveyard, she said, best tomatoes in town; no one can say a word on my tomatoes.

Smoked cigarettes. Rolled them herself. Fingers yellowed as if someone had stained them with a poultice.

She was so skinny that pregnancy didn't soften her angles. You could almost see the face of the unborn child pressing out from inside her. You could feel its little fists and feet pummelling her down.

Her mother threw scraps of bread and oatmeal on the carport roof because the crows took souls to heaven and we should honour them like small gods.

"Look," she hissed as the baby's head crowned. "Look." Edie did and for a moment saw Anne's head bloody coming home from between her mother's black wings.

EDIE

Pulled still as if by a thread toward the end of the hallway, away from the room where her son sleeps. Neither of them says, the children, a long day, much-needed rest, a strange town. Neither of them says, torn stitches, fever, nightmare, blood loss, blood poisoning. The carpet is worn down to its fibres in the middle, brown as a dirt road, and the wallpaper is a mossy green. The carpet stops short of the stairs and she thinks of Slim, of the ice-slicked, broken road disappearing under snow. Small, animal rumblings in her stomach, dollar bills in her bra warmed and softened like cloth by her sweat.

Edie slips her wedding ring off her finger. It slides easily, lubricated by the residue of soap still on her hands. She had meant to do this earlier. She imagined herself flinging it from the train's window but decided to keep it, since it could fetch a small price. Now that she has left the bone on the bedside table, it feels nice to have some charm in her jacket pocket to worry her fingers against.

From downstairs, the Victrola plays "In the Mood," and as she reaches the banister and looks down to the lobby below, she can already see the shapes of people dancing, the whores bright as em-broidered roses.

THE STORY OF THE WEDDING RING

Often, she tried to imagine Slim's mother, the way girls try to picture the faces of their children long before they are conceived.

"Farm. Drought." Slim shrugged when she asked him why he left. What else was there to say?

His mother must have given him the ring to pawn, but he'd kept it all these years. It was worn thin, dented in places as if the hand that had hosted it had deflected blows.

"It'd like to meet her," Edie said.

"One of these days," he said, which meant no, and sure enough even after Belly was born they never visited.

Sometimes Edie sees her, though. Slim's mother looks up from hanging laundry on the line, wipes the sweat from her brow and stares in the direction her sons departed from. Her copper hair has turned silver with the alchemy of dust storms.

THAT TIME THEY WERE WAITING TO HEAD OUT AND ONE POOR BASTARD COULDN'T TAKE IT ANY LONGER

Slim does not see the boy because he is warming his hands on the mouths of cattle in the livestock car. Too busy with their snuffly hot breath on his palms, bristles probing his hands. He walks back and forth across rows of muzzles pressed between the slats, letting them lick the chill from his fingertips. Their ladylike eyes, their long eyelashes, the scent of straw, their shit acidic with fear.

The cattle stamp and low, their mouths always moving. Slim remembers—What? Living on a farm? Watching the dusty hides of the Holsteins turn red gold with sunset? Masturbating in the barn loft to the image of the ruddy-cheeked girl a few farms over? Edie cannot imagine.

Each cow sucks on his fingers to taste some salt or mineral tang before realizing that Slim tastes only of the saliva of the previous mouths and so lose interest. Their mouths and tongues are strong as limbs.

Slim moves from cow to cow with cupped palms—offering them nothing, offering them nothing again—as the boy walks across the railyard staring straight forward, right into the path of the oncoming train.

BELLY

He was not asleep when they left. He watched them go. The bed is so wide, bigger than the train's aisles; in the train he could reach his arms out and nearly touch both walls and now even if he stretches as far as he can he doesn't touch the edge. In her own bed, the girl turns to look at him and Belly gets a shock when he sees her eyes are open. Once, he saw the eyes of a raccoon—"Foul nasty critter," says his dad—in a bush, and the feeling is like that. For the first time, he starts to cry, but the crying stings his face and that makes him cry harder. When you cry long enough you get a tired feeling, like you've been in a warm bath, and then you sleep. Crying, too, is a way to call his mom back from wherever she has gone. She can always hear his crying better than she can hear when he's trying to tell her something. Sometimes when his mom and dad were fighting, he would make himself cry for no reason just so they'd stop.

Already, Belly is thinking of what nightmares he'll tell her he had so that she'll feel bad for leaving. It's a trick that has always worked on her, whenever she's gone and he wakes up without her. It makes her give him apple slices or new soldiers. A monster ate horses and you weren't there, he'll say. But that makes him cry harder, thinking of dead horses. A hoof sticking out of a monster's mouth! Dead horses are terrible things to imagine, but he can't help it; it's like someone else puts pictures behind his eyes.

His mom doesn't come. Instead, the girl Sadie stands beside his bed. She pats his head and he thinks again of horses, live and dusty horses, their eyes big as Belly's fist.

"You're sad," the girl says. "It's okay. You're not bleeding anymore. Perhaps you're hungry. My mother says that when I get hungry, I'm like a bear. I'm hungry. My mother packed some sandwiches. We bought jam at a store."

Belly cries so hard he hiccups. When his mouth opens too wide it makes his face feel like someone's pulling it apart.

"Oh, you're sad," says the girl. She pats his head. He's not sad. He's not hungry. He's something else. There are no good names for what he feels.

At the sound of footsteps, Belly gets ready to say about the monsters he's seen, the dead horses, but the footsteps pass and he forgets
what he was going to say. He makes a fist around his soldier. Thinks
of monsters. Invents all the nightmares he will tell her when she
finally opens the door.

EDIE
It's late afternoon but it feels like night, and they are between destina-
tions in a nowhere town half buried with snow. The day is wrecked,
the night punched through by a rock. What's left to do but have
a drink? Below the banister is a large open room with a bar and a
dance floor and low round tables. Dazed soldiers and civilians clutch
drinks or hunch over plates of food. The room has the night smell of
whiskey and the day smell of toast.

A Victrola perched on a piano jerks out "In the Mood" across the
dance floor. Above, a ruined chandelier, its glass crystals darkened
with smoke, sends a guttering light across the room. Women with
their chests powdered white, as if a fine layer of snow had fallen on
them, snake through the tables patting arms, tossing glances, skim-
ming their fingers along smooth surfaces. They have red mouths and
smoky eyes made darker by the fire-stained light.

"I was right," hisses Vivian, triumphant. "Those are ladies of the
night! I just knew it!" She takes Edie's hand as if they're debutants and
they descend the stairs.

The wall-sized mirror behind the bar is spangled with sunbursts
of cracks, some the size of a fist, one in the exact shape of someone's
skull, so that when the hotelkeeper stands in front of it she looks
haloed. The top of the mirror is fringed with heavy bronzed cherubs
holding up a scalloped pattern meant to resemble stage curtains, and
all the dancers in the bar are reflected in it as if they're in a play.

The mirror projects a larger crowd in the room, doubling the couples dancing and the soldiers perched on their stools, everyone living two lives at once. Edie's own face swims in the mirror's warped reflection. Vivian's too. Edie can hardly bear the sight of her own smooth face when her son sleeps upstairs beside a wedge of glass that was once tucked against his cheekbone. She should be there at his bedside. She should be there — she knows — but hasn't she sat too long with her legs prickling under his weight? Doesn't she deserve this? A plate of food? A moment to go dancing, have a drink? And anyways, he's asleep. Getting the rest he needs to heal.

Her face wavers in the mirror, bluish in the room's strange light as if she's trapped under ice. Doesn't she deserve this? A moment to clear the reek of blood from her nostrils with a drink?

Vivian and Edie sit at one of the tables.

"Goodness," says Vivian. "Let's get us a drink," announcing it to the whole bar.

"We should eat something," says Edie.

Vivian laughs out loud, then remembers her snaggletooth and holds a hand to her mouth. "Ah, but drinking on an empty stomach is so much *cheaper*."

Edie moves to summon the hotelkeeper, but Vivian touches her hand. "Wait," she says and flicks her dress's top button to release it. She tilts her head in a direction so the button can catch the light. Edie and Vivian sit at a table between the bar and the dance floor, Edie facing Vivian, Vivian looking out at the rows of soldiers with a little smile.

"I said *get* us a drink, not buy us a drink," she says. Winks again. "You can buy the food. I'll share whatever you get. Let me take care of the drinks. So," she says, leaning forward so Edie can see the freckles spattered on her chest. "How long has it been?"

"Since?" asks Edie. The hotelkeeper moves against the bar's mirror, past the places it has been cracked, haloed, then not. In the mirror, Edie can see a bald spot where the weight of her bun has likely rubbed. She's hunched forward by the weight of her breasts.

"Since your husband," says Vivian. "How long has it been? Since — you know." Already they are a kind of blood sisters: an arc of droplets of her son's blood still on Vivian's chest, like freckles. The hotelkeeper comes by to take their orders.

"We've got eggs and hash brown potatoes. That's all," she says.

Edie nods. "That's fine."

"Scrambled," says the hotelkeeper. "The eggs are scrambled."

Edie nods.

"Running low on bread. Wish the good Lord would have whispered in my ear that I was going to get a train-full of people at my door. Only He knows what we'll do come supper. Doesn't look like the train's going any place. Conductor wants to wait out the storm. Unload the whole bloody train into my hotel."

"So we're stuck?" asks Edie.

"At least until morning," she says. "Now where's that poor little mite of yours? I might have a sweetie somewhere to get the taste of all this hurt out of his mouth."

"He's sleeping. I'll bring him down when he wakes."

The hotelkeeper eyes her. "Poor little bairn," she scuffles off, muttering. "Trains do take a toll on the poor, poor children."

Once the hotelkeeper is gone, Vivian leans forward again and touches Edie's arms. "Your husband," she says. "So he's passed on?"

"He's dead," Edie says, looking at Vivian's eyes. (Slim's lips blued with cold, the windows open on the coldest day of the year. So, yes, he very well could be.)

Vivian leans in closer.

WHAT SHE COULD SAY

He stood at their apartment door dressed in his uniform. For once he looked right in clothes; the uniform straightened his posture, the epaulettes gave his shoulders shape. He tried not to be flushed with pride as Belly ran in circles around him saying, "Will you shoot a Nazi, will you see any tigers, are there tigers in Europe, what about lions, if you shoot a Nazi will you get a medal, what kind of gun do you have, can I see it, I won't fire it, I just want to hold it, I just want to point it at the wall." He had so many questions he didn't have time to pause for their answers. "Will you bring me a medal when you come back, will you bring me some chocolate, are tigers only in warm places, what about lions?" Finally, Slim enclosed her and Belly in a hug and his arms were long enough to take them both in. He was down on one knee and Edie felt childlike with her head against his neck. They were silent like this for many minutes, though Edie could almost feel the questions spinning around in Belly's head.

Where has she seen this scene? From a poster, she realizes now. The man tender and regal, the woman's face dissolving out of its stiff upper lip, the child's inability to comprehend how long his father will be gone. It was a war bonds poster. And underneath, the words *Buy More to Bring Them Home*.

MY DEAREST EDIE

The week before Slim went to enlist, every movement he made was as posed as a snapshot, as if he wanted her to remember him from every angle. He told stories at a frantic clip and even imagined out loud the letters he would write her from the front. Doing this, he decided, would plant the sound of his voice in her brain, and when she finally received the letters months later, she would feel him beside her. It would be like a telephone call.

So they lay on the bed with the shadows of trees moving like clouds against the tent's canvas, their hair smelling of woodsmoke from the potbellied stove and he told her of the things he would see.

"My Dearest Edie," he would say, and here he would stroke her stomach, as if to convey the emotion of dearness. "Today, we advanced a few hundred yards on the Huns; no one could stop our tanks, which went fiercely across the land firing at will, like prehistoric beasts. The food is decent and we sure are grateful for the socks and cigarettes and chocolate you send from back home, which greatly sustains us in our work. Do send pictures of William Junior and yourself, as I miss you terribly and suspect that the boy has grown to a proportion that defies my expectations. Much love," and here, he stroked her stomach again, "Slim."

As the night went on, the letters increased in their silliness, and they were forced to admit that although the idea was a good one, it was maybe not so practical. "Dearest Edie, We are close enough to the Germans to smell them: twenty-five miles or so, ha ha!" "Dearest Edie, I miss all the parts of you that cannot be named without making the censor blush."

That morning, she made him pancakes with blackberries from their yard and bacon from a neighbour's pig and coffee with cream, trying to fill him up with their home despite the fact that he would not even leave for basic training until several weeks after he was drafted.

After he had eaten, he kissed her on the cheek and left. "My Dearest Edie," he said and smiled, already daydreaming of the heroics he would narrate. Edie did the dishes, thinking of his favourite stories — the story of the dandelions, the story of Trinket the cat — thinking of every time he left them for weeks on end, and knew that the war would do him good. He was built for marching. It was maybe all he wanted. She watched her young son sleeping with his sweet little mouth hung open and felt a brief panic and a desire to smother her child, which frightened her so she went outside and cried until she felt better. She would prepare a party on the weekend to celebrate his leaving.

When she came home from a trip to the town to pick up supplies, she was met with a smell halfway between woodsmoke and what she imagined war might smell: something burned wrong. Something clean but not. It was Slim, scalding his hand with lye, his skin crisped with chemical burn brown and thin as old paper. Rejected: his lungs, his politics, his age, his criminal record. They'd written an *X1* on his hand, as if he were some manner of livestock deemed unfit for sale.

She knows she ran to him, knows she tried to douse the wound with water. Was Belly crying? Was she? What was the expression on Slim's face? Now, it seems important to remember these moments, so that she may one day tell them to Belly when he's older, so that she can have a list of good reasons to tell her mother when they arrive in New Westminster. We left because. We had to because. It is all for the best because.

Even through the burn, Edie could faintly see the blue letters on Slim's hand, as if the failure had been inked into the muscles and tendons below. It seemed likely that Norah would have tended to him — she was, after all, a nurse — and someone — Edie? Norah? Slim? — was embarrassed. Yes, she remembers feeling embarrassed.

BELLY

"You're hungry," announces Sadie. "And that's why you're sad."

In a wicker basket, she's found two sandwiches wrapped in wax paper. The paper has little beads of red jam on it. Sadie lays the two sandwiches on the bedside table, unwraps them and inspects them. Where she holds the sandwich, her thumb leaves a red mark through the bread. It's store-bought bread! Belly knows because of its perfect shape, like no one even touched it, like it came from a special bread tree. He's so thirsty that his lips are stuck to his teeth, but the sight of the bread and the jam—Belly's heard there's store-bought jam but has never seen it and doesn't know if Sadie is saying the truth—brings up the spit.

"You can't eat it yet," says Sadie when he reaches for it. "We have to say grace and wash our hands." She sucks the jam from her finger.

"You didn't wash your hand when you touched the sannich and then you licked your fingers."

"It's *sandwich* with a *d* and a *w*," says Sadie, but she considers Belly's point. "Let's pretend we washed our hands so Jesus doesn't mind. Come here. Hold your hands up." She holds her hands under an invisible stream and Belly follows. "Now make a noise like this," she says and makes a hissing sound that sounds more like an engine than water and rubs her hands together. Belly copies her, hissing and hissing, feeling like a cat washing its paws. This one time, he saw a cat washing its paws, then running them over its head, and this other time he saw a cougar, which looked like a mean cat but had its tongue hanging out because he was shot dead and strung up by his back paws outside the cookhouse.

Outside the window, the snow looks like soap flakes and he imagines putting his hands in them so they'd really be clean. He face is sore and when he hisses he feels a little tugging. He had a cat named Mike once, but he wasn't a real cat at all.

"And now say the Lord's Prayer."

"That's for bed."

"No! It's for food too! And anyways, we were supposed to be in bed and no one made us say our prayers so Jesus is probably quite cross. Get down on your knees." She points at the place he should kneel. "I want to make sure you do it right. Sometimes you don't say your words right."

"It's not bedtime." He feels mad tears coming up. He hates this girl with her weird doll face and how she stands up all straight and tries to look nice but is really so, so mean. If he had a cougar, he would tell it to bite her on the neck.

"How do you know?" And she's right. Outside, it looks like no time at all. It's not dark enough to be night, but it's not daytime because you can't even see the sky. The snow has taken all the weather away and no one knows when to say their prayers.

Sadie dangles the sandwich over his head. Jam runs down her wrist. "It sounds like *someone* doesn't want the sandwich," she says in a mean-sweet voice. "Sounds like you want to go to bed without your *supper*, young man!" Belly reaches for the sandwich but he's too small and she yanks it away from him with a giggly scream. "You can't have it!" She laughs. "Not until you say your Lord's Prayer! I'm the mom right now and you can't have it!"

"I was going to say it! I never—I never—I never said I wasn't!" Sometimes when he's mad his words get tangled up in his brain and this makes him more mad.

"My auntie says that people who don't believe in Jesus will end up roasting forever and she's seen loads of dead people because she's a nurse. She doesn't even like to be a nurse for a man who hasn't taken the Lord into his heart, and she says it's a terrible shame my mother doesn't take me to church, but my mother has to work and says if my auntie's so sold on me being a good little Christian soldier she should take me herself." The jam runs down her arm like a snake. "This one time, a man got both his arms cut off and they had to burn the wounds so he wouldn't lose all his blood. And this other time, a man's guts fell out and they had to put it back together but he died anyways. Lots of times they try to put them back together but they die anyways."

The sandwich looks like it has a bruise from where her finger was. Sadie licks the jam from her wrist and gets a smear on her cheek. "One time I went to Sunday school and the lady there said I could be in a play, but I didn't get to go back. My mother has to work very hard, but when my father comes back she won't have to and she's going to have a career in the pictures or radio advertisement. She's not sure which one."

Belly gets down on his knees in front of the bed. "'Our father who art in heaven,'" he yells. He wants her to shut her silly mouth. It feels like he has rocks in his stomach and they're moving all around like how when you look in a river you see rocks moving over and over. "'Hallowed to be thy name.'"

Sadie smiles at him with her jam-smeared mouth. Belly isn't going to tell her about the jam. See how pretty she looks now, with jam all over her face! "You can just say the rest in your mind," decides Sadie, giving him the sandwich.

The bread is like warm snow and the jam is so sweet that he can hardly believe it and there's a layer of butter in between and he's never had a better sandwich in his whole life. One time, his dad didn't have jam for two whole years when he lived in the work camps and when he had it again his head almost blew up from all that sweetness. Belly eats around Sadie's thumbprint like he'd do if it was a wormhole on an apple, but then he's hungry so he eats the thumbprint whole, when Sadie's not looking. Sadie takes small bites like a mouse, spreading the wax paper on her lap so she doesn't get messy, even though she's got jam on her face. His poor dad: two years without jam and who knows what kind of food they have in Russia. Probably lots of fishes and no jam at all. Russia doesn't seem like a very good place to him. Maybe they eat bears. Maybe they have special animals Belly's never even heard about.

EDIE

They share the clots of scrambled eggs and hash brown potatoes crusted with salt and pepper. Vivian's mouth soon becomes lipsticked with grease. A group of soldiers appears at their table, mild-mannered as waiters. They set gin rickies in front of Edie and Vivian. "For your troubles," one says, without specifying exactly what troubles he's referring to. He touches Vivian's arm.

She smiles at him. "You're very kind. And after all you've *done* for our *country*." Each word spoken as if on the radio: her reflection caught between the bronzed stage curtains of the mirror.

Edie sips the drink. The whiskey has ruined her taste for sweetness and the drink is cloying, but she smiles anyway. "Thank you," she says. She skims her fingers across the elbow of the soldier beside her. Thinks of the limbs from all the many soldiers swaying like fronds in the Pullman car. "We're having a chat right now, but in a few moments we'll need dance partners."

It is not so hard to remember what she used to say. The soldiers nod, retreating to a little knot of men at the back of the room.

"Cheers," says Vivian.

"Cheers," says Edie. They clink glasses, as if there was a reason for a celebration.

"So your husband," Vivian says. "You were saying."

The lie spools out easily in front of Edie. "It's complicated," she says. "He signed up under someone else's name. He'd been rejected the first try on account of some arrests. He was on the On to Ottawa Trek of '35, arrested during the riots in Regina, spent some time in prison—not long and the charges were trumped up, but long enough to get blacklisted—and they didn't want him. So—I don't know how he went about it—but one night he says, I'm shipping off to training next week, and off he goes and soon I started getting visits from an old lady, turns out he'd used her dead son's name, or the name of a friend, it was ridiculous — you can't imagine — but we got money and letters until one day we didn't." She raises the glass to her lips and the burn of alcohol changes her voice into a huskier one. She shrugs. "The old woman never even got official confirmation that — " She gestures. "We heard it from letters a friend wrote back. It's been eighteen months."

Vivian nods. She stares right at Edie, thrilled. "So you're in a bad way then. You can't get the pension until you prove he's dead or MIA and prove he was your husband to begin with."

Edie nods.

"You'll have to get a job. And if you can't prove you're a widow — " she trails off, eyes bright with excitement. "You're in a really bad way."

It all makes so much sense: Slim off under another name, gotten himself killed with his taste for adventure. She must remind herself of Slim unconscious in the axe-scarred apartment, the wood buckling with water damage, the Victrola croaking out a warped melody. "We'll survive," she says. "I'll get a job some place," and for a moment she believes this too.

"What about you?" she asks, leaning closer into Vivian's sweet and dusty scent.

She is gone from Slim and has no good reason. Not a single mark, and Lord knows how many women she's met must come up with stories about how they received this bruise, that puffy lip.

Slim was not mean, he was just gone and then she was gone. She could still pass this leaving off as a trip to see her mother. A new perspective, she would say, a breath of fresh air. Even Slim would think it was planned. They would write it up in *The Observer*: "Mrs. William MacDonald and her son William Jr. journeyed from Ymir to New Westminster to visit her mother. Along the way, young William Jr. was wounded by a rock that crashed through the window while the family slumbered. Mrs. MacDonald was forced to play surgeon and gave her son four stitches in the pioneer spirit those who reside in this realm of the nation are required to possess."

THE PIONEER SPIRIT THOSE WHO RESIDE IN THIS REALM OF THE NATION ARE REQUIRED TO POSSESS

Cupped within mountains, every time she looked to the horizon she saw trees instead of sky. Slim was underground and she was within ground, expecting a lid of earth to close on her any day now.

The tent was an adventure, sure, but even in an adventure someone must brine the chicken, pickle the herrings in their thick secretions, flog the bedsheets in the river, crank the generator, skim the froth from the jellies, punch the bread and watch the indents of her fists disappear. They were far enough inland that the Slocan Lake brought only fog, gave no blue. The lake was only a source of humidity: a film of moss on the tent's canvas walls, which seemed to breathe in the shifting wind.

The tent's generator went out at least once a week and she'd light oil lamps, their wicks blinking like moths trapped in a glass jar. No one could tell her why the war could not spare enough metal to give her some nails to build proper walls. She did not know what made the generator run or not run, nor did she know what made the wind shift just right to fill her tent with smoke. Luck, more than anything. She did know, however, that a woodstove fire must be layered in the right order: wood, paper, sparks, breath from the bellows. She was good at stoking the home fires.

EDIE

Vivian talks in her perfect vowels, telling the story of her husband, Sam. One of the first to sign up. Never one to turn down an adventure. A quick marriage. A new baby. She endured countless silent Sunday dinners with her in-laws, knives shrieking against the bone china as her husband's face smirked over the scene from its flag-draped frame. This last one Edie has invented but feels it could be true. Her mind is too eager. She must slow down and listen to what Vivian is saying.

"Knew him for three years and two of those he was overseas and not exactly a poet either. 'I am well. Kiss our daughter for me. I am well. Thinking of you.'" She toys with the button. "And I think he was well, the bastard! Most men, they don't want to worry you, they could be shot and dragging their arses bleeding through the mud and they'd still write 'I am well. I am doing just fine.' But I think he really meant it. I think he was *actually* fine. Marching and singing. Sniping a Hun here and there. He was built for a war. Just *built* for it." She holds out her hands to indicate the proportions of his body. "Built like a brick you-know-what. You couldn't even stuff his shoulders into a suit without him looking like some kind of animal." She laughs. "My God. He was just *built* for it. So bloody *florid*. A pink-cheeked slab of a man."

She drains her drink, rattling the ice in the glass. "My God," she says.

Edie cannot imagine what to say. When she tries to picture Slim she can only see his arms thin as rifle barrels. War, she imagines, involves a great deal of crouching, something Slim was never skilled in.

"I'm sorry," Edie says.

Vivian laughs. She chews an ice cube. "A slab of a man," she says, trying to keep her voice precise.

Edie glances around the room. A woman in a dress and hairstyle five years old is dancing with a soldier, a widow's band on her arm.

How long has it been since this widow has needed a new dress or an updated hairstyle? She's unsure of what to do with her hands. Edie remembers. It has been ten years and she has never in her life been able to afford a current fashion, but Edie knows what to do.

The woman's arms make sloppy circles, a beat behind the music. She looks at a group of women—her friends, most likely—as if for approval. She laughs. So amazed she is dancing. So amazed that someone has asked her. She wears the band that announces her husband's death as if it was a medal she earned. In Edie's mother's day, people made brooches out of the hair of departed loved ones. Edie carries the spine of a man she doesn't know in her pocket. Sometimes she places it against the knobs of her own spine to see where it would fit.

Edie blinks in and out of Vivian's story: a meat-and-potatoes fellow, a quick courtship. Strange that such a flamboyant woman should have such a mundane tale.

Vivian says, "Just coming down from Salmo. Friend of my husband invited us up. Nice fellow. Free trip, anyhow, thought why not, eh? See the country. Show Sadie. But it's no place to be in the winter. Like a big bowl filling up with sugar out here, can't figure out why we don't get that sort of foul weather in Vancouver. Maybe all the high buildings block us from the worst of it; it's for the birds up there: saw houses with their roofs caved in under the snow. But good to see Fred." She smiles. "Frederick." He took us out for dinner at a little Chinese place. I'd never been, but the vegetables were *lovely* and it was so very *clean*, which I didn't reckon on. Sadie calls him uncle, you know. Uncle Frederick." A secret smile.

Vivian says, "Work up at a sawmill, sweeping up till I'm knotted like a godforsaken cat's cradle but I'm taking these elocution courses, the ones where you write away for records that teach you the proper way to speak. How to train your mouth into the right sounds, speak from the diaphragm, and I expect to move up to the office, secretary work. Hard to get, though, because I won't partake in that special little job interview on the manager's couch. Fred says I should take it up with the union. A bakery's worth of tarts up there! Strutting around, gazing at themselves in the shiny Dictaphones. Can hardly spell their own names."

Vivian says, "You'll just love Vancouver. Lots of places to go. Dancing, you know, men coming back keen on grabbing any old woman. Sick of horse-faced European peasants, I'd expect. And the gals haven't given up the old freedoms, eh? Women drive around in cars they bought and paid for. Riveting work. Putting together big old boats. Ships. Anything, really. Gals did anything. Of course, many of them have gone back to hearth and home, but not all. Not me. Don't expect me to slip meekly back and try to stretch the pension. My little girl's not growing up on cornstarch soup and Fred says she shouldn't have to; he agrees with me. Sadie calls him Uncle Frederick. Not Uncle Fred, but *Frederick*. Such a *serious* child, watching my every move, good *God*."

Edie says nothing. She nods, staring unfocused at the patterns people's bodies make moving across the dance floor until Vivian's words are a kind of pattern too. She could say: My husband wooed me with stories of the On to Ottawa Trek, of riding clean to Regina, of a parade in every town. But what would it matter? It's the wrong kind of marching.

Edie could say: My ma believes that crows take the souls of the dead to heaven. I have a spine bone stolen for me by a prisoner who took a shine to me. Slim was supposed to get his diamond-driller certificate so that we could go all over, mines all over the world want diamond drillers, and when I get to Vancouver I may leave my little boy behind with his grandmother and keep right on going. But why should she tell any of these stories? They've fallen out of their neat packages and no longer make any sense to her.

She is gone from Slim.
Lord.
She is gone.

VERTEBRA

Her father was a policeman and so saw terrible things. On nights
he was home, he loved to tell the stories. Women sprawled on the
highway like dolls, their arms and legs gone double-jointed. Men
with their heads—he finished the story with a finger drawn across his
throat, as if not speaking the words would prevent his children from
imagining them. He saw terrible things and so made it his business to
know the body in a precise way, so as to lend accuracy to his reports.

Each vertebra of the spine controls a different aspect of your life
functions, he told her. One of the twins careened past them, shirtless
and sweating from a bath, and her father caught him around the
waist. He turned him around and the little boy tried to hold still
through laughter. His chest heaved from his running.

Right here, her father said, is for the left side of the hand, and here
is for breathing and here is for the nerves that operate the left thigh.
He pointed with his pencil and the child—she cannot remember
whether it was Paul or Greg—tried not to giggle at the touch. He
spread his arms out to show he could be serious.

This controls the passing of water, he said, and the boy couldn't
help it, he started to laugh and held his hand up to stifle the sound.

Edie stared at her brother's knobby back as if he had grown a tail.
Previously, she had thought of the spine like rungs on a ladder, like
buttons to a dress she couldn't slip out of.

Everything has a purpose, enthused her father, from the base of
your skull to your rump. (The boy giggled at the word.) Her father
ran his fingers up his son's back as if he were playing the slats on a

fence. Both father and son laughed for different reasons. Like a little factory, said her father.

Edie saw now that each bump under her brother's skin was really its own, small brain. For years, she has tried to hold the vertebra up to the light and search for clues as to its purpose. The nerves it held are long gone, but she imagines the electric sparks that used to fill the bone's hollows.

THE STORY OF HOW HE MET HER

Slim meets Edie on the first good day, freshly down from the camps and dazed by Vancouver. Every streetlight a small explosion, all the shrill tramcars throwing sparks that singe lacy patterns on the hems of girls who get too close. The dance is to raise money for the Trek to Ottawa, to bolster strike funds, to shore up support. It's held in the livestock pavilion of the PNE fairgrounds, a round cement building that still holds the musk of animals and straw. The high, creaking lights bleat in the wind and the floors are stained with what might be oil but might also be blood.

The Special Events Committee has strung banners with good-luck messages on the walls and pinned crepe-paper bows to the doors of the holding pens. A band dressed in fifteen-year-old suits play even older waltzes. The music reminds the Trekkers that they used to know how to dance, reminds the townspeople that there was once money enough to sway in someone's arms dressed to the nines.

"I'm not supposed to be here," says a girl by way of greeting.

"Oh yeah?" asks Slim. He holds his punch glass so tightly he worries it might shatter in his palm. How did he used to talk to women? What did he used to say? After years in work camps, he has forgotten how to have the kind of body that looks just right leaning against a wall, talking to a girl by the punch bowl. There's no good place for his arms and legs anymore. His hands tremble from coffee and cigarettes; even his body stammers.

"Caught the tram. Because my father, he says you're ungrateful for what Bennett's given you, eh? Like a roof over your heads and three squares. Lots of people aren't getting that, you know?"

"Lots of people don't, well, lots of people don't—lots of people don't know what it's like living there. No one around. No way out. And just, you know, meaningless work. Bloody useless work—"

"Kind of lonely there, eh?" she asks. When she places her arm on his elbow, he blinks down at her. "My name's Edie," she says.

"Slim." He watches the rest of the Trekkers dancing or eating. There's a sharpness in men: the ribs and hipbones when the shirt's off, the spine taut bending down to pick the dandelions, pick the dandelions, pick more goddamned dandelions. Women, he remembers, lack these angles. Women's bodies are more adept at concealing their bones.

"What's your real name?" she asks.

Slim winks, remembering that was one of the tricks he used to do around women. He used to wink and usually they loved it. "Wouldn't you like to know," he says.

"I would like to know. Mine's actually Edith, but no one calls me that."

"William," he says. "William MacDonald."

"I like Slim better. You don't look like a William."

They dance. She asks him. They waltz, but he keeps her at his long arm's length. She is seventeen years old, pincurls beginning to fall from their combs as they dance, her figure constructed around her own God-given form instead of a corset. His one hand rests on her waist that is so narrow it's usually only seen in women who can't breathe deeply, their bones moulded around other bones. Seventeen. Slender in what he will later learn is her sister's dress, stolen and pinned to the right size. But now, there is no way of knowing that every time he dips her, the pins jab into her hipbones, the reminder of her sister a small hurt.

Slim counts the rhythm in his head: one and two and dip and two and twirl and three and floor and...He keeps a good space between them, nodding to Matt Shaw as he passes between the rows of dancers and heads for the stage. She is pretty enough: too chatty maybe. He wishes for a snort of rye to make himself remember what he used to say.

Edie is such a little bit of a girl and Slim wonders if the ladies he used to know were this petite. Matt Shaw threads among the crowd, pumping hands, clapping backs. When Slim reaches down to sift a hand through her hair, his fingers snag.

"Ow, hey," she says and touches her scalp as if testing for blood.

"Sorry," he says. "I'm—dammit—I'm sorry. Dammit. Are you okay?" Her hair smells burnt underneath the perfume, her curls singed into holding their perfect shape through sweat and the movement of his fingers.

"Fine," says Edie. She pats her head again. "You just surprised me, is all."

When the song ends, Slim stands with her in silence. The other couples, he notices, are doing the same.

"Thank you for the dance," she says. He wonders if she's disappointed in him and has already got her eye on some other fellow. Thinking that makes him like her more.

"Yeah," says Slim. "Yeah. It was. Well, thank you. And sorry about the—"

The music has stopped and Matt Shaw steps up on the stage.

"Well," she says.

"Well," Slim says.

"It was lovely to meet you," she says. "Good luck on your trek or whatever it's called. Your going to Ottawa."

"Yeah," says Slim. "Thanks. Yeah. It was nice to meet you. Maybe I'll see you again sometime."

"When would that be?" she asks. "With all that marching off to Ottawa you're about to do?"

"I guess not," says Slim. He lets the silence be filled by Matt Shaw, who's stoked a real fire in his words tonight. They turn to the stage and forget each other.

"All across our great nation, women are putting away their hope chests and taking up rags as someone's servant girl. Men have confined themselves to the unnatural life of bachelorhood. There is no money for men and women to lead the normal lives that God intended for us." The crowd is already cheering. "Our problem," he says, "is a national problem."

He was supposed to keep marching, Edie thinks now. He wasn't supposed to come back.

BELLY

It's dark and he's not supposed to play in the dark, but Sadie has turned on the light and now lays her toys out in a circle. More small airplanes than he's ever seen. Like someone shrunk down a whole fleet! Belly can imagine tiny little pilots wearing tiny little scarves.

"You were hurt, but my mother and your mother fixed you and now you're better," she says. "Sometimes all the blood can fall out of people and then they die. That's what happens. All the blood falls out. But you didn't die because they kept the blood in."

She's such a strange girl, not the friend he's looking for, because she has airplane trading cards like a boy and when Belly says a Prop B-7 goes *chugachugachugagrrr* she says no, that's a T-28, the Prop B-7 makes more of a *wooshgrrrrr* noise when it's getting up to top speed.

Sadie is no kind of girl because her mouth can make the sounds of engines and guns better than he can.

And she has a circle of airplanes—all sorts of sizes—and a pillow made out of a shirt that Sadie says is her dad, not just a pillow but a piece of her real dad. So she is a dumb girl because Belly was dumb when he had Mike the cat and now he knows that Mike wasn't a real cat. It feels like his cheek is too big for his face and he laughs at the idea: a little boy with a big old cheek poking out there big as a bum. It's itchy too, and this worries Belly because he imagines that there are bugs running along his skin and he can't check to see if this is true because there aren't any mirrors and he can't look in the glass of the framed ladies on the walls because they have eyes like someone took the blood out of them and are probably mean anyhow.

Which is the same with Sadie. The wrong name for a girl like that. All the girls he's ever met in his whole entire life named Sadie have freckles, and this Sadie not only has no freckles but has too-white skin like the creepy ladies who are looking away in the photographs, like they didn't realize someone was about to take their picture and they forgot they should smile. Also, Sadie's nose is wrong. Not that it looks ugly or crooked, but wrong, the wrong nose for her face. Most people would think she's a pretty girl—a pretty little thing, said the lady Vivian, as if that was Sadie's name: Pretty Little Thing. Belly knows better.

"We could play, but I'm not sold on wanting to," says Sadie. She has her hands on her hips and is standing on the bed, bouncing a little: another thing Belly's not allowed to do. "Your mother is very lovely, but you aren't much of anything." She looks at Belly with her soft-mean eyes, the kind of eyes that are sorry because you're too dumb to understand anything. She's shown him a photograph of her father that she carries in her bag of toys and the father has soft-mean eyes as well. Eyes that are so crinkled up you can't hardly see them. He stands on the wing of his plane like it's a stage. Belly's father has a better plane made special for him. The plane is grey and white like a horse but if he flies into blue sky the plane goes blue too because it's special and his dad has a helmet that also changes colour. And there's a special seat for the horse his dad rides when he's on land and a helmet for him with a place for the ears.

His cheek hurts and his skin feels — bad. He can't explain it. Something wrong has happened to his face and is still happening.

Sadie stands on the bed bouncing a little, her eyes crinkling at him. "If you want to play airplane, remember that only I get to be the airplane because I know how to do it the best."

"We can both be," says Belly. As if there was only one airplane in the war! "I'll be a Spitfire and have teeth like this and I can shoot you down and then you can shoot me down and then — and then — and then — we can die." Sometimes he gets stuck finding the right words and his mouth goes in circles before going right again. "I can shoot cherry pits from my mouth like they're from a gun. If you don't have no cherry pits, we could use little rocks from somewhere. We could — we could — we could wash them first." Belly holds his arms out into his strongest wings and flies around the room, sputtering.

"If you don't have *any* cherry pits," says Sadie. She holds her arms out so straight you could put a cup on her fingertips and it wouldn't fall over. "Flying's not like that. You don't know anything about flying, do you? You don't move your arms up and down. The wings don't move. That's so dumb. Why would they move? It's not like the airplane is a bird." His dad says that rich men stand like Jesus Christ himself and Sadie does too, her arms out the way an airplane should be. "That's why you can't be an airplane. You don't know the very first thing about airplanes."

"My dad's flying an airplane." And is probably shooting people dead right now this minute and the people can't tell where the plane is so they can't get away. It's like the clouds are shooting them but it's his dad and you can't run from clouds, like how you can't hide from The Shadow because he knows what evil lurks in the hearts of men.

"So what? Everyone's dad is flying an airplane or on a boat. My dad flies with both the RCAF and he has six medals and they're up in my room. One has a picture of the King on it and the King really gave it to him in person." Belly shrugs. His dad probably has a hundred medals by now, so many he can't even walk without making a clinking noise. "Don't worry if your dad doesn't have any medals," Sadie says. "Not everyone can have one. I bet my dad's been at it longer. How many letters do you get? I get one a week. And I also take dancing lessons down at the community centre and I'm one class ahead of my age group."

Belly can't remember how long his dad has been gone, but it feels like a very long time, long enough that whenever he tries to think of his dad's face, it's a little blurry, like the women in the portraits. "My dad's killed a hundred men," he says and this feels true. "And he hasn't even been doing it for very long."

"My dad's been flying since I was a baby. And he's so good the war couldn't let him go." She drops her arms, hops off the bed and stands in front of Belly. "So I know more about airplanes. At least I know their wings don't move like this."

She flaps her arms in front of his face and Belly can imagine himself pushing her so hard she falls on her back with her prissy little stockings up in the air. Sometimes he gets mad so sudden it's like there's an animal in him. Sadie doesn't even notice how mad he is. She keeps talking on. "So you get to be the hangar. Lie down on the bed. Do you even go to school? I go to grade three at Sir Richard McBride, and my teacher's name is Miss O'Keefe, and in the summer she will marry a young man and then her name will be different and she will no longer be a teacher."

"I want to be the airplane," says Belly.

But Sadie has already gotten off the bed and backed up to the far wall, her arms out straight. "Lie down on the bed," she says and Belly stares at her. "Please," she says and gives him a look that's supposed to be nice, but it's not.

"I want to be the airplane," says Belly. "We can both be airplanes." But he lies down on the bed, feeling mad for doing so.

"The hangar is the place the airplane sleeps, if you didn't know, which you probably didn't. Lie down straight. Pretend you're the hangar." She flounces on over to him—walks like a stupid girl—and moves Belly's arms and legs so they're straight. She has hot, scratchy hands, like claws. His face is itchy and hot; it has a heartbeat in it.

"Why can't we both be airplanes?" he asks. "You're dumb. There were—there were—there were hundreds of airplanes in the war."

"You're the hangar." Sadie begins to run, her perfect wings out wide, making the noise of propellers between her teeth. She does a few circles around the room and Belly has to tilt his head up to watch her. "I've been away for a long time and I'm coming home."

"Planes don't talk," says Belly.

"Neither do hangars," says Sadie, flecks of spit on the corners of her mouth from the noise of the engines. "I'm the plane and I'm bringing the daddy home after a long day of dropping bombs."

She dives on him, her arms still out, her head butting into his chest. They fall together on the bed and Sadie smells like a barnyard, even with her pretty dress on.

"Ow," says Belly. "Ow!" Her stinky hair is in his mouth and it tastes greasy and she just lies there, making an engine sound.

"Be quiet! You're the hangar!" she whines. Why practise your plane sounds if you only get to lie still like a building? This is how Belly knows that Sadie is a strange kind of girl. He's seen other girls play house and one girl is the mom and one girl is the baby and one girl is the daddy, but none of the girls actually play the house itself.

His face is hot from the crash. His cheek feels like it has a little motor in it. Sadie sits up and her hair is so fuzzy and lit up that it looks like smoke's coming out of her head. She pushes her curls off her face and stares at Belly. "When the airplane flies, it keeps its wheels hidden and only puts them down when it's time to land," says Sadie. "If you didn't know."

"I knew," said Belly.

"You're bleeding a little," says Sadie and touches his cheek like she's a nice mom, which makes Belly even madder.

"I am not," Belly says.

Sadie shows him the blood on her fingers, like she just won some big stupid prize. "You are too. See? But now you're not because I took the blood off." She wipes the blood on her white dress and Belly is happy to have messed up her dress because now her mom will be mad. "It was just a little blood. I took it away. My aunty is a nurse and one time she helped a doctor put a man's leg back on."

There are cobwebs like clouds in the corner of the ceiling and the window is so grey that it's like they're in a fog and it must be a good day to have a special plane like his dad's. Off in the next room, he can hear a lady laughing. His mom, maybe, and he wants to hit her face for laughing at nothing when he's stuck here with an engine in his cheek and a girl sitting on him, but when he slides off the bed and opens the door, the shock of colour and noise is so much that it hurts and he must narrow his eyes and shut the door again.

EDIE

An awkwardness now, their stories burnt out, their throats tight from hours of talking. Drinks empty but they sip them anyways for a motion to hide their lips. They take their hands off the table and fold them in their laps like linen napkins, rub their hands along their thighs, sip their drinks. Edie worries that she stinks of the events of the day — sweat, coal, dust, whiskey, blood — and anyone who walks by could read her by scent, the way animals do. A mother who may abandon her child. A mother who has ruined her child because she failed to take the proper precautions. Who has already left him in this small way: to go dancing while he's asleep with a wounded face. From Vivian, Edie catches only a faint odour of talc and a hint of the earthier scent it masks. She looks up at the dancing couples, the sweat between their shoulder blades like shadows, and imagines them caught in glassy spheres of their own scent, impervious to hers.

Above, the chandelier continues to toss its dirty light onto the elderly couple mincing around the dance floor, doing a much older dance that doesn't match the beat. A stiff-backed waltz, lots of tight little pivots. They seem happy enough, though, pleased to be up at this hour, still able to dance.

Vivian touches the button she's undone, rolling it under her thumb. She's taken out a fountain pen and a notebook from one of the pockets on her dress. The dress is of the latest style — a full skirt that defies wartime rations, a row of purely decorative buttons along the collar — and is made of some synthetic fabric that can withstand sweat and weather without wrinkling.

Vivian motions two soldiers over; perhaps the ones who gave them the drinks, but perhaps not. It's increasingly difficult for Edie to keep track of faces. "You're just in time!" The soldiers sit and Vivian leans forward and lowers her voice. "I could use your assistance. You absolutely *must* help me."

Edie doesn't recognize the first man, but the second is the soldier she met in the observatory car. She smiles at him and he smiles back. A strange, one-sided intimacy: she has touched his hand as he plunged in and out of a nightmare, childlike in his terror. He cannot know this, likely mistaking her gaze as simple flirtation.

The soldier laughs. He rests his ruined hands in his lap. "Well, what say? You ladies ready to show these old birds how to dance?"

Vivian laughs. A practised laugh, a twitter in her throat. "In a moment," she says. She touches his shoulder at its starched pleat and lowers her voice in confidence. "I need your help."

The other soldier laughs. "At your service." Every motion he makes is big; he waves his hands and laughs deep from his chest.

They're young and Lord knows what they see in two mothers, Edie thinks. Edie looks as old as she is—twenty-seven, my God—and the men look as young as they are. She doesn't feel any shyness, though, and this thrills her. She should be grateful that during the war she was blessed enough to have been very bored. No one to worry over or mourn.

Vivian sets the pen and paper in front of the soldier. "I need you to write a letter to my daughter," she says. "Her father went down over Dresden and I haven't—It's not the right time to tell her. I'm waiting until she's old enough to handle it." Edie tries to picture Vivian's ham-thick husband stuffed into a craft so tiny the control panel lights blink like fireflies around his knees and he can't reach them. The city toylike and dead as a child's building block set. Fire. His shoulders burn where they touch the metal walls of the cockpit. The buildings growing larger and larger below him.

Edie is a thief of stories. Imagines even stories that are not hers to imagine. Stories she has no right to push herself into.

THE NATIONAL PROBLEM, THE NATURAL LIFE THAT GOD INTENDED

Naked in the river, Slim loves the way the cold of water is different from the cold of wind. They are bathing in Thunder Creek outside of the livestock pavilion where they will be housed for the night and the water still feels glacier-fed, though the day is hot. He'd sweet-talked two more bits of soap from the girl at the railway station and is ridding himself of the traces of Vancouver, the boxcar, Golden, the perpetual boxcar, Calgary, Swift Current, Medicine Hat, now Moose Jaw.

Slim watches Matt Shaw climb up the riverbank. He's not a man who looks deprived, especially not as the water highlights all the muscles on his back. You wouldn't know he'd been starving or cold.

All the other Trekkers are bare too, but they look awkward in their new-clean skin. You would think that years in a bunkhouse with thirty other fellows would have cured their sense of modesty, but they perch on the grass, some of them keeping their caps over their groins.

Matt Shaw pushes the water out of his hair and Slim is surprised to see what the river has done to him: a man standing without scent or dirt, not even much of a tan. His pink skin. The slight hairs on his lower back golden. Matt Shaw wanders over to the tree where he has left his clothes drying on the branches. The garments sway, losing the stiffness that a solid week of rain, sweat and grime brings. The undershirts hanging from the trees are yellow-brown and translucent as the husks of cicadas.

"We have been called agitators, but can you blame us after being condemned to a living hell for four years," Matt Shaw is muttering, counting out the rhythm of his speech with a tick of his fingers. He is practising for the evening rally. "It is not natural or healthy for young men to be deprived of societal influences for so long. All across the nation, women are going without husbands, men are confining themselves to a life of poverty and bachelorhood. Our problem has become a national problem." He pauses, working a tangle out of his drying hair. "Our problem," he says, "has become a national problem."

Matt Shaw leans against the tree and sighs, pissing. "Our problem," he mutters. His body still wet, the piss arcs out of him, the puddles of water by his feet and the one forming by the tree merging, collecting bits of leaves and twigs. Slim floats chilled and weightless.

"Our problem is you never shut the hell up," calls Flash, named for his quick, dark eyes and ability to outrun a cop. Slim doesn't know his real name, since what was written on the work camp register rarely corresponded to reality. Some men changed their life stories after being blacklisted, others simply brushed the foreign soil off their surnames.

Bobbing in the water, so cold he feels absent of body, Slim watches Matt Shaw drying, the way he sighs against the tree, the clothes on the branches growing pale and light as the water leaves them. "Aww, screw off," says Matt Shaw, grinning. "You got the balls to go up there, take the mic, you go right ahead. Be my guest."

"I would too if I had your pretty little face," says Flash, not looking up from the words he's tracing on his sweater. He drops his tone to a radio host's baritone. "Tonight, we have with us the baby-faced spokesman of the On to Ottawa Trek. He's leading an army of unemployed men across this great nation to confront Prime Minister R.B. Bennett and bring him a message from the people. Yes, ladies and gentlemen, despite his youthful appearance, Mr. Matt Shaw speaks with the wisdom of the ages."

Matt Shaw grins. He has grey eyes that never tire of grinning. "Just jealous," he says. "Not my fault I got the looks, the voice, not to mention this baby right here." He gestures, shaking out the last of the piss.

"Ah, but do you have a lady friend, Mr. Boyish Good Looks, Mr.

Voice of the People? After four years picking dandelions and wanking off in the middle of nowhere, what do you have to show for it?"

"Aww," says Matt Shaw. "Screw off. If you're so lucky with the ladies, why are you still here watching me take a leak?" Slim laughs and Flash laughs and Matt Shaw chuckles, his eyes camera-ready before he is even clothed.

HOW THEY MET AGAIN

Without the crowd of marching men, Slim looked thin and pink and unsure of what to do with himself. Cleaner than the first time she met him and stiff in his government-issue suit—the kind they give to prisoners when they're released—he was reading a newspaper on a park bench. She knew all about that, having watched the men shifting in their cheap-shiny suits by the Pen bus stop, their cardboard suitcases sogging in their wet palms. It was November, but he sat there as if it was a summer's day. She recognized him because of his height and his red hair.

"That On to Ottawa Trek," she said in greeting, as if it was his name. It was the right thing to say because his neck snapped up from the newspaper he was reading on the bench. He looked pleased. The newspaper was folded into neat, manageable rectangles.

'Right!" he said. Those clean blue eyes. He smiled. "How'd you know?" His voice was thinner than she imagined, as if he needed to cough.

"We danced at that fundraiser last May," she said. Anne was whimpering, tugging on Edie's arm. She refused to be carried and so Edie had to do everything at the speed of a child's small feet. Anne quieted when Slim smiled at her: already such a ham, loving to charm any man.

"Oh!" he said. He tapped the newspaper in his palm. "Right! That fundraiser!" He didn't recognize her and she didn't mind.

"How'd that work out for you anyways?" she asked. "That On to Ottawa thing?"

He stared down at the newspaper, as if seeking his name in the headlines. "Don't you read the papers?" He coughed, but his voice stayed scratchy, as if it was being forced out of a small space.

"Hah. Barely got time to breathe. Sister to take care of. Chores. Cooking. Ma's going to start a boarding house, now that my father's gone."

"I'm sorry to hear that."

Anne pulled on Edie's arm, finally wanting to be picked up at the least convenient time. Edie picked her up and the fur-lined hood of the child's coat irritated her neck. "Oh, no, he's not dead. Just—" She waved her free hand, vanishing him with a gesture. "But what I meant to say is," she said, recovering her expression, "is that I don't have time to read the papers, but I do have time for a soda."

"Oh," said Slim. He blushed and she loved it. She could see all the veins on his arms as if he didn't have any skin at all. Now that the layers of dirt had been scrubbed from him, he looked like an entirely different person. He stood and gave her a little bow. "How am I to deny two lovely ladies a soda?" Even his voice was different, as if it had been scuffed up by his adventures.

And that was the last of the awkwardness between them. They had sodas at the pharmacy, and Anne spun her stool around and around, laughing, ice cream sticky all over her face. Now, Edie forgets what they talked about but remembers that his voice kept blanking out and he would touch his throat as if it were a motor he could get running again. He coughed, winced at the cough, covered his mouth. While she sipped her soda, he drank hot water, which he said was the only thing that could revive his voice.

"Tear gas," he said. Edie leaned in as he swallowed more hot water, readying his voice to seduce her with the story of the dandelions, the story of the riot, that time they all went marching.

HER FATHER

Because she was her father's favourite, he would take her to run errands on the back of his motorcycle and buy her small treats: egg creams, marbles, tiny paper fans with flowers painted on them.

"Share with your brothers and sister," he would say, but they both knew Edie was meant to keep the treats under her bed and only bring them out when she was alone.

Once, he took her to visit a lady and left her there for a few hours. The woman was nervous. She kept waving her arms into loops and arcs as she spoke. Now, Edie can't remember what she looked like but recalls those hands drawing the shapes of birds in the air.

The woman made her a grilled cheese sandwich, but the cheese was white with blue streaks and tasted of coal. Edie suspected that it had gone off, but minded her manners.

"That's special cheese," said the woman. "Your father likes it that way."

"Thank you," said Edie.

"Does your mother make it like that?" The woman stopped waving her hands and smoothed her skirt, then rested her hands on her knees.

"No," said Edie. "Differently."

The woman let her pick a chocolate from a little cut-glass dish and Edie almost cried when the taste of the chocolate was ruined by the sharp aftertaste of the cheese still in her mouth. Then her father came to take her home.

"How'd you like that lady?" asked her father, and Edie knew this was one more thing she couldn't share with her siblings. She could only guess at the relationship between her father and this woman. She could only imagine what happened.

EDIE

The soldier's hands are not so damaged that he cannot hold a pen, but his handwriting is that of a young boy. (Edie thinks of the rows of pupils bent over their chalkboards as she marched down the aisles, watching the scabs of horsefly bites on their shorn scalps. Chalk tapping and shrieking against the blackboards. "Loosen your grip," she would instruct no one in particular. "If your knuckles are white you're holding it too tightly.")

The soldier frowns, biting his tongue a little in concentration as he makes the curve of a *D*. The pen is heavy and wooden in the stubs of his fingers. Vivian hasn't noticed. He's so handsome she likely sees his hands as whole. If Edie hadn't found him wandering the observatory car, perhaps she would think the same.

"I've met lots of fast friends, but I do so miss you and your ma," says Vivian, reciting the letter, oblivious that he's stuck on the first word.

The pen wavers in his hand like a gramophone needle. The soldier hunches over the paper, concentrating hard. Ink pools on the paper by the *D*. *Dear*, he writes, the ink fattening the letters until they're illegible.

"I can do it," says Edie.

Vivian pats the soldier's arm and the pen leaves a spike mark from her contact. "It needs a man's touch." She cocks her head and flutters her eyelashes in a grotesque imitation of something she's seen in the movies. Her lips try to smile in front of her snaggletooth: to hide it and keep smiling.

The soldier doesn't look up. *Dear*, he writes again in letters so rough it's as if he wrote them on a ship during a storm. *Dear*, he writes again. Tongue out. Hand clenched. Beside him, the other soldier prattles on to Vivian about his plans for the future.

"Uh huh," she says, beaming at him. "Sounds swell. Sounds just swell." The soldier has his arm in front of the paper so that Vivian cannot see his words. "Did you get that?" she asks him. "The part about missing me and her."

Dear, he writes. Crosses it out. *Dear*.

THE ORCHARD INTERNMENT CAMP SCHOOL

Edie does not know why they hired her, except that she had nearly a high-school education, was female and was married: all the qualities necessary to bestow a civilizing influence upon children. It didn't matter, apparently, that Edie lived in a tent or that her husband was often away and the whole town whispered about where he was and most of the women smiled close-lipped at her on the street and twittered later in their parlours over eggless, sugarless, milkless tea cakes—Victory Cakes!—that she just *lets* him go, she just *lets* him, if he were my husband I'd have handcuffed him to the *radiator* by now, not that they have a radiator, mind you, ha ha, but it *can't* be good for the boy and he looks just like his *father* too.

The children sat in rows in their little desks, even Belly, who was too young for school. All the boys had shorn heads. She read to them from donated books, many of which were scribbled on so that the blond boys had horns and difficult words had ghost traces of erased pencil circles. Inky thumbprints in the margins from children who were long grown and now in possession of much larger hands. The books had many stories, but one of Edie's favourites was about orphaned children who lived in the woods. The students liked it too; it reminded them of their disrupted lives. Like animals, the orphans seem to require nothing but berries, riverwater and songs to subsist.

"'Mary gets the water from the river,'" she intoned.

"Mary gets the water from the river," the children replied.

"'Robert found berries on the bush.'"

"Robert found berries on the bush."

"'They sang as they worked.'"

"They sang as they worked."

"'They all had a lovely meal.'"

"They all had a lovely meal."

The children repeated whatever she asked them to. They bowed their heads in concentration and followed the words with their fingers.

EDIE

The soldier puts the pen down. He stands, his cheeks high with colour. "I just don't think children should be lied to," he says. "It's filthy to lie to children." His hands dangle by his sides and are lovely, the scars like chisel marks, as if someone's carved them out of a tusk.

Vivian stares at him, her mouth open a little. "I'm sorry?" she says, not an apology but a question.

"Now who the hell wants to dance?" he asks, reassembling his face. There's ink on his hand and all the prophetic lines stand out in stark relief. Edie imagines they depict a map of a dangerous, river-strewn country that someone has etched in his palm to assure him safe travels. Maybe the scars were done intentionally. He was a spy, she thinks, carrying maps on his hands behind enemy lines.

"I do," says Edie, taking his ink-blotted hands. Vivian tries to recover her laugh, and her snaggletooth glints behind her red lips like a little jewel. The soldier's friend takes the pen without comment.

"What do you want said?" he asks. The soldier's palm is wet and the ink seeps into Edie's palm, lending her his map. But no, she thinks, this is wrong. He's merely injured. Maybe the injury predates the war. A farming accident, a run-in with a thresher. Or maybe he's one of the countless boys who lost arms and legs while riding the rails and he wore gloves to scam his way into the armed forces. Maybe the war does not mind men with ruined hands so long as they can still hold a gun. Maybe it's only the lungs they worry about, or the politics.

The soldier leads her past the windows and across the dance floor, almost strutting, over to the Victrola. His hand is hidden in Edie's grip. Outside, it's properly night. She missed the sunset completely, or maybe the blizzard sloughed it away.

With his better hand, he lifts the Victrola's needle and the music sizzles to a halt. The dancers stop in a strange tableau, crying, "Hey!" at once, as if that were a chorus to a folk song they'd been singing. The soldier doesn't seem to mind. He grins at them.

"Forgive me, gentlemen," he cries. He raises a glass half full of amber liquid that's not his. Someone's left it to go dancing. He raises the glass and the rum touches the rim but doesn't spill. "I promised this lady a dance and by God she's going to get it." His chest puffed out, his hand hidden in Edie's grip.

He sifts through the records for an appropriate one and everyone cheers because he's in uniform. Because he's coming home.

HOMECOMING STORIES NO ONE GOT TO TELL

Slim travels with men from towns with the names of gorgeous ladies: Nicola, Belcarra, Rosalind. They speak of their hometowns as if they were speaking of women, talking so low and gentle that Slim imagines that each house hosts a perfectly lit window where a girl sits combing her hair for hours until it falls in an endless frozen sheen. He imagines that the towns are just waiting for the men to return, knock on the doors, and take the women in their arms. When the Trek is over, he thinks, perhaps they will be welcomed back with parades.

But what did he think of his own hometown? Edie imagines red dirt, for some reason, cows wandering like town idiots across the pastures, hemmed in by some sharp-eyed sheepdog. These are stories Edie has never been told. When she tries to picture his parents, she thinks only of her own.

HOMECOMING

He stood at the door and laid his chaps and his jacket and his helmet on the radiator. He faced them. Edie and Kate stood up, as if at attention. Tom seemed nonplussed. They stared at him and he stared back. This was the first time he'd left and Edie was genuinely relieved that he had returned.

"Well," he said. He uncrossed his arms.

Edie couldn't figure out what he wanted. They stood there. Her mother rushed in from the bedroom, a pillowcase still in her hand. She threw her arms around his neck and he nodded.

"You're back," Edie's mother said. "You're back."

"Girls," he said. They took small steps toward him. He opened his arms, though their mother still clung to him. He wanted to be congratulated for the act of coming home, for the implication that he would stay there.

THE WAR

Moons waxed and moons waned. She kept her vegetables in a copper kettle hanging engorged and metal from a tree limb like a moon. The moon, too, seemed engorged and metal, and after '43 they lived in a tent so it was the one light. They wanted a house, but the war had taken strange things: nails were hard to come by, every scrap of metal gone from their lives save what the men took out of the ground. The moon seeped through the holes in the canvas and rolled along her skin like small, cold pearls. In the summer, the tent glowed green from the trees above and Edie could not stop thinking about the sea. Women wanted their husbands back and men wanted to escape the war alive and whole-bodied and all Edie wanted was the sea, which she'd never longed for when she lived only a few hours away from it.

Slim came home with half-stories, useless trinkets, apologies, trembling hands. He came home and came home and sometimes he didn't, but she knew where he was. Once, she got word that someone had drowned on a fishing trip and feared it was Slim, but it was the town doctor. Slim returned after a few days and that was the most she'd ever worried about him.

In town, every woman was pregnant and couldn't stop touching their bellies. So proud of themselves. So big and damp, hot even in winter. Though Belly was still a baby, Edie could not imagine she'd ever been in that state and had no desire to do it again. It was a mystery why she became pregnant once and a mystery why she did not conceive again, but she thought so little about the subject. One war baby was enough and she figured one child to two hands was the right equation. She still had the upper hand. Slim came and went.

The war went on. Belly grew, talked, grew some more, talked some more. Reached for her, always grabbing and pulling and talking. "Up," he would demand. "Up, Momma." It was one of the first words he learned. Babies were born. Many women left to be with their mothers. Slim wanted to enlist, but they wouldn't take him and so he stayed. Some women stayed too, and Edie imagined them looking out their windows during 3:00 a.m. feedings, expecting that knock on the door but seeing only the miners passing for the early shift, stooped as if ashamed, stooping to ready themselves for the small spaces they worked in.

No one in her family wrote her, but she received letters from childhood friends and the odd aunt or cousin. Maybe Tom was at war—it seemed likely—but no one mentioned him, so she set him out of her mind. Sitting on a rock with her legs bare to the sun, she replied to their letters. Condolences, mostly, in the neat script she remembered from back home. She got a job teaching at the internment camp and Belly picked up Japanese quicker than his mother tongue. Got sullen in English. Slim came and went. In town, toddlers staggered around bearing the names of their dead fathers.

BELLY

His face is dizzy. He spins in tight circles. Sadie spins. The game is confusing because they are airplanes, but they are also in a big airplane and Sadie says some airplanes are big enough to carry other airplanes inside, but Belly doesn't believe her. The walls here look like they have round windows with old grey ladies staring out, but it's really just pictures in frames. Airplanes have round windows. Also, in airplanes, there is a round place that holds the man who fires the machine guns. There is a special name for this man, Sadie has told him. Her dad is the man who hangs in the round glass and fires the machine guns. Belly feels a little sick.

"I feel sick," he says. From the spinning.

Sadie looks up and stops spinning. He can hardly look at her they're up so high. Being up high makes you feel sick. So many men have tossed him up high and their hands were rough and they caught him again. That's what men like to do; they throw you up in the air and catch you again and make you feel dizzy. Sadie sways, like how when you're on a train you walk like you're dancing and everything is wrong just a bit.

"I feel sick," he says.

Sadie stares at him. "Don't upchuck!" She giggles.

"I feel like there's some sick in me," says Belly. He was on a train and now he's in an airplane; he has been so far in just a day. He throws up and is amazed that only water comes out and a few chunks of white and pink. Airplanes don't need to eat. They eat gas and Sadie has said that they eat the gas by burning it and that's why smoke comes out of an airplane's behind and makes clouds. He is an airplane and he is in an airplane. He can make the right noises, no matter what Sadie says. He throws up again, more burning water. There's one square window and it's cool and has tears down it. Belly presses his dizzy face there. Outside, clouds.

EDIE

He swings her, and the fabric of her skirt and jacket resist. She takes off the jacket and drapes it over the back of a chair and through the blouse's thin fabric can feel the sweat of his palms against her lower back. She doesn't know the dance steps, but she trusts his arms. The stitches of her skirt strain as he dips her.

Beside them, a whore is pressed up tight against a soldier, and Edie moves in and out of the radius of her perfume. Edie's shoes are stained and warped from snow but she's light in them. She remembers the steps easily despite the damp shoes and the skirt that was designed for waiting patriotically for a husband to return, not for dancing.

Where has the soldier learned to move this way? Practising with whores, maybe. She wants to lay her head on his shoulder, but he keeps spinning her this way and that at the wrong tempo for the music. Her hair snaps against her face and some tendrils stick there with sweat. She tosses her head. The soldier looks beyond her, over her shoulder. His eyes are glassy, his cheeks flushed with drink. He watches nothing.

The whore brushes Edie's shoulder as her dance partner dips her and Edie sees a bruise on her chest as if someone's drawn a rough circle there, grey under the powder. The soldier pulls her back close, then twirls her away.

Edie can hardly hear the music for the thrumming in her ears. She has given up on counting the steps and instead trusts his movements and her own memories of being swayed light and easy in the arms of a man. (Slim's hands tugging through her hair, pulling the comb she'd stolen from her sister. The stick pins jabbing the small of her back, the reminder of her sister such a small, insignificant hurt. Her arms light because she does not have Anne in them.) She can still do this. She smiles at the soldier. He returns her gaze long enough to smile back. She can still do this.

NEW YEAR'S EVE

Every couple dumped their children at Mrs. Saundrette's house, as if they were overcoats to be flopped down in the back bedroom. Mrs. Saundrette was too big in her pregnancy to go dancing, but somehow they thought she was not too big to mind a few dozen children. At the dance hall, Slim was on the piano so Edie arranged herself on the smooth, cool lid, her heat leaving a smudge of condensation in the shape of her body. Slim was too shy to sing, so Edie tried to channel his brain into her voice. Her vocal chords hummed as if slack.

Her voice's grit was never strained out by church choirs and she sang loudly but inconsistently. Slim made up for her lack, keeping a steady beat on the piano even as she wavered across time signatures.

The guests laughed, loved it, because she was singing like a boy. They called her a card and didn't mind her lack of pitch if she would strut like a man, wink at the ladies with her hip cocked out. Hey gals, she would cry in her lowest voice, and everyone would cheer.

Slim once told her that for years he had no piano and so played scales on the roof of boxcars, tabletops, hard-packed ground. When he finally sat down to a real piano, he was momentarily shocked by how the keys gave way beneath his fingertips, surprised to hear music that wasn't in his head. He had remembered the shape of the keyboard incorrectly and now reached for notes that didn't exist.

"This one here's for all you pretty dames," she cried in the deepest voice she could muster and thought of her body boy-shaped under the work jumpsuit, tucking herself into the smallest chiselled spaces. The miners went wild at her vamping, but Slim pinked with embarrassment. I like it best when you sing right, he said.

MATT SHAW

Faces must not look human from that height. A crowd made quiet as children, the scent rising up from their salt-crusted hats, their undershirts decaying in the body's acid sweat. Maybe Matt Shaw sees the crowd's heat as a shimmer above their heads. In Golden. In Kamloops. Now in Regina. The men shift their pains from hip to hip, listening. The women cross their arms under their ribcages. Once, in Vancouver, Matt Shaw stood on top of a statue of a soldier whose bronze patina reflected his own tan. From that far up, he could not see each head nodding, only a current of assent that rose through the mass, heads dipping as if to drink from a trough of water.

Now, he cannot see their faces. The microphone, big as a dinner plate, likely shows him a slice of his own reflection: an eye, a flash of teeth, his hand stabbing at nothing. The spokesman of the Trek, the voice of the Trek. He drinks his honeyed tea by the fire: this one small sweetness the men are proud to give him. Slim stands at the side of the stage by the photographer, coughing from the tang of the camera's small explosion. The smell of the press gallery is half fire and half sweat.

Slim's job is to count the crowds. His height allows him to see over the stooped farmers and miners, but if he could just get up on stage he could warrant a better guess. A photographer's camera flash brings the smell of burning. "Takes a good shot," the man says. "All that pointing."

"Looks a little like Mussolini from the wrong angle, though," another says.

"All across the country, women are closing their hope chests. Men are living the unnatural life that God did not intend," Matt Shaw shouts. Maybe five thousand people. Maybe six thousand. The Main Street square is filled and all the side roads. "Our fight is your fight. We are linked in this common struggle. And now, here to tell you a little more about our cause, please welcome Comrade Slim." Arthur-Slim Evans, of course. The leader of the Trek, jailed twice, shot in the leg at Ludlow. For a moment, though, Slim imagines that he was the one called up. He freezes and the camera explodes into light again. Slim cannot imagine what he would say were he called: trapped in all those gazes, in front of all those thousands of uncountable eyes.

EDIE

Maybe this dance does not even exist. She knows all of the old ones and some of the new ones. She has been within a radio's range and imagined how people would move to a certain song. Her pelvis strikes the soldier's in a quick spark and the song's tempo does not quite match up. The wrong steps for this song, but still Edie lets him twirl her.

"Where you headed?" she asks him.

His response is lost in the music and his habit of speaking into her hair.

"I'm sorry?"

He looks down at her. "Probably South Westminster."

"Probably?"

He shrugs, almost in time to the music, and twirls her. A haze of cigarette smoke clouds the bar and the mirror is beaded with condensation, as if it's raining indoors. He twirls her back, dips her down low. The chandelier above lurches from the storm. The ceiling is patterned with stamped tin and she grows a little dizzy from all that light and metal.

"Old man wants me to work for him on account of my brother being gone." He trips over the word. "The insurance business. Not gone. Waylaid." Edie thinks, Gone. POW or MIA at the best. She tries to imagine Slim tucked into a Spitfire, his knees at his chest. A plane lean as he is. She cannot imagine him hunched in a ball turret or at a control panel. Wings on fire, smaller and smaller circles.

"I'm sorry." The soldier's scarred hand is slick in her grip. Do scars sweat? she wonders. Would it be wrong to ask him that? She's drunk, holding on to him so he'll guide her body through the music.

"POW most likely. You read about that in the papers, some poor widow gets word her husband's dead and he turns up years later with a whole new family, claiming not to remember. Or it just takes them a while to find their way back." He twirls her again, not because the song calls for it but because he doesn't want to look at her.

She doesn't know what to say. "He'll come back," she says, too bright.

The soldier doesn't say anything. Twirls her away from him. Edie is dizzy. He has blond eyebrows and blond eyelashes, the structure of his face barely demarcated. Watery blue eyes. The old couple still dances. Their posture is perfect, their steps almost military. Edie thinks of marching. She thinks of Slim. Is always thinking of Slim. She's twirled and Vivian laughs far away, a high laughs that cuts through the music, is its own music, a harmonica in the wrong key.

Edie has been through the war and every movie hero she knows wears a uniform but still she thinks of her husband with his useless fight. When she thinks of marching, she thinks of the most impotent kind.

THE TIME WE ALL WENT MARCHING

They write their ambitions on their backs as they march. All they want is an easy slogan. All they want is the same as anyone else. Work. Wages. Homes. They write this in neat block letters, practising their script on scraps of bark since it's been years since their fingers have needed to remember the exact curve of a *w* or how to spell *demand* or *Ottawa*. They want pretty girls to be their wives and they want well-cut suits and they want jobs that make good use of their bodies and they want to dance in bars just a little drunk, but they can't fit those into the slogans.

They stick their tongues out in concentration like schoolboys and squint into the fumes of the shoe polish they apply with twigs to their sweaters. *We Want Work and Wages,* they write. *Down with the Bennett Starvation Government,* and soon they are their own advertisement.

The letters crack and flex around fibres, shrink when in rivers, flake off during heat and marching. At each stop, they must wipe soot off the lettering so the message is not hidden. They brush one another's backs until the words appear again and they can run their fingers along their demands — *We Want Work and Wages! End the Slave Camp System!* — until the words are not letters but textures, a smoothness against rough wool. They remind one another this way, by seeing the message expand and contract with the breathing of the men standing in line in front of them.

While they march, they read between one another's shoulder

blades. Because of the cold and burning heat and wind and smoke-stack fumes, it's hard to go unclothed and since they are without mirrors they must ask each other to decipher what is written on them so they can remember what slogan their own back demands. They wear their sweaters until the letters bear their scent, until the sweat bleeds the message imprecisely onto their damp skins.

POLLEN

In the lobby of the Saskatchewan Parliament building, Slim shifts on a glossed leather chair. Behind the conference-room doors, voices rise and voices fall: a noise like wildlife.

"Sit down, Mr. Evans."

"I will not sit down!" Arthur-Slim Evans, jailed twice, shot in the leg at Ludlow.

"Mr. Evans. Mr. Evans. Please be seated!"

"I have been mandated by the people of this nation——" It goes on like this.

The lobby's scent is of lemons and darker fruits Slim has never tasted. In the months to come, he will know this odour as a mixture of waxes and polishes, will find it in courtrooms and first-class trains and other expensive places that lead to trouble. But for now, the scents seem to be from a jungle, and Slim searches for the flowers or fruit they might belong to.

The mirror rests in dark, wax-fragrant wood. Slim is stunned. Has he ever seen himself this clearly? Even when he lived with his parents, he cannot recall a mirror, only ponds rippled with wind, the polished shard of tin his father looked into while shaving.

Slim peers at his reflection, unable to believe he has this face. Hears "government," "a bloody foul conspiracy perpetuated against the people of this great country," "sit down, Mr. Evans." Slim's eyes are deep in the socket, scant-lashed. He can hardly host a beard. He bends closer. His sun-chapped skin moulting away. Little black specks in his pores. He pinches his cheeks again, amazed at the image.

"Sit down, Mr. Evans!" Premier Gardiner's voice is plaintive, as if he were Arthur-Slim's whiny son, and Slim feels pride in this. He pinches a pore between his nails and it releases a small golden seed. Thinks of Matt Shaw's candle-pale skin: so many tiny scars on his face he looks almost albino. Slim holds the seed on his fingertip. It might be coal dust or sweat or grain or chaff or pollen.

"You ain't fit to be prime minister of a Hottentot village," yells Slim.

"Sit down, Mr. Evans. Mr. Evans, the government has nothing to offer you. In these times, it's ludicrous to imagine that we'd place the demands of foreign transients ahead of the needs to our own —"

It's going badly. Slim was brought for another body: a big guy raised on the land's grain, a native son.

"There is nothing to be done," says the voice.

Slim is out here, a closed door between. There is nothing he can do. There is nothing to be done.

EDIE

"Maybe he'll come back," she says again as one song blurs into another. She has lost track of how long they've been dancing.

The soldier nods. They've talked too long for her to ask for his name without being embarrassed about not asking it sooner. He keeps twirling her, even though the music has slowed into a swaying waltz. She wonders if her blouse is translucent with sweat, if he can see her undergarments. His hand worries over her brassiere's clasp but lacks the dexterity to release it.

He twirls her harder, a flick of the wrist so her body snaps like the sail of a ship. Pulls her in closer, lets her hip bones strike against him. She's drunk. Has missed being drunk, her limbs tingling as if emerging from cold water. He pushes her away and reels her back in. Pushes her away, then dips her down low. She feels her skirt rip along a seam that has been mended many times, but it does not matter; it could not possibly matter. After years of mending, it is important to stay like this, flushed and warm in his arms. Her back arches and she looks beyond his too-young face to the chandelier, which tosses its smoke-ruined light against the haze. Outside the window, flurries of snow, as if they are aloft in clouds.

Saw the ceiling blurred and dizzy from dancing.

Saw an old couple foxtrotting at 3:00 a.m.

Saw a man with half-ruined hands holding me and pushing me away, holding me and pushing me away.

And the hours pass like this: twirling in his arms, dipping in and out of the present moment.

BUT THIS ONE TIME, OH CHRIST, GOING ACROSS THE CROWSNEST PASS

The craggy hills, the river still dusty with grey ice and the hills crusted too, old snow tarnished within the radius of the train's smokestacks though it is June. The telephone lines are taut and following them endlessly, other people's conversations moving faster than locomotion, until they reach the Crowsnest coulee and are oh Christ aloft. The train is in the sky. Slim is in the sky. The train is in the sky, its metal blanched the colour of sky and Slim can only hold on, hold his breath, since holding your breath across a bridge is good luck, like how letting your clothes fall to the ground means that you will fall too. He could fall at any time. The train rattles on. Below him, the river is a daubed smear, the trees small as eyelashes, and Lord he can't look down. Looks up. The wind flattens his shirt against his chest and he imagines himself stripped bare, even as the sheer freezing wind cracks his lips. It is summer but impossibly there is snow. Slim is so high up he is in a place where summer doesn't exist. He lifts one hand from the guide rails. Wind at his fingertips like catching something and letting it slip over and over. Does not fall. He lifts the other hand. Slim does not believe in God, but he believes in this.

EVER ONWARD TO VICTORY

There are people born with a wildness driven deep in them and most of these people are men. Sometimes they are women; once, Edie was one of those women, who slipped into her sister-scented bed right before dawn with straw still in her hair, bruised lips. Who lay there touching her pulsing mouth that had been kissed and bitten and sucked and knew that her sister dreamed of gentler suitors. Even as children, these untamable people will follow the path of a frog along a riverbank until they are miles from home. They will stare out a window when they should be mending or sweeping. They can never sit at a family supper table without jostling their knees, their eyes on the door. There are those who want to ascend in life and those who want to move straight and fast as far as they can go: those who seek clouds and those who seek the sun setting along a horizon they will never touch. Edie believes that the world can be divided into those who dream of walls and those who dream of trains.

WILDERNESS

Every night, she could hear the train's whistle over the mine's infernal noise. At first, she mistook the sound for an owl's hoot. Later, it was a reminder that 12:04 p.m. existed, even in a place where time was kept haphazardly by a fifty-year-old pocketwatch. She imagined the train's headlights spraying through the trees, all the animals watching as it passed, leaving a radius of soot on the white snow.

BELLY

Belly cannot count high enough to number all the horses he's seen. Horses have more muscles than you can imagine. They can go so far on all those legs. Belly is hot and feels like he should be naked, which is bad because you're supposed to hide your parts when there are girls around and Sadie would probably scream, since girls have a trick of screaming and laughing at the same time. Once after a bath he stood under the fan and it felt like someone was patting him over and over, but his mom came in and said time to get dressed or you'll get your death of cold. You must get dressed and stay dressed, Belly knows, or you might catch a death.

"You can be the daddy if you want," says Sadie. She kneels in front of him with clouds around her hair. Her voice is sweet for real. "I'll be the hangar and you can be the daddy coming home. You can be whatever plane you want."

Horses are hot with their many legs and all that hair and Belly cannot tell her that he isn't a plane. He is a horse, can run like a horse, fast on many legs, has a face big and hard as a horse.

"There's the Lancaster and the Spitfire and the Hurricane and the B-52, but only the Yanks use that one," says Sadie. "But you can be the B-52, I don't mind. I won't say nothing about it." Her too-nice expression makes Belly feel wrong. "*Anything* about it," she says. "I mean, anything about it." She touches his face and her hand is cold and wet the way a window is cold and wet.

"You can be whatever you want. I don't even mind."

His face prickles. She's being too nice and he doesn't want to make her sad, but his face is changing. Belly is growing a muzzle and knows the prickling on his face means he will get bristly hair and more legs than he can imagine.

"You can be whatever you want," Sadie says. "You can be whatever you want."

EDIE

"I'm sorry to hear about your husband," the soldier says as the last song dissolves into crackle and fizz. "And now what's happened to your little boy." His breathing is soft against her hair; he's standing so close. She can feel the heat coming off him, strange against the bursts of cold from the open door. Some soldiers are drunk and laughing, running outside. They dive in the snow, these men in uniform making the shapes of angels in the white banks. She watches with the soldier from the doorway.

"Come in!" cries the hotelkeeper. She, too, stands at the door as if on the edge of the sea. "It's too cold! You'll catch your death of cold! I won't waste good whiskey heating you back up again! Not even the bad stuff!" They are young and coltish, drunk, but stand carefully so as not to disturb the angels they have made. They scoop handfuls of snow and throw them at one another, the balls bursting into powder on one another's coats. They laugh at these minor explosions.

The soldier holds her hand with his ruined hand, the half-fingers soft as fins. It's as if he'd dipped his hand in acid and part of it disappeared. (She thinks of Slim rubbing the lye into his hand and the smell of the skin curdling into a burn. He was calm as he scarred the pen marks away. The *XI* scrawled on his hand that said he wasn't fit, that his skills were needed in the mine so he couldn't even be a bloody secretary in uniform. They looked at my teeth like I was a horse, he said.)

"How's your little boy doing?" he asks. Both their hands are grey with ink and sweat. The soldiers are singing a song — "'Dear Lady Astor, you think you know a lot... standing on that platform and talking Tommy rot'" — swaying together with burrs of snow on their jackets. "'You're England's sweetheart and her pride... We think your mouth's too bloody wide... That's from your D-Day Dodgers in sunny Italy.'" Loud and happy as boys. Well, she thinks, that's what they are. Nineteen or twenty. "Hold the fort for we are coming," she thinks. "Union men be strong." "Did you get the glass out fine?"

Belly. When she was pregnant, she used to have dreams that he'd already been born and she'd forgotten him down in the mine. In the dream, she would be anxious to get to the surface and only when she reached the sunlight would she realize her arms were empty. "He'll be fine down there," Slim would say in the dream. "We'll fetch him tomorrow." So strange, she thinks, that she always imagined her child as a boy, that she always suspected that she would leave him.

"He's fine," she says, bright as music. "Four stitches, less than I thought. I'll check on him in a minute, but he's sleeping. Children that young, sleep is the only medicine they need. It's all you can do for them." She cannot imagine stepping out of the shimmer of warmth that surrounds her now to go upstairs and check on her son. The soldier's eye would surely wander to other women and Belly is fine — probably sleeping — and Lord knows the child does not suffer in silence and would find her if he needed to.

"If only you'd seen what I got into as a boy. It's a miracle boys make it to men. That's what my mom always said, must have scraped all the skin off me a dozen times over," agrees the soldier. Maybe he ruined his own hands so he wouldn't have to fight but they made him ship out anyways. He gazes at her tenderly and touches the small of her back. How long has it been since someone has touched that indentation? That particular curve. Right there. "But anyways, I'm sorry to hear about your husband."

Edie looks away, to the old couple taking a break, dabbing the sheen on their foreheads with napkins.

"It's fine."

"Where did he go down, if you don't mind me asking?"

"Well, it's... I mean, it's a strange thing. He signed up under an assumed name. There's been no official word, just rumours, just talk. The war wouldn't take him so he had to fake his way in. No widow's pension, nothing."

"Then how do you know he's dead?"

(His lips blue with cold as she shut the door, the windows open and the heat turned off on the coldest day of the year. His heart gone lazy with booze.)

"I know and I don't know. It's a strange thing," she stammers, trying to keep the story straight. She has never managed to tell a story that didn't tangle or loop in wrong directions or cut off before the best part. "We heard through word of mouth. It's a long story."

"Your boy's so young. This whole war was just—What part of the service was your husband in?" He almost coos the phrase at her, sweet-talking her with the death of her husband.

She is hot and she is drunk. She stares at the handsome profile of the soldier and cannot remember what she has already said. Outside, Vivian's shrieking laugh has gone unhinged from the one she practises. Edie glances toward the door and sees her lifted in the arms of a soldier, soaking wet, the bodies of the snow angels dismantled with their scuffling. Her dress is wet, the skirt damp against her legs. Her new stockings must be in ruins.

"Can't we try to make this a good night," she says.

He is so warm, his uniform damp. Runnels of sweat cut down his forehead. He gazes at her with a dreamy, trusting look and she presses herself against him in a brazen way she's never done before, not even with Slim. He gives a little grunt of shock but does not move away.

THE FIRST GOOD DAY

After an awful night, the town of Golden in sunrise and the miracle of soup and bread. Volunteers are ready with breakfast at the station. The Trekkers descend, blinking through a crust of soot on their eyelashes, mouths rank with the taste of charcoal. Slim can hardly believe it: breakfast, townspeople with banners, pots frothing, the train steaming innocuous white puffs. Women sweat even in the morning chill, their lovely pink arms stirring a bathtub full of soup.

"Hold it up high now," he hears one lady chide her son, forcing a sign into his grasp. "High so they can see it."

OUR BOYS, says the sign, an old sheet stitched with letters cut from rags in a way that makes Slim want to weep. All that time that could have been devoted to the family's own mending. After they're gone, the loose baste stitches will be plucked free, a child will sleep under this sheet, the letters will be balled into a woman's fist and used to scrub filth from the sink. (Likely Slim does not think of this, Edie realizes. He was used to work camps without indoor plumbing, left home at fifteen.)

And now, Jesus: OUR BOYS. Soup. Bread with a thick crust that Slim imagines is still warm on the inside. The Trekkers stand fidgeting in their ranks away from the food tables as if at a Sunday dance before the first nip of rye.

An older woman approaches Slim. She looks like his ma, everyone's ma, could fit right into the photographs many of the boys have tucked into the bottom of their rucksacks wrapped in waxed paper.

The woman takes his face in her hands, testing the sooty oil on his cheeks between her thumb and index finger, then runs her hands along her apron.

"Look at you," she says. "Black as a little pickaninny." She stands on her tiptoes and dabs his face with her handkerchief. "We got a basin where you can wash up. Good food." She pats his stomach. "Good home food."

He thanks her, calls her ma'am. "This is God's country," he says to her, will say again on the many stops toward Ottawa to the many women who take his face in their hands and look for traces of their own absent boys. But here, he truly means it: the mundane miracle of a bathtub of soup, its odour of earth and roots, the morning smell of wet grass, a woman who has been stirring since before sunrise. People arrive with loaves of bread, cans of tomatoes, baskets of produce fresh ripped from the ground.

On a platform by the railroad tracks, some union leader gives a speech. Welcome, he says. And something about fighting the good fight, not wavering. Something about the city's own sons gone long-haired in hobo jungles. Slim cannot help but stare at the women raised on grain, their hair the colour of it in the early light. Soup. Bread. A trough of water for the men to wash the soot from their faces and hands.

At a trough meant for horses, a girl hands out brown curls of soap, which Slim whips into a froth that's already greying in his palms. He dips his face into the cold water, comes up to lather, dips his face again. He uses his never-clean palms to scoop the water into his mouth, then spits the blackness into the dirt. Swallows again and keeps the liquid between his cheeks until his teeth ache. In the water, Slim tastes a salve of metal and grass, the salt of his own raw face. He stares at his reflection. Sunburned. How did that happen?

Later, Slim is sated by the taste of herbs picked by hand, potatoes with their tang of local minerals. When a girl comes by to take his empty bowl, he refuses to give it to her until the ceramic's last warmth is gone from his fingertips. Some of the boys will no doubt linger their gazes at the breasts of this serving girl, but that's one rule Arthur-Slim Evans and Matt Shaw established early on. Hands off the ladies. Instant dismissal for any man caught getting fresh.

Call it a publicity ploy, call it what you will, Slim thinks, but you don't need to read Marx to know that people like their town left clean and their daughters buttoned up. It's a rule that causes the most grumbling. All those men. All those years without women. Years and years. Slim suspects that Matt Shaw will recruit him to walk like a school marm among the Trekkers trying to waltz at the dance tonight, making sure they keep their gentlemanly distance.

THE FRASER VIEW CEMETERY

As a child, Edie loved to watch the long black cars sliding smooth as eels up the dirt road to the gravestones, sliding out the sleek coffin, lowering it to the ground. She loved the pastor's murmured incantations and the movements of his hands over the open earth. Old women with veils and flowers, dressed up prettier than at a wedding, stood for hours at the fresh earth. Edie was young. What did she know of grief? What did any of it mean to her?

When Edie was fifteen, the older cemetery by the river flooded and convicts bore the stinking bones up the hill to the Fraser View cemetery. They carried the skeletons wrapped in cloth, then stuffed in a sack so that the smell of putrefaction would not ruin the interiors of cars or horse carts.

The convicts bore the bones up the hill. Most of them were old men and looked so sad and gentle under the weights of the skeletons.

For three days, Edie was kept indoors while the men formed a long line, sun-up to sundown. She was fifteen, restless and the house reeked of putrefaction despite the closed windows and rags under the doors. Her mother sweated out the last of her pregnancy dizzy with the stench, running a shard of ice along her face.

The convicts carried the bones up the hill and laid them gently on the ground. Crows followed them all the way and the sky was thick with their wings and their greedy noises. The men kept their eyes downward, stooped under the weight of the bones, and the crows hovered above them, all the way up the hill.

BELLY

This one time, he ran through big grasses squishing apples that had gone mushy on the ground and smelled sweeter than the good apples and he was a fast runner; no one could catch him; he was probably the fastest boy ever. Cherry pits became bullets in his mouth. He likes the way people's mouths look when they eat cherries, how even their tongues get bright and red like they're covered in blood, but not in a scary way. Now, he pretends that there are horses running across the snow and counts them in the words that feel right to him.

His dad will bring him a horse after he's done with the war and doesn't need one anymore. The horses are fast. Belly is fast. He counts in the language of small boys everywhere—*yi, er, san, shi*—special words so that boys can talk about secret things and their moms and dads can't understand. Maybe when you get old you forget how to say things right. Maybe you have to stick to one type of word.

His dad is gone and his house is gone and his friends are gone and his mom was gone and then back and now she is gone again. *Sensou* means war and *tomodachi* means friend and *uma* means horses. *Sensou* means war and *tomodachi* means friend and *uma* means horses. *Sensou* means war. *Tomodachi* means friend. *Uma* means horses. These are words that his mom will not allow him to say.

He finds the door. He opens it. Outside: a shock of light and music.

"You can't do that," says Sadie. "We aren't supposed to go anywhere." She is somewhere beside him. Downstairs, big people are laughing too loud. "If my mom was your mom, she'd whip you for sure. You can't go down there."

He will find his mom, he thinks. There is a hurt on his face and his mom will know what to do. He wants to make a big noise when he finds her. He wants to make her feel bad for leaving. When his mom and dad were hating each other, he often would cry for no reason or make a loud sound so they would remember he was in the room and not say terrible things.

EDIE

Once, when she was boy-shaped, she swam with her friends' brothers in the Fraser River and tunnelled into its sand dunes. Now she has a different shape and can only watch the adults cavort in the snow, though it is counter to everything their mothers have told them about catching their deaths of cold. It is night, but it has never been day, and no one will sleep until they're safely in the civilized train with its neat, school-like rows.

Edie and the soldier watch from the door. Edie holds her jacket, not wanting to lose it, but not wanting to put it on and blunt the touch of the soldier's hand against her back. It seems as if all of the train's passengers are outside. The civilian men's black coats look like wings as they raise their arms. Boggled by the room's heat and the lack of a true day, they dive into the snow and emerge damp and laughing. Vivian dove first. Maybe she suggested it. She laughs her screeching laugh and remembers, though drunk, to put a hand over her snaggletooth. Edie leans into the soldier. He is warm but straight-backed; his hands stiffen to hold her tight. Outside, women and men jump into the night-blued snow, immune to the temperature, their silhouettes blurry with snowfall. They make a lake within this landlocked place. The snow is so fresh that the train hasn't had time to sully it and the only other houses are so far away they cannot be seen, so the landscape feels like an ocean, the train station and hotel small islands.

The light from the door is the one stain on the snow, and Edie and the soldier stand in front of it, their shadows projected huge and many-limbed on the snowbanks, over the snow angels and the backs of the tussling people. Someone sings a drinking song. Someone sings "Nearer My God to Thee." The whores do not get into the act, not wanting to ruin their faces, and Edie watches them cluster with their elbows on the bar in the empty room. Outside, women's mascara runs down their cheeks; the men do not care if they tarnish their watches. The soldier holds her tighter. His hands are on places that have not experienced a steady touch in so long. Slim's fingertips trembled so much it was as if she could feel the electricity in his nerves. Her thin-skinned husband.

"Foolishness," he whispers. "These grown people!" His fingers in the spaces between her ribs, calm and solid as wood. His hands are so warm they feel whole, though she can picture the missing fingers, the lattice of scars. Soon it will be morning and the storm will abate, letting them pass through. Already, she can hear a scraping sound of railway men clearing the tracks with shovels so the train can get its start, points of moving light from their cigarettes and lanterns in the distance. (She thinks of Slim's road going nowhere, vanished under the snow.) Vivian's laughter. Other laughter. The shape of angels left in the snow. In a snowbank, someone mimes a backstroke. Even the old couple takes part, balling snow into their fists and tossing it at each other.

"Like children," whispers the soldier. "It's a bit frightening. Some of these people are upper class. They'll be sorry when their rings and watches are lost." Edie thinks of her own ring still in the pocket of the jacket she holds over her arm. The bone is on her bedside table and she has nothing solid to move her fingers against.

"Just like children," repeats the soldier. One by one, the lights in the hotel come on as other guests cluster to the window to see what the noise is about. A sizzle, a pop: the power goes out. A little gasp, then silence. In darkness, the figures stand up one by one, brushing off their snow-burred clothing.

"That's what they get," the soldier whispers, then kisses her as dozens of people shuffle past them, their shoes squeaking on the waxed floor. By the time Edie opens her eyes, candles are lit and there's a wet patch up the stairs, some embarrassed murmurs, as the passengers file into their rooms to get changed before the train brings the morning. She kisses him again.

Saw grown people cavorting in the snow with their clothes wet against their bodies and their laughter stretched weird in the wind.

Saw a soldier with a hand like a fish.

Saw a snowstorm so bad that it took away the face of a whole town, so you could have been anywhere.

GOING STRANGE

In the work camp, a boy of seventeen or eighteen hung himself. Slim forgets his name. He went strange, he told Edie. What does that mean? she asked. He was depressed by the conditions or what? No, he went strange, said Slim carefully. You know. It happens. The isolation. You know what I mean. She didn't. Not when he first told her.

BELLY

Downstairs, they must be dancing and Belly moves away from the music and light and the mean-laughing voices that adults make. When big people go dancing it is sometimes scary because they act like children and smell strange and find everything more funny than it is supposed to be. Usually, you know what a mom will do and what a dad will do, but at nights when they are dancing you cannot always tell and this is scary. Back home, he often snuck out of rooms where he was supposed to be sleeping and saw his mom and dad and many other big people throwing each other around and touching each other's arms and the smell was wrong and he didn't like any of it.

Now he moves to the closed doors, where he thinks she will be. She cannot hear him because the door is shut. She must have fallen asleep somewhere. She did not mean to fall asleep. She was probably just so tired because it has been a long day.

Sadie follows behind him saying, "You can't go in there, you can't do that, you better stop right this instant." Saying his name as mean as she can. The lights pop and then it is dark and there is no music. Sadie grabs his hand. Her hand is dry and rough as a bird's leg. He felt a crow's leg once when it was dead and his mom said don't touch that and washed his hands until they hurt.

Belly moves away from the adults making strange sounds. He opens a door. He walks in to more darkness and sees the light coming blue through the window. "You can't do that," Sadie says.

EDIE

And how does she sleepwalk from there to here? And how does she decide yes and did he lead and did she follow? Her brain works in flashes: the soldier groaning into her hair, his half-gone fingers trying to distinguish between her own bones and those of her under-garments, neither of them saying anything. From the smell of snow and whiskey, up the stairs to the empty hotel room, which neither of them has rented and which has a woman's coat slung over the post of the bed and a tiny valise in the corner. The bedframe is bowed from years of moving bodies and the pillows smell of hair cream and cologne so that when she turns her head to the side she breathes in other people's odours. The walls have the same framed portraits and her own face ghosts across the glass.

Even as it happens she cannot quite recall how she got here: naked on this bed. The buttons on his trousers were different — this, she remembers — and were not like the overalls that Slim wore, which would unhinge with an oiled snap. So the buttons were different. So he was shorter; she could almost look him in the eye. The shock of looking him in the eye. His ruined hands pressing but not gripping. His ruined hands blunt of feeling, pressing too heavy on her, the knuckle where the fingertip should be and the scar tissue pearlescent in the light so that the tips of his hands seemed to be faintly glowing. So yes, she remembers his hands, but not how they reached the bed, how they lay down upon it, whether he slid her stockings off or if she guided him.

He says her name or he does not say her name. Perhaps he does not know it. She leaves her eyes open or she shuts them. He strokes her hair, her cheek, along her neck, and his fingers briefly encircle her throat. He is fucking her the way the war has taught him: to aim first for the body's vulnerable hollows. The pressure around her neck makes her vision burn over with darkness like a badly developed photograph.

His hands move to her breasts and remember again how to stroke without bruising. She breathes. She presses her heels against his lower back and they fit so neatly together and they rock like this and it is easy in a way it has never been easy before. He thrusts into her and her memory flares and gutters. She is hollowed out. Cored. Glows like an egg candled in the light. She is not reminded of anything. There are some people who go their whole lives without wanting this, she thinks.

BELLY

He touches the bed in the dark room and the bed is empty. The window is very blue. He is awake or asleep and his face feels huge and has his heart in it. His mom is not here. Sadie is here and he doesn't want her to be. Outside, there is a long hallway with many doors. He is cold and then he is not cold. He cannot even imagine where his mother might have gone.

EDIE

After years of apologetic sex — the mother-of-my-child gentleness, the eyes looking elsewhere — she has missed this. The pulse in the stomach. The sex that is like opening a door and walking through it and finding that there are other such open doors that you could just keep walking through.

Up close the soldier's young face makes no sense. He runs his hands along her upper arms as if expecting a widow's band to be burned there. Some trace of her husband, some medal for valour tucked into her undergarments. It's too dark for him to see the stretch marks her son has left on her and so her body must seem to him to be an expanse of unbroken whiteness, as if the marks he leaves when he grabs her hips or takes her breast in his mouth are the first wounds she's ever received.

Her muffled brain is quiet the way a road is silent after a snowfall. Is bright and shining. Snow on the window frame like ash.

BELLY

"This is a bad place to be," says Sadie. "This is someone else's room. They will be so mad to find us here. We have to go back straight away."

Belly could open the window. He could sputter and make all the right airplane noises with his arms out perfectly straight. The air would cool his face and stop the thumping inside of it. He could shoot cherry pits and his mouth would be a terrible gun. He could pretend he flies a special plane and that he is a father coming home.

Belly presses his face against the glass. He knows that there must be a latch. When they moved into the apartment he was so amazed by windows—how bright they were, how you could just look outside whenever you wanted or even when you didn't mean to—and he kept opening and closing the one in the kitchen whenever his mom wasn't looking, loving how the wooden frame would squeak as he did so, loving the click that the latch made.

"Get away from there," says Sadie and her voice goes higher and higher. "Mother! He's going to fall!"

He finds the latch and it is smooth and cold. The click it makes when it opens is the best noise. He would like to fall. It would feel so lovely to land in all that snow.

EDIE

When the lights come back on, the soldier freezes above her, still inside of her. The feeling of being caught. (She thinks of her sister screaming as the prisoner backed away; "I thought he was killing you," she said.) They look at each other perfectly still and she is cold where his body is above her and hot where they are joined. The whiskey on his breath. His nose flaring with the effort of keeping himself aloft. The new light blots out his face's shadows so that he looks overexposed, all shiny forehead and pale eyebrows. From downstairs, the music begins again and they move in time to it.

As he thrusts into her, he grabs at her hips for curves that aren't there, runs his hands along her breasts and seems startled when they fit in his palm. He is fucking someone else, the ghost of another woman who lies fleshy and soft between them. Edie can almost see the woman's outline shimmering around her own, blunting Edie's sharpness.

He is close to climaxing and she does not stop him. There is no way, she thinks, that a child could be born of any of this. Her body is a lone thing: pared down, war rationed. Nothing can take root in her. She's so light she feels bloodless.

After, she does not mind when the young soldier, who is suddenly blushing, covers her with a sheet as if she were sick. Her lips pulse where they have been bitten. The soldier hides his hands under the sheet and lies beside her, staring at the ceiling. She thinks, finally, of her husband and the many hotels and knows that sex is just another form of leaving. She does not think of her son until the soldier says, "So, how do you think that boy of yours is doing?" in a way that is both gentle and an accusation. She is amazed at how easy it is to do what Slim did, to remember only in fragments, to blank out the guilty parts.

THE GIFT OF STORYTELLING

One night, she asked him to tell her about the other women. She felt that it was her right to know.

"Describe them to me," she said. "Tell me about every one of them."

He rolled over in bed and stared at her. "I don't know what you mean," he said. She knew that there were scratches along his back. She could so easily picture the lacquered fingernails that caused them.

"Tell me about them. You can at least be honest with me. If I'm going to hear about you from every smug housewife, you can at least tell me to my face."

He stared beyond her as if trying to conjure the women up. "I'm not sure what you want," he said.

"What they looked like. What it was like. What it—" she made a gesture. She lowered her voice. "What it felt like."

"Jesus, Edie," he said. "Our son's here."

She could feel the other women in the room: prim war widows still brittle with grief squeaking out their husband's names as they climaxed; the booze-fattened whores with their hair crisp from home permanents. If he wouldn't tell her, she would just imagine them and that would be worse. Night after night, she stayed awake inventing the faces of the women who had fucked her husband.

"He's sleeping," she said. "He won't hear anything. I want to know. I won't hold it against you. I want to know."

"Who says there's anything to know?" She could feel his hands damp on her back. He was holding her against his body so she couldn't see his face. A tremor that was either guilt or booze buzzed from his hands down the small of her back. "It's not right. It's not natural for a woman to think things like that. I don't think I could tell you even if I tried."

"Try," she said. What else had she ever asked him for?

He was silent for a long time. Moths hurled themselves against the tent's canvas walls, their shadows huge and prehistoric. Belly snuffled in his sleep. Edie lay pressed against Slim and she could feel his mouth moving against the side of her cheek, testing the words out.

"Even if I could remember," he said finally, "I couldn't say." And now — lying in the sagging bed next to the soldier, feeling her heartbeat everywhere in her body — she knows that he was telling the truth. If someone came to her years from now and said, "Tell me about the time that you came down from Ymir," how could she possibly respond? The only words that feel right are stuck in her head. Her brain is flooded and submerged. Her brain is candied, heavy with sap. How could she be expected to remember, let alone tell?

MOTHERHOOD

For five years they made love and she did not even imagine that a child would come and a child did not come. Though their bodies struck together like flint, there was no tinder between them. Nothing caught fire.

And then local boys started dying in the war and she quickly became pregnant, as if the world was evening itself out. The pregnancy began as a dizziness. Blood rushed to her head when she stood and her vision pulsed with flecks of light. In the mine, the odour of molten rock and wet stone made her gag; she could hardly stand the smell of ash in Slim's hair.

When she could not hold down her morning coffee Slim wondered if she might be pregnant. She had not even considered it but knew at that moment that it was true and thought of her mother swollen and unwashed staring out the window, moored in the rocking chair as she waited for her husband to return and leave and return again.

When Belly arrived, she thought that other children would follow but none ever did. Sometimes, though, she feels herself surrounded by dozens of tiny sparks. All those unborn children circling her, unable to land.

BELLY

Sadie screams, "Mother" and no one comes. Sadie screams, "He's trying to die. Mother. Mommy. He's trying to fall out the window," and no one is there and her voice is like an engine. She is so good at making sounds.

The window swings open and he almost falls but doesn't and the air is so cold it feels hot and it tastes like water. Back home, the wind smelled different: of smoke or coal, of burning. Sadie screams and her hands are on him. He is dizzy from being up high, from the wind going and going against his face, from the air that is good and cold. The wind is like big hands pushing him back and if he jumped now something would catch him. A boy like him would probably fly.

"I don't like you at all," Sadie says and she is crying now. Her voice has hiccups in it. "I don't even like you a bit."

And then there is a crackle and he sees light under the door. And then Sadie is at the door, her body dark around the door's light, and then she is gone and he is alone with only this throbbing in his face and the music starts again. He kneels on the windowsill — the wood prickles against his legs — and holds tight to the window frame as the wind puffs his shirt out around him and makes such big noises. He looks down through the snow for a place to land, and knows that if he said "Mom" right now no one would come.

EDIE

Standing with the soldier outside the hotel room door—dressed now, her body tucked back into the slim skirt, the mended blouse, sharply cut jacket—she tries to make herself want to go down the long hallway to Belly's room to check on him. She feels very far away from him. She tries to picture her son, but he does not make sense without his father beside him. She imagines Belly's red hair and sees Slim's. She imagines her son twirling his soldiers through the air—loving to make them fall from a great height—and can almost see the scar on his hands where the *X1* would be written, as if Slim's failures would emerge like freckles through Belly's skin. She is terrible to think this. She is unnatural.

He's just fine, she tells herself as she heads down the staircase to get another drink. He's just fine. He's just fine. The decision is not about her. It's about Belly, the life he deserves and she can't give to him, a life with someone who will put him in a routine and keep him there, who will be good and patient and rub poultices on his chest until his lungs glow a new pink.

The smoke-blackened chandelier hosts clouds of cobwebs between the crystals that sway with the storm. A high whistling of the wind making itself known. The passengers have freshened themselves up and returned to the bar, though they talk in lower, nighttime voices, and Edie cannot decipher how much time has passed since she left with the soldier. No one even looks up at her.

"Well," says the soldier as they reach the bottom of the stairs. He stands with one hand on the banister, as if posing for a photograph. Edie looks up to the top floor where her son sleeps, willing herself to climb back up the stairs, to open the door, to bring Belly a glass of water or a sandwich, to lie down beside him so that he falls asleep to the rhythm of her breathing. Under her dress, Edie's breasts are throbbing. Her chin is red from where his stubble has rubbed against it. How can a woman like she is be any kind of mother? The life she wants is no life for a boy of Belly's age.

Upstairs, a small white figure is moving down the hall with her hands folded in front of her body. Sadie. Her white dress looks unsullied from this distance. The little atmosphere of heat Edie feels bursts, nothing but a soap bubble.

"Sadie," says Edie as the little girl makes her way down the stairs, hands steepled in front of her, eyes straight ahead. There's an arc of blood on her chest, like the drawing of a rainbow. Edie bends down to Sadie's height. "Did you have a bad dream, love?" As if this is a child she has always known, not one she's met today.

Sadie is crying, despite her stiff posture. "Your son won't play right," she sobs. "He won't even talk the right words and he got sick-up on his shirt and he has got the window open and he's going to jump out and then he will be dead."

The hotel is slammed by a gust, rattling the storm shutters. Roofs can cave in under the weight of snow. Once, in Sandon, a whole family was crushed because the father built a level-top roof instead of a peaked one. Didn't want to live like a bloody Scandahoovian, he said, and his whole family was smothered, their backs broken under the timbers the man had sawn himself. (She thinks of the siren like screaming, all those beams that Slim had laid, had believed to be the right course, had gone wrong. The weight of earth like the weight of snow in the damage it could do.) How did we survive in a tent for that many years? she thinks. How did we even live? What would we have done without Norah and Red to take us when it got too cold?

"He won't speak right," Sadie says. "We were just playing. I said he could be whatever airplane he wanted. He won't even speak right. He won't even speak the right words."

Vivian comes through the front door with a soldier. Her dress is wet and there's snow in her hair. The last to come out of the cold.

"Kitten," she says. Sadie stares blankly at her mother and Vivian looks ashamed. The sodden fabric shows outlines of her breasts and ribs and Vivian tugs at the front of her dress. The hem is grey with mud. Mascara on her cheeks.

"He won't speak right and I couldn't find you and he's going to jump out of the window," sobs Sadie. She moves to bury her face in her mother's shirt but recoils at the sensation of wetness and cold and so stands there with her elbows tight against body, her fingers linked tightly together.

The room keens in the wind; the lights spark and die out, and before her eyes have a chance to adjust to the darkness Edie is already running up the stairs, listening for her son or the thud of a crash that would tell her it's too late, oblivious to who might be following her.

WAR WIDOW

So many animal cries could be mistaken for the cries of wounded children. The newspaper said, "Fifteen Men Killed in Air Attack" and she found the bruised imprint of a woman's teeth on her husband's thigh. The newspaper said, "Women and Children Feared Dead in Bombing of Britain," and she slept with her two hands around their flashlight as bears tried to bat their garbage down from the tree. The radio named the dead boys — all those family-worn names — and she could just picture all the James MacKinnon Jr.s and Robert Smiths and knew that their school friends must have called them Mack or Smitty or Bobby and waited for her husband's footsteps along the gravel and for the familiar rage to flare up in her and for Slim to avert his gaze as he ducked into the tent bracing himself to be struck by her, but she never did, only stood there taut and shaking, saying, "Well then," saying, "so nice of you to finally join us" in the meanest voice she could muster. She wanted to strike him square in the hollow between his ribs, but none of what she felt meant anything when the radio named all the dead boys and her live husband stood trembling in front of her.

AND HERE CONTROLS THE HANDS AND HERE CONTROLS THE BREATHING AND HERE CONTROLS BODILY FUNCTIONS LIKE THE PASSING OF WATER. SO, YOU SEE, EVERYTHING HAS ITS PURPOSE

Live men bore cursed bones up the hill. Edie would watch them; how could you not?

A man confined to a patch of soil, a square of concrete, a place on a chain gang with the others. She pitied him. Shackled, his arms could not stretch to encircle her. She leaned against the gravestone, pinned against the outstretched arms of a bronze angel, and he stood in front of her. Perhaps the name of the dead woman and her birth and death dates would be branded into Edie's back, in reverse. She was hidden by the sheer size of him; they had only a few minutes; the warden would find them. His mouth tasted strangely of tea.

"What did you do?" she asked.

She was concealed by the angel's bronze wings, turned mossy with oxidization so they felt live. A rusty stink. His shoulders were thick, but he touched her lightly. She felt charged with static. His warmth in front: sun-warmed metal behind.

"Jesus," he murmured. He smelled of sweat and mould, tasted like tea. He was damp with heat.

"What did you do?" she asked. The chain between his handcuffs clinked against the angel's wings.

He touched her breasts and she reached out toward his groin and was shocked by the heat, took her hand away. She looked at him, his expression like kindness gone wrong, like reverence, like something. She was too young to know. She put her hand back and kept it there.

"Got caught," he said. He placed his hand over her hand. His wrist was bruised from where the handcuffs had strained in his eagerness to touch her. The chain between the handcuffs gave him just enough room to dig potatoes from the ground, not enough room to touch her the way he wanted to. He was bruising himself over her. Harming himself. He couldn't get enough. Edie thrilled at the idea that she might be the last warm thing he would touch.

BELLY

His face is wet with snow and the wind makes a low sound—part animal, part engine—in his ears and the light has been on and now it is off again and he is not sure how far down he could fall. He knows the sound of her feet before she arrives. She carries a light and her face floats like the ladies in the picture frames and she pulls him from the window frame so hard it's as if the wind blew him backwards.

"Belly," she says in a voice that is mad and not mad. He was going to tell her something, but the words he remembers are not the words she knows. Something to make her sad. He was going to tell her about horses and the open window and how soft he would land if he fell. He was going to make her sad for going. He wonders if she can see how his face is changing. He wonders if she can look into his head and if she would be mad at the terrible pictures he makes in his brain.

EDIE

Belly stands naked in front of her, sheen of sweat glowing in the candlelight as if he's lit from within. It's like seeing Slim at a distance, if Slim had her brown eyes. He's slick with sweat, mottled shades of red, white and pink. Goosepimpled all over. Bruises on his knees from where he's knelt against the windowframe.

Belly has a fever and Edie is still a little drunk: hot in the core but cold in the limbs. (In the mine, half drunk and pressing herself into the tightest space to feel her heartbeat in her wrists, in her chest, in her stomach, as if she had many hearts. Heartbeats wherever she pressed against stone.) A spray of snow fans out on the carpet below the window. She kneels in front of him, wavering a little. Lord, she cannot even keep a sober expression in front of her own child. It's a shame that he will have to witness her like this and cannot imagine how Slim lived with the guilt of returning ruined to his family.

The women in the photos look toward heaven, but their faces are streaked with grit and smoke. Sadie runs past Edie to Belly and begins picking up his clothes and handing them to him, one by one. She stares above him, polite, pressing the garments into his hands.

"Your pants," she says, as if teaching him the word. He drops them. They crumple at his feet. He mutters to himself, imagining the other side of the conversation, sliding between English and Japanese. Edie catches only a few words: "horse," "airplane," "crash." Half singing, half talking, his vowels sliding around.

"Your underpants," Sadie says, and he drops them. She does not look at Edie, who kneels in front of him, feeling the heat rolling off him. A furnace of a child. The string they've stitched him with can barely hold him together. It's dissolving into his skin, like a vein, only the edges sticking out. Edie cannot believe what's happened to him in such a short period of time. She was only gone for, how long? It feels like only an hour or two, though it must be much longer because it was day when she left and now it is the middle of the night. And now this has happened. And he was supposed to be sleeping.

Edie closes the window. She locks it. She can stand between her son and the window—can protect him in this one small way—but she has no way to cure what is happening inside his bloodstream. Vivian leaves a puddle where she stands in the doorway, her dress so slickened to her body it's as if she's naked and she knows it. Goosebumps on her arms and legs. She leans against the doorway for support, staring at the ground. Every few moments she opens her mouth to speak but closes it again.

"Your shirt," Sadie says. Helpful. As if he's a room she's tidying. A pool of vomit by the window and the acid stink of it like the stink of whiskey. Maybe whiskey is taken in through the skin like a mustard poultice and he's drunk. She imagines her son's limbs hot from whiskey, the way Edie still feels the heat in her own stomach.

The soldier also stands at the door beside Vivian, unsure of what to do with his hands. She didn't realize he'd followed her up the stairs. "He's taken sick," he notes. "Poor fellow. All this and now he's taken sick."

Belly stares beyond her, babbling. He has the same bone structure as Slim: the ribs jammed high against his shoulders, a little cave sunk in his solar plexus. The hole was the size of a man's fist and Edie often teased Slim that if only he had a heart, he could use it to fill the gap.

THE GRAVEYARD

It was late fall the last time she saw him. Her back was cold and her stomach was hot. Soon she would be caught and shamed. She pressed her pelvis against the prisoner, feeling the handcuffs between them, the chain stroking her knees. They would never have a private moment together. He would never have a private moment with anyone. She was the last warm touch for him. Of course, she was being dramatic. He would be out in ten years, but Edie couldn't imagine waiting that long for anything.

"Jesus," he said and reached to put a hand under her skirt. The handcuffs jerked him back and he stopped. A sore thin as a bracelet around his wrist from his straining to get to her.

"I'll come tomorrow," she said.

"Come tomorrow," he said. "Make sure you do."

She could hear someone calling for him. He would go back to the Pen and she could go anywhere: down to the riverbank, catch the tram to the drugstore, anywhere. Her mother was confined to her bed, her belly like a sack of rocks she'd strapped to her chest, and until the child was born, Edie could roam wherever she wanted.

BELLY

He was wrong to name the horses because they are better without names. You don't see a cougar with a name or a fox or even a spider. All the big people have lights around their faces and the little people must stay close by so they are not lost because it is dark. Belly has his mom's light around him and the man's and the lady Vivian's, so he is lucky this way.

Once, he called his friend Chinky Chinky Chinaman and his friend punched him in the nose. Belly had never been more surprised, since it seemed like a nice name, like a song a girl would sing while jumping rope. His face feels like someone split it open. Maybe he has said the wrong thing again.

He will jump into the snow or into the clouds that look like snow. Anything cold. He tries to take off his clothes, but they're already off and his stomach is slippery like he's wearing water instead of clothes.

"The boy's taken sick," says the man. His dad, maybe, come home from flying. Belly has taken sick, as if sick was something you could steal and swallow before anyone could catch you. Like the peppermint he found between the seats when his mom wasn't looking that was dusty but tasted like a clean mouth. Like the window he licked, expecting it to taste like ice, but it didn't and he gagged. Like the apples all smeary and sweet on the ground that you're not supposed to take, even though you can reach them, because they've gone bad and you'll get sick if you eat them and deserve whatever happens to you.

EDIE

An aureole of red around Belly's wound, starburst streaks branching out and following the path of veins to his heart. He sways a little and his hands trace out a language of shapes. The story his hands depict is made huge on the walls behind him, blinking in and out with the guttering candlelight.

There are only so many cures she knows. His face is swollen as if he'd been punched and he stares angrily at her, his cheeks a high, drunk colour. Mustard poultice for ailments of the chest. Camphor for a cold. Cod-liver oil for general vigour. Cold water for a fever. Hot compress to draw out the pus.

What is penicillin meant to cure? she wonders, having heard it can save people from all manner of afflictions of the blood. People who previously could not be saved now live. What path has the drug travelled in its civilian use? Has it gotten this far inland? In Vancouver, maybe every child is cured with a drug bred for soldiers.

"Belly," she says. His whole body is flushed. He shakes a little, goosepimpled, his gaze beyond her. "William," she says. He ignores any of his names. "Belly." When she gingerly touches his cheek, the skin is hard as wax. A white imprint of her thumb lingers: a bruise in reverse. Cold water for the fever or a hot compress to draw out the pus?

Children go blind and children go deaf and children go missing and children die of diarrhea and children choke on vomit and children go lame and children go mute and children lose fingers and feet and legs and children drown and children have their skin burnt to bubbling and children die of a ruptured appendix and pox and influenza and measles and mumps and children step on rusty nails and poison their blood and children drink rat poison kept in a pretty bottle and children are hit by trains. It is amazing that any of them grow up at all. Graveyards are filled with millions of small white headstones to mark their brief lives—infant son of Mary and James, beloved daughter of Matilda and Howard—the same shape and shade as the markers for soldiers whose bodies were lost to the war and so could not be properly buried.

THE GRAVEYARD

The children's bones were the saddest, said the prisoner. Thin as fish bones. He wanted to do a good job with those and would often cross their little arms over their little chests and put a dandelion or something bright between their fingers.

Each grave was topped with a white cross and none of the crosses had names. None of them had names before. The prisoner was doing his best, he said. He wanted to do a good job, especially for the babies.

WHY SHE STAYED

Slim called the keys of the piano "teeth." The black were rotten teeth and the white were good teeth. He was self-taught and found it difficult to let go of the names he'd created when he first learned.

For the first five years of their marriage, he brought her everywhere, taking literally the vow that had soldered them together. He took her even to places she wasn't supposed to go: bars, union meetings, down to the mine. She loved him for this. He never imagined there were places she wouldn't be welcome.

Later, someone had to stay with the baby. The walls of the tent undulated with wind, the yellow canvas stippled brown and red with shadows, and Edie felt she was in the belly of some great animal.

She sat on Slim's lap while he played piano, her small hands piggybacked on his as they moved through the music. He whispered the lyrics in her ears and she sang them out loud. They shared hands and throats. Her hands mute overtop of his. His voice mute except to her ears.

WHY SHE LEFT

There was no why. There was no reason. There is still no good reason. Something between them was simply crushed to a fine powder, as if ground in a millstone. Something solid turned to sand. She thinks of love as hard as a tooth or bone, forged out of the body's own mineral toughness.

No good reasons. Many small ones, but not a single good one. He'd given her an apartment, finally. Years later than promised, but still. He'd gone off on a drunk, spent a week up at Pecker Point, sure, the smell of perfume in his sticky pubic hair, okay, but that's a common story. She has only the right to be angry, not the right to leave, but she did. She's gone.

Often, he'd come home from a drunk with ridiculous gifts for them. A pencil, an apron with someone else's name embroidered on it, a basket full of carrots still hairy with roots, an empty beer bottle filled with dandelions, a chunk of broken saw, a pocketful of the same stones that were outside their tent for miles, the dirt still on them, a gas rationing book for a car they didn't have.

Her magpie husband proud as bloody Santa Claus, still shaking as he pulled the treasures out and set them on a table. Overeager. Trying so hard to make amends. "Was reminded of you," he'd say, and Edie liked to imagine that the moment her name entered his mind he'd grab whatever was nearby. Maybe once he'd drag back some whore whose face reminded him of her own.

A can of beans. A matchbook from a hotel three towns away. Once, a box of Jap oranges, though those had been lovely, each one nestled in green paper so they were a gift you had to unwrap twice.

Now, she could grind her teeth into a fine powder. Her head is stuffed full of stories that will impress no one. They are private things, might as well be secrets. Most of them aren't even stories, just fistfuls of images, anecdotes that get their charm from the way he told them. The stories never feel whole when she replays them in her mind now. A head full of stones. Mouth full of sparks. Good thing you ain't got more minerals in your bones, the foreman said, or else you'd be mining yer fingers and toes. She has no reason to be gone. Keeps going.

TAG DAY

Slim unlatches the gate, walks down the path and plucks a white blossom off a tree whose trunk is made hunchback by the weight of the flowers. The blossom is fat as an apple and the petals bruise with the slightest touch. Now, she thinks of Belly: the way his swollen face holds the imprint of her fingertip. On the ground, fallen petals are scarred with the diamond imprints of boot soles.

Slim is selling paper tags. SUPPORT THE TREK, they demand. ON TO OTTAWA! When the woman opens the door, the house stinks of vinegar. Her hair is tied with rags into a nest around her skull. When he offers her the paper tag, they both blush, though perhaps the woman is just pink from the effort of cleaning. Slim would not think of that, though. He would believe she blushed for him. He cannot meet her eyes. So long without a woman's gaze and he feels like a ridiculous suitor.

"We're raising funds," he stammers. "For the On to Ottawa Trek. You may have attended our parade this morning."

The woman stares at him, one hand on her hip. The ink of the tag is smudged with his sweat, the word *Ottawa* barely discernible. They might be going anywhere. Slim imagines her hands throb from vinegar in the splits of her skin. Or maybe he imagines nothing: simply wants to get on to the next house, the next woman, to bring the loot back to Matt Shaw so they could march to the next town, so they could keep on marching. "Would you like to support us?" he asks.

The blossom is creased along the lines he has bent it. She leaves the doorframe wordlessly and he watches her disappear down the hall, whose floor shines in wide swathes, the light showing the places she's missed. The woman returns with a bag of pears — their skins pockmarked by birds, he will later learn — and a few pennies. He hands her a paper tag, maybe not even caring to give her a fresh one so she can show her husband what she has purchased.

"Thank you," he says. "Some people pin these on their jackets."

She nods, crushing the tag in her work-reddened hands. Slim moves to the next door to ask for donations, though what has he ever had to offer?

BELLY

When you don't know what time it is, you get sleepy. That's why cats are sleepy. They can't read clocks. At the Orchard school, his mom played a game with them called Dead Lions. "'Dead lions, dead lions, we fall on the floor,'" they would sing. "'Dead lions, dead lions, we don't make a roar.'" Then they would all lie down and if you moved even your nose you'd be out and you'd have to get up and sit at your desk with your head down. There wasn't a clock, only a bell that his mom would ring when it was time for recess or lunch or when it was time to go home. She knew when to ring the bell somehow. Mostly, Belly fell asleep during the game. As did all the other children.

EDIE

She carries him down the hall. Vivian clips along beside her, sobering now, tugging at her drenched clothing. She carries a clean dress but keeps dabbing her arms with it and leaving wet imprints on the cloth.

Edie follows the rut worn on the runner by thousands of people leaving the sins committed in the bedroom to stoop over the basin. Belly flails and his hands twist into shapes through her hair, tugging at her haircombs. When he was a baby, his fingers would move unfocused this way, yanking her hair from the scalp with a strength he seemed too young to possess.

"You're being very brave," she tells him. "And we're going to get you cleaned up and then you won't feel sick."

"I got sick on myself," Belly says, surfacing from his fever long enough to be ashamed.

"We'll get you all cleaned up. We'll make you feel all better," she says.

"I wasn't sleeping and I was trying to find you and you weren't there," he says.

She strokes his hot little head. What else can she possibly say to him? Her mother would know the cures for fever: the right medicine or at least a good potion. "We'll get you all clean and you'll feel so much better," she says, repeating the phrase like an incantation all the way down the hall, past the sounds of the music, glass being broken, someone fighting behind a closed door.

THE WEDDING NIGHT

The sound of broken glass from the next room. A couple was arguing, the woman's voice cracking as its pitch reached toward the ceiling. "Wretch. Cad. Monster," she kept repeating, higher and higher. The man's voice was a soothing hum. "Wretch," the woman shouted. "God-damned stinking bastard."

The bedsheets smelled of starch but were off-white. Slim had a strawberry stain on his collar. They'd eaten at a restaurant for their wedding supper—her first time—and neither of them knew what to do with the many different forks. Edie was embarrassed by the waiter's sardonic little bows, as if he knew that bending to serve people like them was a joke, knew that they knew it, and reminded them of it each time he smiled while calling them sir or madam with too much formality. When someone found out they were newlyweds and sent over a pavlova to the table, neither of them could figure out whether they were meant to pay for it, though eventually decided to eat it anyways out of courtesy. Edie was thrilled at the meringue dissolving in small bubbles on her tongue, reminding her of the bone and its hollow, water-smoothed places.

And now the hotel room. Such a dizzying speed. They'd known each other for three weeks, eloped in Spokane and now they were married. One moment she was in her old life and the next she was pulled clean out. He had a contract up in Zincton, that was the reason for the haste. If he got his diamond-drilling certificate, he could go any place in the world—to Africa or Brazil or anywhere—and she would go with him.

"Cad. Wretch." The woman's voice sliced through the walls. Slim had carried Edie over the threshold and laid her on the bed, undressed her slowly, fumbling, undressed himself. The callus on his fingers left faint bramble scratches on her cheeks and breasts and stomach, a reminder of where she had been touched.

She felt old, felt panic, felt young. Which she was. Seventeen years old. His arms made the arc of wings as he shrugged out of his suspenders and her mouth tasted impossibly of metal. Next door, the woman cursed in time to the movement of their bodies, as Slim worked with gentle but furious effort. He was so tall she couldn't see his face and a drop of sweat fell off his nose and landed on her hairline. The pain was brief, then Slim hunched as if he was coughing.

He lay down next to her, looking ashamed. "It's been—you know. Years and work camps and then." He fell silent, then coughed. Edie was cheered: he was so much older but didn't seem to be any better at this than she was. Slim could hardly look her in the eye.

He fell silent. The fan lapped warm air against Edie's body and from the next room she could hear broken glass, a sob, the thrum of a man's baritone voice saying, "Jesus, Lucy, you get so worked up." Slim nervous beside her. He was too tall for the bed and had to bend his knees to lie on his back. He coughed again.

"Married," he said. "Married." As if to give what they'd done a name. The next day, they would leave by train for Zincton.

Two weeks later, Slim would get a letter from Matt Shaw, asking him to come to Spain to fight Franco. All the Trekkers were signing up. Like old times but better, he said, because here's a place we can make a difference, where something real can be done. But Slim couldn't go. Edie said he could, but he shook his head. It wouldn't be fair to her; he couldn't afford a train ticket down there; he was a newly married man.

"Justice starts at home," he told her.

"Oh darling," Edie said, throwing her arms around him. "There will be other wars!"

CAUGHT

The long grasses were releasing their down, and pollen stippled the inscriptions chiselled into the stones. Edie's sister was about to be born and Edie could see her moving like a weather system in the atmosphere of their mother's belly: quick, alien rumblings under her nightgown. Edie imagined the child's fists and feet.

Her mother had taken to her bed, and the house smelled of dust and turned meat. Kate was the good daughter: bringing basins of water, washcloths, carrying the stinking water out again, bringing trays of food, sitting at the bedside and patting their mother's hand reassuringly. "There, there," Kate murmured, small mother already. Already promised to an engineering student. Their father was gone — for good, everyone said it — and their mother's face was a storm of hormones and grief.

Edie walked the twins home from school. They ran ahead, then looped back around the metal gates of the cemetery that were lit like fuses in the September sun, taking the long way home past the convicts tending the vegetable garden on the graveyard grounds. Once inside the cemetery, Edie would let her brothers race each other home. They wove strange paths among the stones, disappeared into the long grasses by the hedge, emerged over the fence, waved goodbye.

Alone now, Edie would saunter past the garden, loving the way the convicts stopped their work as she passed and pressed their thumbs against the skins of the tomatoes and peppers. Their eyes followed her as if charting the arc of a plane. When the baby was born, either Edie or Kate would drop out of school to care for it. Her mother couldn't be expected to.

How did she single out that one particular man? Go to him again and again? She cannot remember what pulled her. Cannot recall how he got free of the group and came to her. But it happened, she knows. Against the bronze angel. Now, little motes of pollen were stuck to its wings, as if it were sprouting real feathers. There was no good reason to, many good reasons not to. Lots of boys her age were sweet on her.

But it happened. Against the bronze angel, the prisoner pressed himself against her, then fumbled his shackled hands in his pocket.

"Reach in there," he said, finally, and Edie thought it was a trick to get her hand on his groin but did it anyways and was surprised to find an object the size of a shooter marble. An oddly shaped bone. The prisoner flushed with pride. What else could he give her? The scabs on his wrist oozed fresh blood: her fault. He smelled like sweat and his mouth had the pale, milky taste of tea.

"Doesn't even look like a piece of a human," he said, which was true: the bone was shaped like a puzzle piece. "Thought it was an ankle bone, but someone said no, spine, that's how you bend. They're all linked up together."

"Thank you," she said. And meant it. How often do you get to see the inside of people? How often do you get to hold it in your palm?

Someone screamed. All the prisoners turned like startled birds and he backed away as if Edie had scalded him. Her sister: her neat white blouse, her long skirt, hair pinned and burned into prim waves.

"Get away from her," she screamed. The prisoner staggered backwards as the warden tugged him by the shoulders. Edie slipped the bone into her own pocket, though it was evidence that would be used against her. Her father had told her all about the lengths people went to in order to hide proof of their crimes. Women ate coins and jewellery. A man once swallowed a knife and died from the wounds.

"Oh my word, oh my word," Kate whispered all the way home. "I thought he was killing you. Oh my word. I thought he was killing you."

When they got home, Kate disappeared into her mother's bedroom and closed the door. Edie listened outside. She was bruised in small ways: the neck, the collarbone, the place where the handcuffs pressed into her abdomen. She rubbed the bone in her pocket like a lucky coin. Edie knew exactly who would be made to care for the baby.

DOESN'T MATTER IF I DON'T HAVE A CERTIFICATE; PENMANSHIP AND ALL THAT LA-DEE-DAH AIN'T AS IMPORTANT AS YOU THINK. WHERE'S IT EVER GOTTEN YOU, EH? THOSE THREE BLOODY WEEKS TAUGHT ME ALL I NEEDED TO KNOW AND MARX SURE AS HELL TAUGHT ME THE REST.

Years later, he will wonder how they started in a straight line and ended up circled in Regina, how someone managed to add the word *cannot* onto both *stay* and *go*. The reasons — government, police, newspapers, Red Scare — will not seem to be enough. These explanations are faceless things, lack arms and thighs, have never been marching. And strange, too, that the Trek ended on the Prairies against the rambling horizon that seemed to say, *And then and then and then.* The river twisted away farther than he could see, always finding an ocean. Highways and train tracks went on and on. Even after the principles of math course the mine paid for him to take when he was working on his Stage 2 certificate, he never wrapped his head around ellipses, parabolas, the arc of a flight path. All his life he'd hoped for the simple math of *A* to *B*, ever onward to victory. He did not expect his straight line to curve like a pencil in a glass of water, like just another trick of the light.

BELLY

One time Belly woke up to find his dad sitting on the side of the bed, so that Belly was tucked against him the way dogs sleep. His dad put his hand over Belly's face and the smell was bad. Belly had his eyes open, but his dad didn't notice his eyelashes scratching against his hand. He patted Belly's head. Patted him again. His dad could almost fit Belly's head in his hand.

Then his dad picked him up and held him under the armpits. Belly wasn't scared. No one was as tall as his dad, so he was the most high-up boy in the world at that moment. His dad looked at him. Belly looked at his dad.

"You're awake," he said.

Belly didn't say anything. The floor seemed very far away. Belly couldn't believe his dad got to be up this high all the time.

Now his mom carries him and his feet almost scrape on the ground. His mom is kid-sized and Belly is getting bigger, so she is slow when she walks with him, wherever she is taking him. One day I will be bigger than her, he thinks.

EDIE

There are too many people in the tiny bathroom, and Edie lets the water run brown, then yellow, then clear, Belly on her hip. The soldier and Vivian still carry their candles like altar boys, shifting from foot to foot, staring at walls. Sadie pushes between them to get a better look at what Edie is doing. The only thing she appears to be scared of is the dark.

On the walls, stains where the water has found the wrong way out of the pipes make the shapes of continents. The mould and the rusty water give the bathroom the odour of stone underneath the human

stink. Edie feels underground. The pipes knock as if there is someone
trapped nearby, tapping out a code, waiting to be saved.

The bathtub fills in gurgling bursts. Belly is hot in her arms, babbling into her shoulder, his mouth moving against her collarbone and
creating vibration against her chest. It makes her squeamish. She can
sew his face, wipe pus from his wound, but the feeling of his chapped
lips moving against her shoulder, whispering against her neck, gives
her goosebumps. (Once, she tried to slap the English back into him.
That's not how nice boys talk, she said. What would people say, if
they heard you talk like that?)

Lord, the child is burning up, little animal, his cheeks flushed and
soft as bruised peaches, a small drop of pus between each stitch. How
has all this happened so quickly? Sounds of wind and music come
from the heating grate in alternating bursts. The water sputters out
of the tap, hairs floating in the tub, but there's no time to care about
that; nothing is clean here; nothing has been clean anywhere they've
lived; there is nothing to be done; snow is the only whiteness for
miles and even that will be greyed by dirt and soot come morning.

Vivian and the soldier stand as if waiting for a tip, the candlelight
projecting their shadows into stains on the wall. Maybe she should
take Belly out to the snow; she imagines a snow-angel shape the size
of his body melted into the banks.

Belly takes ragged breaths. She thinks of his young brain boiling
in his skull. Children go blind and mute and lame from the smallest
things. Children go deaf and dumb. They fall into rivers and are never
found. She does not want him thrashing alone, shrunken in the big
tub, the knobs of his spine bruising against the porcelain. Better she
should cushion him.

"Can someone get us a glass of water?' she asks and all three of
them look for a glass, find nothing, hold their candles.

Edie doesn't notice she's naked until her clothes are off and she sees the downcast eyes of the soldier, looking furiously elsewhere, jiggling his knee as if marching in place. She wants him to look at her, but he won't. Her body still pulses from the places his mouth was on her. Vivian glances at herself in the mirror, maybe comparing herself against Edie's shape. Sadie is the only one who stares. Edie holds her fever-flushed son and Sadie does not look away. She picks up the clothes and tries to fold them.

"Can someone find us a glass of water?" Edie asks again, wanting the soldier to look up at the sound of her voice.

When Sadie holds Edie's jacket upside down, the wedding band pings on the tile floor. Such a small sound, softer than a coin. It rolls across the floor against the tub. And at that moment the lights crackle back on, so that it seems as if the ring has conjured the light with an electric energy of its own and Edie stands there naked, wondering if she is glowing in the new brightness, watching the ring glint as it rolls to a stop beside the bathtub.

Neither the soldier nor Vivian says anything, but she knows what they must be thinking. Why hide your marriage in your pocket? Why not wear a ring on your finger or on a chain? Why not put it behind glass as if it were a medal you earned?

PLANS

When they lived in Ymir, Edie once drew houses on the tent's canvas walls in chalk, imagining where they might live. Taking inspiration from borrowed editions of *Chatelaine* and from Norah and Red's house, she sketched floor plans of where their new walls would be: how many rooms, how many perfectly angled corners, a space for each person in her family like slots in a jewellery box. Belly's room—though she had no way of representing it—would be blue to remind him of the ocean, a colour he would never grow out of. Slim would have a study to study what? Something. It seemed that easy: draw a study and your husband will fill it with a white-collar job and a certificate to hang on the walls, though it's classist, Edie knows, to place a white-collar job above a day's honest wages, to expect Slim to betray himself and join ranks with the bosses who are like a different species they think they're so far above the common man: half carnivore, half parasite. It wasn't the job she sought, but the change of scenery another job would bring.

Sometimes, she drew the facade of the house as viewed by a visitor—little palm trees flanking the sides—and in these she was less successful. Those drawings were childish; it was hard to create the right sense of perspective. She left them on the tent anyways and Slim came home to many possible futures. Palm trees. A study. A room for Belly that he had no way of knowing would be blue. Anyone can draw a diagram, Slim chided her. Any old child can doodle a floor plan—even Belly could—but that doesn't give us a house now, does it? Where's the electricity going to go? Have you thought about heating? What about the pipes?

But her imagined rooms were not lit by lamps or bulbs. They simply glowed. She did not care where the gas and spark and heat came from. It seemed as if the house would figure that out somehow, that the presence of the structure would be enough. While she drew, Edie never imagined Slim's opinion. She was not trying to shame or prod him. Nor did she expect her drawings to be granted even the permanence of paper, let alone a blueprint. She did not expect real walls. What Edie did imagine was the lines of her floor plans projected onto the landscape by the stove's glow, haunting the rocks, re-striping the fur of raccoons. She drew lines onto the wilderness, imagining where all the perfect homes would never be.

EDIE

The soldier bends down on one knee to pick the ring up and hands it to Edie without looking at her. It looks as if he's proposing, but he won't make eye contact. She can feel his anger, can sense the way Vivian tries to twist her feelings of betrayal into an attractive expression, her hand covering her snaggletooth. There is nothing to be done.

She puts the ring back on her finger and it settles in its old spot, as if a groove had been worn for it over the years. Why not be married? Why leave? How is it possible to consider giving up your child after all these women have lost their husbands and all these mothers have lost their children? Why would you lose someone by choice?

Until tonight, has she ever been naked in front of anyone other than Slim? (In the lit-up tent, the shadow of her naked body stretched longer and thinner on the ground until it might have been the outline of a tree. Men could come by to see the pantomime: wait for her to turn sideways and betray the outlines of breasts and hair.) She can't remember when. Even when she shared a room with Kate, they undressed with their backs to each other.

She looks down. The redness left from the soldier's mouth and hands is no longer visible, but she can see pink seams on her stomach and thighs from her girdle's ribbing, the elastic of her panties held on by safety pins because elastic was another one of the thousand minor things the war took from her and has been slow to return: elastic, tires, bacon, metal. Strange, she thinks, what the war needed. The dollar bills are still pinned to her brassiere, soggy with sweat but intact. Vivian takes the clothing from Sadie's hands and drops it on the floor.

When Edie lifts one leg over the tub, she is shocked by the porcelain's coolness. So many years swimming in mine-ruined rivers, rivers that were too fast to be warm even in the summer, her feet slipping over algae-slickened planks from where men had tried to direct the water into a more convenient path. Humming to Belly, she squats down into the water, supporting him as if he had an infant's lolling neck. When she peels him off her chest, his body makes a sucking noise, a glaze of sweat having soldered them. She sets him in the water—he arches his back in shock, then relaxes—then lowers herself into the tub, into water so cold she gasps.

As a child, in the sand dunes by the river, she jumped into the snarl of water in her undergarments, when she had the right body to do so and no one stopped her. Why think of this and not the wellbeing of her son or what it might take to cure him? What use are all these bits of stories? They are soothing, she supposes. They are fortunes and lullabies and forecasts and incantations. They are all she has to show for the past ten years.

She pulls him on her lap in part out of modesty and looks up. The soldier stands at attention, hands behind his back, guarding the door. He's younger than her brothers. Vivian stands beside him flushed with drink and candlelight, her arms loosely around Sadie's shoulders.

"I can get the water," says the soldier.

"Why doesn't Sadie do it?" says Edie.

"I want to watch," says Sadie.

Vivian taps Sadie's shoulder. "Go on," she says. The soldier looks toward the door, following Sadie with his eyes as she runs down the hallway. Edie sinks lower into the water so that Belly is submerged up to his neck.

Light wavers across the ceiling from the reflection of the water and the room sways in the storm. The music from downstairs has wound down into lazy waltzes. She anoints Belly's head and he flinches. She anoints him again. The water goes filmy with what has sloughed off their bodies, warming with the heat of her furnace son.

Do you suck the pus out of a wound as if it was a snakebite? If the poison comes from his own blood, should you still suck it out? She would do that for him. She would put her mouth to the wound.

Such a thin child. He was pudgy once. When she was still breastfeeding, he was so chubby he looked boneless. She had to use a washcloth to wipe hidden crumbs from the folds of his fat little neck. Some of her friends bottle-fed — that was the clean thing to do, the latest thing — but in that dirty refinery town she didn't trust the water and decided to take her chances on what she could make on her own. The nurse placed her fingers in Belly's mouth like she was feeling for a pulse there. "He latches on," she said and yanked Edie's dressing gown down and arranged the baby around her. They joined and Edie was surprised at the pain. Since weaning, she has been feeding him whatever she can find and wonders if she's been starving him ever since.

Now, her son wavers underwater, pale. His bony fingers churn up bubbles, his ribs stick like islands out of the water.

"Mommy?" he asks.

"Yes?"

He has no question. He's making sure she hasn't gone anywhere.

WILLIAM "SLIM" MacDONALD

She loved to kiss his stomach. After swimming, he would stretch out on the sand and there would be a tide pool of water cupped in the hollow of his solar plexus, his heartbeat flicking beneath like a minnow. He was slight but could hold her aloft. How could he be so thin but still hold her aloft and for so long? Muscles around his arms like vines. He would carry her over thresholds, into bars, once down the whole trail leading down from the tent when she cut her foot.

At night, he read her Marx or *The Worker's Voice*, a rush of words against her bare skin — *proletariat, manifesto, bourgeois, feudalism* — like songs or foreign languages. Now, she cannot hear those words on the radio without feeling a spark, as if they were erotic terms meant to be whispered. Why is it she remembers his body and not the sound of his voice? Why does she remember his stories as images, detached from his accent and his habit of scratching the back of his neck before he spoke?

He carried the scent of ash in his hair. Chapped skin by his knees. Stooped shoulders. His hand sheened with scar tissue where he burned the *X1* off. In the mine, his voice boomeranged back to her. He played the piano but was too shy to sing. A voice lost to whiskey, lungs lost to the Trek and the mine, wife lost, son lost. You could look at his naked body and see every disappointment he'd ever experienced.

In the tent, he stroked the handle of the generator each time it shut down, called it Old Bertha. "Come on, Bertha, sweetheart, give Daddy some sugar," he would coo. His fluttery lungs hated the damp mine. "Let me fell trees or build boats," he used to say, "anything. Let me do anything else," but no one could read the rocks like he could and he always ended up underground, too tall to stand up straight, chasing the lucky veins of gold, silver, lead, zinc, galena. Tungsten when the war demanded it.

He wanted to do anything else. He wanted to do *something*, but he didn't have the schooling, the opportunities, the luck. He wanted to be Matt Shaw. He wanted to be Arthur-Slim Evans. He wanted to carry a gun. He wanted to save someone from a burning building, write a manifesto, have his name in the paper. He made such big hand gestures when he talked.

Why does she try to recreate him from his red hair down: the Slim who isn't a fallen soldier and isn't a spy on a secret mission? Crooked pinkies. A creak in the mattress springs when he eased himself onto the bed at early light, trying not to wake her. The milk from her breasts that once tightened shiny against his stomach from where she pressed against him, saying, "Why won't it stop crying? Such a little thing and such a big noise. Do you think it's cold? Lord knows I'm cold." Even with the stove on. The generator humming. Naked as he held her. Why does she eulogize her live husband? Why does she press herself into stories that don't belong to her? Why does she remember him by what he lacks: flesh, solid walls, known relatives?

How long has it been since she's tasted the salt tang of the ocean or the salt of her own man that always reminded her of the ocean? The smell of the miner's carbolic soap might be the one thing that could bring her to tears because wherever he went, people could smell it on him and so know him by the thing he hated most about himself.

She sees him unconscious on the bed and warms him up, puts the pink back in his lips, wipes the frost from his eyebrows, massages his limbs until the blood flows right in them. She places him in Africa inspecting a mine with a tan and an extra ten pounds of muscle, blows the smoke from a cigarette in his mouth to burn away the taste of whiskey. She straightens his posture and breathes on his hand as if fogging a window, rubbing away the scar there. She gives him a story that begins with the word *today*. "Here is what will happen," she imagines him saying. "Here is what we will do." She makes a version of her husband they both could live with.

He carried a newspaper clipping from the *Winnipeg Star* in his back pocket that listed the names of all the men arrested during the Regina Riot. His name underlined twice. The clipping was soft as cloth as he unfolded it and showed her when she doubted elements of his stories. "Wasn't I there? Read this, right here. What does that say? Isn't that my name?"

When Belly was first born, he held him stiffly in the crook of his arm as if posed for a studio photo.

"Well, Ma," he said, giving her a new name. "How about that? Look what we did, eh?"

Edie looks down at Belly—whose name was meant to be William Jr.—his arm raised from the water and flung over his eyes as if shielding himself from a blow. Look what we did, she thinks. Look what we have done.

THE NIGHT BEFORE THE REGINA RIOT

In Regina, snow. Clumps of it fall like windfall apples on the stadium grounds and the Trekkers are joyful until the cold works into their boots. From the roof, an effigy of Bennett turns grey with ice: a snowman suspended in air and twirling against the lighter grey sky, the snow fattening it until its painted red eyes are crusted pink. Inside the stadium, the Trekkers play poker with cards so worn that they have no numbers or faces. Effigies themselves, the men wake straw-covered, stiff-armed.

The Trekkers sit in their divisions and now and then a bout of song flares up. "Comrade Hold The Fort" and that bloody concertina, its song box made rheumatic in the chill. "'Hold the fort for we are coming, union men be strong.'" They sing with their arms around each other, snug against each other's tenors. There is no shame in this because contact is a matter of warmth. Outside, police officers patrol the fairgrounds. Cars drive past at odd hours of the night, slow down, speed up.

The night before, Matt Shaw washed his overalls and they froze solid, which is what he gets, said Red, for being so fussy about his looks.

"Will you look at that," Matt Shaw said and knocked on them. "Frozen stiff."

"'Bout the only time you're hard in the crotch," said Red Walsh, to laughter.

Now, they must squint to see the numbers on the cards, the queen's face blurred like a photograph of a woman turning her head at the last moment out of shyness. Like the women they see from trains, waving before returning to the chores of the day. Outside, snow softens the barbed wire and rubs out the lines in the parking lot. The boys in Division One have a snowball fight against Division Three, leap and fall hard, the snow's cushion making them fearless. The expanse of white becomes scuffed with their tussling.

But, no, Edie must be mistaken here. The Regina Riot was on July 1, so this would be June 30. Nights still have teeth that far north, but a week before weren't they swimming in the Elbow River?

She remembers the story so clearly, though: Matt Shaw's face ashed by the snow's light as he knocks his boots against the door frame and enters the stadium. His eyes that so many reporters described as "steel-grey" or "sleet-grey." (Once "grey and cool as a fall morning" by a reporter more ambitious with language.)

"Well that's that," he says. The fight gone out of his face. All the hard camera-ready angles slackened. He picks up Slim's cards, shakes his head at the luck of the hand, drops them. "That's it. They stopped it. Goddamn bulls are cracking down on the trains and they're pulling our fellows off the trucks. Cosgrove and the Reverend — Reverend East — the 'we're going east with East' fellow, both of them arrested. Arrest a bloody reverend, why don't you? A man of the cloth. Throw him in the pokey! That's it." What do you say to a speech like that? By a man whose fine words were reprinted in newspapers across the country.

All the men look up startled, and for the first time, after nearly three months in the company of thousands of men, there is genuine silence. Matt Shaw paces. He crushes his cap in his hand, then slaps it against his thigh. "One word — that's it — one word. Stop. Old Iron Heel just had to raise his bloody pinky finger and the whole works grinds to a halt. They could have stopped it wherever they wanted. Whenever they wanted. Might as well have not even left Vancouver."

Matt Shaw, the face of the Trek, the throat of the Trek, overturns the card table and stands panting as, outside, snow pads the effigy of Bennett until he's huge and frozen, so heavy the rope snaps, but this is wrong because it was not snowing, because Matt Shaw was not even there. The night before the Regina Riot, he was in Toronto getting ready to speak in front of a sold-out crowd at Maple Leaf Gardens, totally unaware of what was about to happen.

Edie imagines it was cold then because she is cold now and cannot imagine not being so. Because she has lived years in a tent where there was always a draft and she was perpetually aware of the pattern of sweat on her skin from the wind against it. And so she has brought winter to this story. And so she has brought Matt Shaw back into the scene. And so she has frozen Slim's stories in the literal sense of the word.

It was June 30, she reminds herself now. It was summer. She must try hard to put the warmth back in.

BELLY

He is hot even in cold water. He is hot because he has a new face. All the people watch him because he is a different kind of boy. Because his mom sat on him and put a needle through his face and he could see everything she was doing to him. Because his mom made him hurt and he still hurts and something bad has happened to his face and still happens. Below him, he feels her hip bones stabbing his back, one more small hurt, one more wrong thing she is doing to him.

EDIE

"We need some hot water," Edie says, releasing them from the room. "Can someone get a cloth and a basin of hot water?" Vivian and the soldier leave, grateful to leave; they don't look back. Vivian places her candle on the sink and walks close to the soldier, almost touching his arm. She hears them whispering their prognoses: "Fever," she hears him say. "Infection."

"He's only how old? Four? Can't be more than five? That was her wedding ring, wasn't it?" Vivian asks brightly, and Edie can't hear the soldier's reply.

"Some dead husband," Vivian coos. "I just met her. She's not even an acquaintance. Some people need all the sympathy, even from those of us who have been through real hardship." Edie can see Vivian's wet footprints as she walks on the hardwood floor beside the carpet. And now the door is unmanned. Anyone could walk in.

Belly shivers. She scoops palmfuls of the greying water and douses his hair. Rubs soap bubbles along his face to wash away the creamy tears of pus on the wound, trying to be gentle, trying to keep soap from the wound, knowing lye's power to scald. He flinches and moves his face away from her. She needs a compress to draw out the pus: hot water in a metal basin that keeps the heat, towels that smell of bleach. She needs cold water for the fever. Hot compress to draw out the infection. Belly's hair is dark with water and she imagines his young brain cooling. Bone holds heat, she knows. It can be worn down by your fingertips. Surely the skull can hold coolness as well.

On the surface of the water, other people's hairs float trapped in soap bubbles. This cannot be helped. There's an acid reek of shit, the ghost scents of hundreds of patrons, but this cannot be helped either. Edie's skin grows a shell of goosepimples, her nipples hard and rough as scabs or stones. She bathes her son, feeling her own heart slowing with the cold. (Slim's heart, booze-sluggish, and she shut the door and she left.)

She wished her son gone. When he was a baby, she let him cry for hours, though that was what you were supposed to do to mature a child in the correct way. You weren't supposed to give in. Everyone told her to do that. From the day he was born, she imagined how her life would be if she were alone. Endless dreams about the mine and its many corridors; endless dreams of trains and horizons. While he played in the forest, she kept watch only out of the corner of her eye and sometimes not even that. She's unnatural. She wished him gone. Now, she should feel more terror; she should know what to do; she should never have brought him in the first place. He will be better off with his grandmother, who will never let him out of her sight.

He is still except for the fingers he swishes through the water. She has nothing to give him but cold water, hot compresses, the most basic of cures. They are not soldiers. They lack this century's wonder drug.

"Mom?" asks Belly. His tender shoot-green voice, the thrum of his words between his shoulder blades.

"Yes?"

"Where is this?"

"I don't know where we are. Some town. I don't know the name."

He turns to look at her: his fever-glazed eyes, chapped lips. He's disgusted with her, she can tell. "No, *where*? Where *should* we be?" When he furrows his brow, a bead of pus forms between the stitches. It's been just a little more than twenty-four hours since he was injured and look what has happened. She hadn't thought that an infection could occur so quickly, but who knows what sickness he already carried with him? "If." His words are staccato with shivering. "If we weren't here. If we didn't stop." His brain cools enough to find sentences.

"New Westminster. Where Mommy was born. A big old house with your aunts and uncles and your nana. You'd be all snuggled up in bed."

He waves his arms through the water. "Newest Minster," he says, testing out the name.

"Right. New Westminster." She scoops more water onto his head, made sober by cold and adrenalin. "With your uncle Paul and your uncle Greg and auntie Anne and your nana and maybe a dog. Your uncle Tom is probably all grown up and far away, and your auntie Katherine has her own family, but they might come to visit and bring you all sorts of cousins to play with. Did you know that New Westminster was one of the first cities to be built in the whole province? And it was built by special soldiers the King sent?"

What else can she tell him? The story of Trinket the cat? The story of the nowhere road? What do those stories have to do with the places they're going?

He cranes his neck to stare at her.

"Maybe a hundred years ago, before your grandmother's mother was even born, the King sent special soldiers called sappers and they were big and strong and cut down all the trees and made roads. Their camp was near where your nana lives, which is why it's called Sapperton. New Westminster was supposed to be the capital city, people call it the Royal City, but something happened and it didn't get to be the capital."

These are the kinds of solid facts she gives to her schoolchildren. What else is there to say?

Sadie returns with a beer mug filled with water held with both hands. The water is yellowed with either dregs of beer or candlelight. She sets the mug down on the lip of the tub.

"Look," says Edie. "Sadie brought you some water to make you feel better."

"I brought it because you told me to," says Sadie.

Edie raises the mug to Belly's lips and he drinks greedily.

"Slowly," says Edie. When she pulls the glass away, he reaches for it. "Just take sips. Hey, just take small sips." He drinks more, quickly, and gags. "Slowly," says Edie. He swallows. The water stays down.

"Sappers don't build cities," says Sadie. "They're the ones who take away bombs." She lowers her voice. "It's terribly dangerous. My aunt's a nurse and she served on the front lines, so she knows. She's seen them. Sometimes they get so hurt that their bones fall out."

"This was a long time ago, sweetie, in peacetime. You're a very smart girl to know so much about the war."

"My aunt's a nurse and she tells me. She sewed a man's leg on once but it fell off again and he died. Lots of people die."

"My dad's flying a plane right now," says Belly. "His plane can disappear whenever he wants it to because it's special."

"No he can't," says Sadie. It's just camouflage. Camouflage is when you paint something to look like something else, if you didn't know."

"Belly's right," says Edie, cupping water into her palm and anointing his head. "His father has a special plane. A special disappearing plane. That's exactly right."

Belly vomits again into the water and Edie feels the curdled heat of it on her leg.

THE STORY OF THE CITY

Everyone knows the legend of the sappers and Colonel Moody. It is not a legend but the truth; you can read about it. The sappers were fine, strong men brought from England to graft Colonel Moody's dream of Old Westminster onto the forest and call it New Westminster, the Royal City, the capital. The sappers laid neat lines. They timbered the city's bones. All the avenues were numbered and all the streets were named. Parks were cleared—Moody Park, Queen's Park—and soon women in high-collared white dresses sweetened the grasses with the roses they'd nurtured through the long boat ride over.

Everyone knows the city's birth story, how the sappers came from inflicting all that order on the forest to sleep in a tangled hovel at the top of the hill, where they could brawl and drink and watch the grid they had built expand. The sappers stunk of pitch fire, tar, wood, metal, oolichan grease, sweat. Their hands were ruined. Hard to be clean while doing the Lord's work of nation building. They felled trees so big that five men could stand on the stump and did once in a commemorative photograph, their chests puffed out as if posing with the head of a dragon.

Every year on Dominion Day, Edie's Sunday-school teacher took them to the section of the cemetery where the sappers were buried. Some died of sickness brought from bad water and some died when trees fell the wrong way. The ones who didn't die went back to England or scattered themselves around the country, so there were only a few names left behind to remember all those men. They had names solid as stone, names from the Bible, and the headstones were so old that the *f*s looked like *s*s and the other way around.

Once, the stones had been laid in neat rows like the map of the city itself, but many had grown crooked over the years. Most of the inscriptions were eroded. The men felled the trees and the tree roots buckled the stones and shifted the earth around them. Years later, the prisoners would carry the tangled, floating bones up the hill to rebury them in streets and avenues.

SECTION 98: THE UNLAWFUL ASSOCIATIONS ACT

Official negotiations. Arthur-Slim Evans, Red Walsh, Matt Shaw and the rest of the executive committee sit in rooms with their elbows smudging the sheen of long tables smooth as wet stone, their own scruffy reflections in the gloss. They negotiate with all levels of government—municipal, provincial, national—practising their poker faces on tall, dour officials. Premier Gardiner, especially, likes to crinkle the skin around his eyes into something meant to resemble sympathy. In their hatred, the Trekkers imagine these men practising this look in mirrors, like dreamy girls, for Chrissakes. Premier Gardiner, Mayor McGreer, Old Iron Heel Bennett. The same university-coiffed excuses. Bennett with a diamond stick pin at his throat.

But Slim, of course, cannot recall these conversations. He never stood in a pair of starched overalls purchased new for the occasion by the Women's Solidarity League. The official business was merely a buzzing overhead, beyond his concern. Slim was busy counting the crowds, parading, bathing himself in the river and singing around the campfire, "'Hold the fort, for we are coming.'" All that endless marching. "'Union men be strong.'"

So when the Trek was noosed, it was a blow that Slim had not seen coming. And here the story veers into newspaper headlines. Prime Minister Bennett invoked the "unlawful associations" clause in section 98 of the Criminal Code to make it illegal for the Trek to stay in Regina but also illegal for it to leave. July 1st, Dominion Day. Market Square, Regina. 7:45 p.m., 1,600 miles from Ottawa. Headlines and photos and editorials. They were going to give in. It was illegal to stay and illegal to go. What more could be done?

From his place on the flatbed truck loaded with the speakers in Market Square, Slim counts the crowds: less than some of their earlier speeches but a good night. The crowd is fanned star-shaped in the square's five arteries. The speaker hisses and pops. It's hard to get an accurate estimate because of the market's irregular shape. Posters stapled to telephone poles warn residents of criminal prosecution if they aid or abet the illegal Trek. Stores are closed, a boy sells buns in paper bags — his high, thin voice competing with the speeches — police tap their billy clubs against their thighs. There was no reason for things to happen the way they did. Even the government inquest could not find any.

Gerry Winters is speaking, waving his cap around. He's angry. Everyone's angry. Many Trekkers couldn't stand to watch the final speech so they'd snuck away to a baseball game they'd received free tickets for.

At 8:17 p.m., a whistle blows. Police stream out of delivery vans parked around the square, waving billy clubs, shouting. Two of them grab Arthur-Slim Evans, two more grab Comrade Marsh. They stuff them into the van. Slim heads toward the fray.

There is no good reason for any of this to have happened, since the Trek's leaders had surrendered, but it happened anyway. It was illegal to stay and illegal to go; what could they do? The Regina Riot. The Market Square Massacre. Trekkers gone missing outside the official body count. Detective Charles Millar dead, his little girl learning the news from a paperboy's cries the next morning. Edie imagines the child waking up in a house free of the musk of sweat and wet leather heated over a radiator.

Slim does not remember what he did next. Does not even remember the canister of tear gas that must have landed at his feet. Somewhere, there are photographs of these moments in newspapers across the country, but Slim was arrested and never saw them, so cannot tell if he appeared anywhere in print.

BEING THERE. TAKING PART.

And this is Matt Shaw's best day. The moment in which he shines and dreams about later: Maple Leaf Gardens; a crowd of six thousand; Matt Shaw, the elected voice of the Trek with top billing; a podium erected over the place where men skate fast and rough. His words are punctuated with camera flashes, each gesture preserved in black and white. His words are the perfect words, the ones he has been rehearsing for months in front of farmers and housewives with the air golden from the sun filtering through the dust kicked up by their shifting feet, the smell of straw, sweat, manure. But now he is on a proper stage. He does not even tremble. He has always wanted this. The men who elected him to go wrote his name over and over on their ballots—*Matt Shaw* spelled many different ways in many different scripts—his imaginary name so much better than Matthew Surdia, the one he was born with, the one he shed at sixteen when he left home with a face made pale by thousands of tiny scars. *Matt Shaw*: the crisp syllables of his new name like camera flashes. He wishes he could see himself.

From the loudspeaker, his voice echoes back on a two-second delay and seems to belong to someone older, maybe an actor in a radio play; he speaks the perfect words he has practised; he is better than Tim Buck or Reverend East. In the stands, the women are wearing fur stoles even in July and he hates them for this but loves to imagine the *shushing* sound the fur must make against their thin summer dresses and bare arms. Their rouged mouths hang half open listening to his every word, and he is so perfectly in the spotlight that even the smallest hairs on his arms must be brightly lit. When his speech is over, all he can do is say thank you and a few seconds later muffled by the din of applause, his words return. Thank you.

He does not know what he is missing. He does not know that the photos in the newspaper the next day will be of blurred men throwing stones. He does not know that sixteen hundred miles away, there is tear gas instead of words and Slim is choking on it.

Because Slim was there. Because Slim took part.

BELLY

The last time Belly saw his dad, he was practising disappearing. He was lying very still. There was snow on his eyebrows and on the quilt. His lips were white, which was a good trick because if he was hiding in a snowstorm no bad people could see his face.

EDIE

When Vivian returns, she has changed her dress and wiped the mascara from her cheeks. Her face is pink from cold cream and she smells of powder and soap. New stockings: a gift from Fred, perhaps. Edie cannot adjust to the notion that you could afford to ruin a pair of stockings.

The soldier has disappeared. Vivian carries a steaming metal pan full of water like it's a birthday cake. Under her arm are some off-white towels with the hotel's name branded into the corners.

"Here we go!" exclaims Vivian. "We'll get all that mess out of you, darling!"

Belly looks at her a little dreamily, the fever glazing his eyes. His cheeks are still flushed.

"I can do it," says Edie, sitting up as the water sluices off her breasts. "Why don't you take Sadie and go get some sleep?"

"I've been helping," protests Sadie.

Vivian shrugs. Her new dress, which is made from a fabric that must defy wrinkles or stretching, shows no signs it's ever been in a travel valise, except for the scent of lavender sachets. "Sadie, why don't you go to sleep, kitten?"

"I can help. I brought the water. I didn't spill any when I carried it up the stairs."

"Sadie," says Vivian, and Belly flinches at the tone of her voice.

"I'm always going," Sadie sobs as she leaves. "I'm always having to go."

Vivian smiles, her lip stretching over her snaggletooth. "She's fine. You tell her to beat it and she'll entertain herself for hours. She'll just put herself back to bed. It's like blowing out a candle!" She sets the steaming pan down on the edge of the tub. "Thank goodness!"

Edie dips a washcloth in the water, her hands shocked with heat. The cloth steams as she lets it cool.

"Some medicine for your cheek," she tells Belly. Belly flinches but lets her. He trusts her. She holds the mug up for him to drink. "Lean back. Hold still. Why don't you get some sleep, Vivian?"

Vivian stares at Edie's naked body, unabashed. Her own form is hidden within the clean dress, her own scent delicately spiced with rose water. Even the freckles on her chest are safe behind buttons. "No point in sleeping. Train leaves in a few hours. And thank *goodness*! I personally am good and ready to *leave*. I'm sure you are too. Get this boy of yours to a *doctor*!" She laughs too loud for the little room. "You're lucky no one came barging in on you like this! Can you *imagine*? Someone barging in on you?"

"Get some sleep," says Edie. "He's my boy. I'll take care of him. It's not fair to impose on you."

"What happens if someone has to use the facilities? They'll be storming the doors!"

"We're nearly done," says Edie. The cloth over Belly's face has a yellow blot of pus that spreads.

Vivian narrows her eyes into a version of meanness that looks rehearsed. "What would your husband say? You know, your *deceased* husband? All these men tromping in here? Can't imagine that your dearly departed husband — your *deceased* husband — would fancy that very much. Or at least mine wouldn't. My husband who is actually — " she stops and looks out the door to make sure that Sadie is out of earshot — "My husband who is actually dead."

Edie cannot feel guilty because she cannot even imagine Slim in a flag-draped casket. She cannot imagine receiving a pink telegram, sinking on her knees in grief or falling to pieces in the arms of friends and neighbours. She can only see his waxy face, snow in his eyebrows, his hand extended as if he was trying to give her something.

THE UNION FOREVER, DEFENDING OUR RIGHTS

"We could go to the Interior," he said, like a question. His scarred voice made everything a question. They sat at the pharmacy, sharing an egg cream, though Slim said he felt ridiculous sipping a drink like a teenaged boy when most men his age had a mess of kids.

"You just going to cart me up there like a little maid girl?" she asked.

"We could get married, you know?" he said. There were no sweeping gestures, no long gazes. He didn't even look at her.

Edie had been twisting on her stool and became aware of the creak of metal, her feet hooked around the base because she was too short to reach the ground. She stopped turning. She couldn't believe other people in the pharmacy were still yammering on at a time like this. "Say it properly," she said. "You want to marry me, you got to say it the right way."

Slim blushed right down to his chest; maybe even his stomach was pink. She couldn't imagine him bending down on one knee. "Aww, Edie," he said. "A progressive marriage is equal, isn't it? No one stoops." They had known each other for a week. He coughed.

"I need a ring is all I'm saying."

Slim traced his finger around the rim of their shared egg cream. He looked up at her, at the people shopping for health tonics and Aspirin at the opposite end of the pharmacy, back at her. "Fine. I know you'll marry me, I'll get you a wedding ring. Most people, Matt Shaw, you know, he doesn't even believe in marriage. Says that when the new era comes, people will live collectively and raise their children as a whole, no mom and pop."

"Then fine. Then don't marry me. You don't want to marry me, don't marry me. I'll stay here."

Slim rubbed the back of his neck and coughed again. "That's what Matt Shaw says, not me. I'm just trying to give you some global perspective about the way things are heading. But I'm thinking, there are so many fellows who are too poor to afford a wife, much less a family. I sure as hell was, living in those work camps, never saw a woman for three years. And here I am able to go from job to job. Even in a time like this. I'm thinking it's a right to get married. That was one of the reasons for, well—" He gestured, repeating the whole story of the On to Ottawa Trek with a flick of his wrist. "'Wasted generation' and all that. And now sure as hell isn't the good times, but if you can afford it, it's like getting what you deserve, eh? Don't you think? Getting what's owed to you."

"I don't want to marry you if you're doing it as some sort of political statement. Get one of those hairy Marxist girls with glasses if you want that."

Slim sighed. "I don't mean it that way, Edie. You know—I want to marry you." His red hair and his pink cheeks and pained expression: how could she say no? She was thinking of the train ride, a new town, maybe another town after that. And maybe that was romantic too: marriage as a right.

"I want to marry you too," she said. "I want to be with you too. But we have to do it right."

"We'll do it right," he said, lifting her off the stool as the entire pharmacy started to clap, the eavesdroppers around them first, then the whole store. That was movie-romantic. That was something. "We'll do it up properly," he said. "We'll do it right."

The next day, he gave her the thin and dented ring. Two weeks later they eloped in Spokane. Two days after that, the train arrived in Zincton.

BELLY

He is cold and then he is hot and then he is cold. The water is cold and it feels fine. His cheek hurts and then he forgets it hurts so much and then his mom put some hotness on it and so it hurts more. His mom is warm below him and stays warm, though her bones are too pointy and hurt him where they press. And then she lifts him out of the tub. The air is cold and stays that way.

EDIE

Stretch marks like the lines the tide leaves when it retreats. On her breasts, her hips, her stomach. Hip bones bruised. The water sluices off her. She wraps Belly in all the towels Vivian has left. The candle has burned down to a stub, its scent smoking out the other odours of the room, but the hallway is lightening. It must be near morning.

Still naked, Edie carries her son down the hall through the calm blue light from the window at the front of the hall. Silence except for the murmurs of a few low, pillow-talk voices. By the staircase, a haze of cigarette smoke dissipates like mist. Has she ever been naked in front of an open door or an open window or a place where other people could see?

The door across from Edie's room opens and one of the whores slips out, her makeup smeared below her eyes, lipstick bleeding into the lines of her mouth so her expression is imprecise. She holds a broken hair comb in her hands, trying to fit the pieces together. Shrugging at Edie, she turns back to the hair comb as she heads down the hall.

Inside the room, Vivian lies with an arm loosely around her daughter. This woman she does not know has seen her naked, has held her hands as she plunged a needle into her son's face.

Edie sets Belly on the bed and he lets her, trusting that she will return. She is so glad that he cannot read her thoughts: to see the selfish life she is already imagining for herself. When she stands, the small, wing-shaped bones of her spine shift one by one. The blue light, blue mountains in the windows, blue snow, blue trees. The underwater dawn of winter.

Edie looks toward the walls. Her body is reflected in miniature over the disappointed expressions of all the long-dead women. From within his nest of blankets, Belly stares at himself in the mirror above the bed. They both watch themselves in faraway mirrors, their faces carved and sharp in the strange light.

THERE IS POWER IN A UNION

Slim searches himself for the places he has been wounded and finds none. His hands search and search and his split knuckles are minor but bleed more than they should. A gash, a laceration: there must be something larger he can staunch. They are warm and bloody, his hands, and they smear this warmth, this blood across his own chest and neck. Anointing himself. Outlining his own muscles so it must look to others as if he's been carved from soap like one of Matt Shaw's creatures. The lines Slim's fight-bloodied hands draw shine in the strobes of searchlights and project his inside hurts outwards. Outside wounds are so easy to mend. They can be fixed with a lady's sewing kit. Another Trekker wears the torn hem of a skirt across his eye and the fabric is crusted with blood. Some lovely girl has bared her legs to him behind a car, doused his wound with alcohol, said, "Shhh, this will hurt a bit," perhaps kissing the spot to make it better after she'd mended him like a housedress.

Slim has a mouth that is home to burning. His throat is wreckage and metal and gun and riot. It must bubble like the paint on the car he saw lit. He gags on his own scalded lungs as if he is gristle that cannot be swallowed down. Other Trekkers have bullet wounds, black eyes, legs swollen double from billy clubs. Slim can spot their injuries from a distance. But no one can name what has happened to him. No one is there to say, "Tear gas," since Matt Shaw's golden voice is thousands of miles away. There is no one to suck the poison from his black, black throat.

THE NATURAL LIFE THAT GOD INTENDED

Matt Shaw's eyelashes were too long for his face. They curled a little, like the lashes of dolls. Edie imagined that he carried a cloying scent, more sweet than musk. His blond hair brightened with streaks of silver, he dusted off a chair before sitting down and Slim snuck a glance at Edie, chiding her silently because the tent was never clean, but how could it be clean when the mine churned soot all day? In that town, the glasses were turned over so they wouldn't fill with ash. You could have a mansion with a thousand maids, blow your nose and it would still be black.

"Nice set-up," said Matt Shaw. He perched on the chair, completely at ease, a handsome scar above his eyebrow. Maybe Vancouver is a brighter city, Edie thought: one that allows his shirt such whiteness, like the inside of a loaf of store-bought bread. Some woman must have scalded her hands with lye to get his shirts to that shade.

It was a windy day and the tent's walls undulated: a whistling noise from where the canvas met the tent's metal frame. The sound made voices staticky, as if Matt Shaw's golden voice really was coming from a radio show.

"Thanks," said Slim. "Was meant to be a temporary measure, but with the war and the rations—. Roughing isn't so bad though, eh? Keeps your spine straight. And it's good for the boy to be out here in nature." He shifted from foot to foot like some ridiculous crane, stooped so he didn't hit his head on the ceiling. No wonder he hated to spend time at home. Only Edie and Belly fit there. Slim looked more natural in front of the Salmo Hotel's piano with his arms extended to their full wingspan over the keys. "But I've got everything here: warm bed, nice stove, all the little luxuries." He patted the canvas wall, which vibrated with his touch, then withdrew his hand as if surprised at its give. "Edie, get Matt Shaw a bar of soap, will you? Maybe he'll carve something nice for William."

Matt Shaw fished out his pocketknife. "Don't let me ruin your household goods, Edith. From my work organizing mines, I know that people here need all the soap they can get. In fact, many housewives such as yourself are worried about the increasing cost of lye, which is something I've personally lobbied against in my fight for price caps." Everything he said sounded like an advertisement.

Edie found a slab of soap. "We can spare some," she said. At that moment, she hated them both: Matt Shaw with his spotless shirt and practised voice and not a hint of manners, Slim aiming to please.

Matt Shaw rubbed his fingers in the faint dusting of ash on the table. Slim stood over him flushed with pleasure. "It's a nice place you've got here, Slim, my boy. Pretty wife, handsome son. And you still haven't gained an ounce." He leaned back in his chair and tapped Slim on the stomach. Slim looked down at his hand. "If I had a wife like this, I would be fat as a barrel. Edith, love, you've got to put some

meat on this man! He'll freeze down there in the mine!" He patted
Slim's stomach again and grinned at Edie, those long lashes working
away. He laughed. "I'm joking. I'm sure you pump him full of love
and the fat of this fair land. Why, back when we were fighting the
good fight, we never imagined any of us would have some nice lady
to cook us supper. It's the skinny ones, eh? All the fire of class struggle
just burns every last ounce off 'em, that's what I've always said."

Tipped back balancing on two chair legs, he stared up at Slim,
whittling a hunk of soap with little mincing gestures. "Well, I'm proud
of you, my boy! Of all of us, you're the only one who looked domesti-
city in the eye and said, 'Yes, this is the natural life that God intended.
This is a good and noble existence, perpetuating the bloodline, all
that.'" He chuckled to himself. "While the rest of us were getting our
asses shot full of holes by Fascists and trying not to get the clap from
the senoritas." He cast a glance at Edie. "My apologies, ma'am. I am
used to knowing Slim without the company of the fairer sex."

Such a small man and such a huge voice: a handkerchief folded
neatly in his pocket. She needed to get out.

"Looks like time for me to call on Norah and Red. I'll leave you
two to catch up," she said. "It was good to meet you, Mr. Shaw."

"Tell me about Spain," said Slim, his birdlike shadow cast on the
undulating walls. "I read everything I could in the papers. Was itch-
ing to get down there, but you can't exactly leave a wife, eh? Got some
letters from Red Walsh and he said it was a heck of a time."

Edie found her coat and Belly's coat and got ready to go. If she
tripped over Matt Shaw's chair leg, he would go flying. Land on his
milky face, stain that lovely white shirt. Matt Shaw's carving released
the scent of soap, so it seemed as if he'd cleaned up the tent by his very
presence. Belly was still sleeping, two years old, heavy in Edie's arms.

"Still a war, Slim. No picnic, that's for sure. But I've always maintained I would rather be a socialist with my feet than a socialist with

my mouth, you know. I can do radio shows until the cows come home, but it was there—" He flicked the penknife as the shape of an animal slowly emerged, a snowstorm of shavings collecting in his lap. "It was there—and you must remember that I saw Guernica first-hand, dead old grannies with their arms blown off— that I thought to myself, this is what the common man must do. Their fight is our fight. Paddy O'Neal, God rest his soul, gave his life to Spain and I can think of no greater honour."

He pointed his penknife toward Slim, who stared at him with a look that Edie could only see as longing. The white scar on his hand looked whiter as the knife cast light on to it. "You were there when Paddy died?" he asked.

Matt Shaw startled from his monologue. "I was farther up north, making contact with a native brigade. I learned the language. Spanish. I was needed in that capacity. A shame, anyways. Paddy O'Neal. A good comrade."

Slim nodded. He rubbed his own shoulder. "You could tell by the way he was on the Trek that he would be a good soldier."

Matt Shaw shrugged. The wind picked up, making the tent keen at a higher pitch. "Trek nothing. Only thing the Trek and the Spanish Civil War have in common is that they both failed." He set the knife down and stared at the canvas wall as if there was a window there. "People died in the war. Trek wasn't anything but a fancy parade."

Slim coughed into his handkerchief and Edie watched him hunch. He was maybe ashamed of the noise in his lungs and the blackness he coughed up. "A parade that cost me my breathing. Cost some men their walking right, cost two fellows their lives and who knows how many more? That Ralph fellow from Division Two never did turn up."

Matt Shaw shrugged again. He gave the soap creature eyes and sharp ears. "That was the cops and the government doing what the cops and the government always do. Wasn't a war because we couldn't win it. Wasn't a real war anyways. Besides—" He set the finished animal on the table. "You can't exactly blame tear gas for your lungs when you've been down in the mine for most of your life, eh?"

EDIE

Edie's mother will be the fixed point Belly needs. She will never leave. Every day, the crows know where to get their daily bread. Every day, the bread will be there at the same time, no matter where the crows are returning from. Edie's mother will be fixed as the sun. Children need something to orbit around.

Now, she lies with Belly in the same bed, side by side, fused by sweat as his body tries to purge the infection. The mirror reflects their unsleeping faces back at them. She is trying not to think of maps and train tickets, of young soldiers and small apartments. She is trying not to think of her son waking up in his grandmother's house without her, waking up the next night without her, and the next night after that. She is trying not to compose a letter to him in her mind that will explain her actions. *Stability*, she will write. *The most difficult decision of my life. A life I couldn't give you. Not because I didn't love you.*

All of it sounds melodramatic. There is no way to explain any of this to a four-year-old. *Dearest William*, she would write. *Dear Billy. To my darling Belly.* She crosses the phrases out in her head and starts over. None of it is any good. *To my son. Dear Belly.*

Belly rests and does not rest; he twitches against her, claims he is too hot then too cold, wants the blankets on then wants them off. His body swings from landscape to landscape. The stitches she neatly sewed have come loose and his wound remains open, like an eye.

TRINKET THE CAT

Arrested, Slim can hardly breathe. The jail's stink is acidic in his torn throat. Red Walsh sits hunched beside him, bleeding from minor cuts, dirt all over, a sleeve torn off.

"I hope she's okay. I'm sure she is. Smart little thing and used to fending for herself, eh? Cats will live through the bloody Armageddon and maybe it's good. Maybe it's the right thing. I mean, where am I going to go after this? Maybe when they let us out I can go to the square and call her, find some fish heads, she's probably starving, or maybe she's been adopted by some girl or boy. Cats are fine. Cats are always fine. The noise must have scared her. And thank God she wasn't on me during the fighting, poor thing, she must have been terrified with all that racket."

Red Walsh stares at Slim. His eye is pinked with blood from his split eyebrow and his eyelashes keep sticking together whenever he blinks.

VOCABULARY LESSONS

"Did you know that the word for a group of crows is a *murder?*" said her father. Often he would call her over to his easy chair and give her a single fact, as if it were a peppermint.

Edie nodded. "A murder," she said.

"A murder of crows," said her father.

Her father told her what to call the crows and her mother told her how we should feed them sweetened crusts so when we die they will not forget where our souls should go. The hearses slid up the path with their black, liquid finishes; the coffins went into the ground; Edie's mother made an altar on her carport roof for the creatures that flew above the line of men stooped under the weight of bones, singing dirges to carry them home.

BELLY

There are two Bellys: the one on the ceiling and the one on the bed. The boy on the ceiling is Belly's reflection, but he imagines him to be someone different. He tries to put his eyes into the other boy's eyes. When the other boy is in him, he's hot; his body is crowded. When the other boy is gone, he is cold because his skin is baggy and the air blows through.

Belly slides in and out this way. In the bed and then above it. It is both pretend and not pretend. In and out. Here and then not. He gets this gift from his dad, who people say is so skinny he can turn sideways and disappear. Cats can make their bones small. Snakes can get out of their skins. His dad lands his plane on the snow, turns sideways, disappears.

EDIE

In the morning, Edie and Vivian dress for the day with their backs to each other.

"Is Belly feeling better?" Vivian asks stiffly.

"I'm not sure," says Edie. "It's hard to tell." She looks to her son, who is sleeping fitfully, all of his features pursed together.

Sadie flops over in her sleep, a thicket of curls around her face, arms around the pillow made of her father's shirt. Her lips are pursed in concentration.

"What are you going to do with him?" she asks.

"I was thinking he should stay at his grandmother's house, you know. Because of school. He'll start school and there's no need for him to be carted around from bed-sit to bed-sit, to be stuck with a babysitter when there's kin around and my sister's old enough to mind him." Edie picks the bone up off the bedside table and feels the indent her thumb has worn. "Just until I get on my feet. It's not fair to lug him around until I get on my feet."

"I meant about the doctor," says Vivian.

Edie looks down: small burns on the carpet, places where water has stained and buckled the hardwood, splinters. "The railroad said they would see to it."

Vivian chuckles. "On your feet. Darling, if I ever get on my feet, I won't be able to help it. I'll just keep going. No one will ever be able to catch me if I get upright long enough to bloody stand. You get on your feet, hon, you'll never come back."

Edie places her folded clothes on one side of the valise, Belly's clothes on the other.

BRUISES

On the train home from Regina, Slim is unbruised but gagging. His throat is lined with hundreds of blisters tiny as pearls, and every breath has a burnt metallic taste. He is like the men who are smothered by fine sand pouring through the mine's timber walls, wrecked without a mark on them. He might as well have spent the riot out dancing.

Slim sits there shifting on the red velvet benches wondering if he's ever been in a place as nice as this, aware of the scent of his papery undershirt and his overalls stiff with sweat and weather. He leaves grimy fingerprints on the white tablecloths in the dining car and a dusty shadow on the seats in the shape of his body. Such a lovely train. So much for him to ruin.

Beside him, Matt Shaw is already telling the story of what happened to a pretty girl in the opposite aisle, even though he was not there. He'd been arrested in Toronto and brought to the jail by train, where he'd received a handsome black eye from an overzealous police officer. Edie thinks of Slim's unruined face pale in the train's weird light, his chest heaving as he struggles to breathe in the smoke-curdled air. She thinks of Matt Shaw and his tidy little wounds, the black eye turning abalone shades of blue and yellow and green, the woman giggling as she touches his face and says, "You poor thing. Did you get in a fight? Did you hit him first?"

"A fight of sorts," Matt Shaw says, readying himself to launch into the story of the march toward Ottawa, the thousands of men on boxcars, the rallies and parades, the riot, the arrest, the government's free ticket home. "Maybe," he says, "you've seen me in the papers."

Reporters came to see the train off and Slim suspects that he, too, will be in the paper: his startled face a foil to Matt Shaw's steady grin. And the headlines: FAILED TREKKERS HEAD HOME, VOW INQUEST WILL EXONERATE THEM. WILL THIS CONTROVERSY BRING DOWN THE GOVERNMENT? Slim wants an open window. Everyone can hear his breathing; it annoys them, he's sure. As Matt Shaw prattles on, Slim opens yesterday's paper and finds a list of names: those arrested, those charged, those released, those injured. A ledger of endings. He is pleased to find his own name. He tears the page out and underlines it once, then again. He folds the paper and tucks it in his wallet. He will carry the clipping in his wallet for years to come, pressed between sheets of waxed paper like a corsage.

Next to him, Matt Shaw lets the woman touch the outline of his black eye. Slim could drown in his own flayed breathing and would be left without a telltale mark. Matt Shaw, though, will tell the tale of his marks and his body will heal his wounds smooth and white-silver as coins and he will dine out on this story for years to come.

EDIE

When the repaired train stokes its engine, time starts again. "9:04 a.m.," says the porter when he comes to take their bags. The train brings 9:04 a.m. Their suitcases ballast him as he balances through the snow. Edie sits in the lobby on a balding couch waiting for the train to load with Belly in her arms as if he were a younger child. People stream past them, sheepish with hangovers. The hotelkeeper has brought them a glass of water and some sandwiches, neither of which Belly is interested in. She doesn't see any soldiers. Maybe they were needed to uncover the tracks. She imagines their shovels sparking as they strike metal.

Edie and Belly will board last. Rumours of his fever have spread throughout the hotel. Even the whores pat his head as they pass and Edie smiles to imagine her son as pillow-talk fodder. Do whores have pillow talk? Maybe some of these women know the story of the dandelions, the story of Trinket the cat.

Belly is bundled in his coat and several blankets. He keeps scrabbling his fingers around his coat's button to take them off. Edie folds his hands in his lap; he moves them to the buttons; she slaps his hand; he cries; she soothes him. It goes on like this. He is not well. The passengers stream whispering past them: "The boy who got hurt by glass," they say. "An infection," they say. "Fever." They tell their own stories of a neighbourhood boy who stepped on a rusty nail and died of infection, of a housewife who stepped on glass and passed away a few weeks later.

She raises the water glass to Belly's lips; he tilts his head to drink; he lays his head down; she slaps his hands away from the buttons; he cries; she soothes him. She holds him in her lap and sings there is "'power in the factory, power in the land, power in the hands of the worker.'" A simple song with its lullaby melody. Most of these union songs come from hymns anyhow. She has kept him alive through the night and soon there will be a doctor, maybe penicillin, a nurse who will hold Belly's split face in her hands and will be scornful at the shoddy job Edie has done.

She rocks him, staring out the large windows at the blue mountains, unable to see the sky from this view. The mountains seem to move toward her slow as glaciers. There is no demarcation between the bar, the restaurant and the lobby, and the detritus of last night is scattered throughout: plates scraped clean, empty glasses, teacups full of ash, ashtrays full. People still eat as if they're starving. They clean their plates, leaving only ash, as if the food had been burned away. Every glass is drained dry. Every plate is empty.

The porter arrives. Edie tips the glass of water to Belly's lips; he swallows; she tips it again, he swallows again, the rest pooling by his collar. He is just old enough that he will remember this. Years later, this is how he will remember her. His long-absent mother stitching sickness into his face. She can barely look at him.

"All set!" says the porter.

"Ready?" she asks Belly brightly, as if they were at the beginning of the journey instead of its strange middle.

A path to the station has been cleared by all the passengers before her. The snow is piled up a several feet high, the edge shining blue with ice, and Edie feels as if she's in a tunnel. A few buildings sit off in the distance, so obscured by snow they look like rabbit warrens. She carries Belly, whose feet skim the sides of the snowbanks. He is almost too tall to be carried.

BELLY

The door is open and there is only one path for his mom to go. He feels as if he's grown big just since they've been here. There is a long, dark road in the snow, so there is only one way his mom can walk. Soon, they will be on the train, where all the doors will be closed, and she will never leave him and she will always be there and then the train will stop and they will be in another place and something will happen and then something will happen after that.

EDIE

Belly's small fingers dig into her collarbone and the plans unspool in front of her: the remaining thirty-six dollars will buy how many nights at a bed-sit; perhaps she could find someone to bunk with; she could buy a loaf of bread and some cheese and that would last her for days and wouldn't cost much; she could get on as a waitress somewhere, everyone needs waitresses; how far could she go by train and still have enough money left over to make do until she found work; where is the farthest she could end up? Edie cannot help but imagine how, in perhaps just forty-eight hours, there will be no warmth from someone else's skin pressing against her.

But now, she carries Belly into the train, where all the passengers are already neatly tucked into their seats. It's impossible to tell that anything happened here. Thirty-six hours later and the window has been boarded up and sealed, the glass swept away. The train looks the same but brighter in the snow light. Not even a crumb of glass marks the place where Belly was injured.

As they enter, the passengers begin to clap for Belly, many of them still drunk. Some stand up, then some more, until everyone is on their feet as if cheering for an encore. All the passengers have wan, hopeful faces, tender for her little boy. They imagine that his injuries and his fever are heroic.

"Look, darling, they're cheering for you," she whispers, and he raises his head, waving gallantly even through his sickness, which makes them clap and laugh. Sometimes, he used to play "parade" with his father, so he has learned the right way to wave.

"'Hold the fort, for we are coming, union men be strong,'" sings

Belly, swinging his hands as if marching. The passengers love it. The train hoots long and low. It pulls away down the track. His gaze flicks from side to side, beaming at the crowd. Belly imagines he is marching.

EDIE IMAGINES WHAT HAS HAPPENED, WHAT MIGHT HAPPEN

At 3:00 a.m., as Slim was getting ready for work, Edie would be up to fix his coffee and eggs or pound dough for cinnamon buns so they could rise while she napped. In her nightgown, hunched over the stove's light, her shoulder blades were winglike as she pummelled and kneaded. Slim would creep up behind her in his longjohns and undershirt and slide his cold hands against her waist until she'd whirl around—"Hey now," she'd whisper, "you'll be late." "Slim," she'd say, "Love. It's nearly four"—and swat his arms or rest her fingertips on him. Her words overpowered by the processor's grinding.

Hours later, six hundred feet below dry ground, he would wipe sweat from his eyes with his forearm and smell cinnamon where her hand had been. Under the headlamp, he could make out her prints bright with lard, the scent of yeast and spice. Sometimes it was rosemary and chives for herb bread. Once it was the milk from her breasts that tightened shiny against his stomach where she had pressed against him and said, "Why won't it stop crying? Such a little thing and such a big noise. Do you think it's cold? Lord knows I'm cold. Even with the stove on." Naked with her breasts dripping as he held her, mad as a March hare.

No cinnamon when he wakes and there is nothing of her on him. No spice or polish or yeast, just the winter odour of snow and ash. When he flexes his elbow, his shirt creaks with cold. A down of ice shining along his body. Why not be bright everywhere when she has touched him everywhere?

"I have half a mind to stay the night," he said to Matt Shaw when the train stopped in New Westminster on the way home. This was how many years ago? Eight or nine at least.

"You have half a mind," said Matt Shaw, trying to smile, his yellowing shiner narrowing one eye. He passed Slim a cigarette.

There was no obvious destination: after years of boxcar riding, he could barely remember his hometown and he had no particular job lined up. Edie likes to think that he picked New Westminster because of her — the memory of a girl he danced with on a good day — but this is vain to think. It could have been any reason. Slim had no history to return to. He got off the train. He walked clean into a new life.

Waking again to music and the absence of music, the warped song of a record that has been set off-kilter by cold. The gramophone skims over bars of some blues, knitting its own melody, the music wavering too fast or too slow and maybe he, too, is off-balance because of this chill. The processor's own guttural rhythm plays backup to every song.

In his hand, a soggy photograph is wrapped around his finger like a poultice. He peels it off with his teeth and it's an eye, a hand, a dress. Her face looking up at him while his hand was around her waist and this was before they left the Lower Mainland when she was how old? When he was how old? Nearly a decade ago.

Matt Shaw waved goodbye at the station, his bruises darker from the train's weird interior light. Whatever he said was lost by the closed windows, but hadn't it been many years on top of the boxcar, words snatched up by wind?

═╎═╎═╎═╎═

Too long being still and if he doesn't move — he realizes this in a spark that's brighter than these memories — he will die. The Victrola rasps out random phrases of a woman's blues voice warped slow and husky. "'Oh baby,'" she sings. "'Oh pretty'" — and a pause — "'oh pretty — oh pretty'" — and the needle is stuck. And now he is cold to an extent he knows is dangerous. Since her hands have not been on him anywhere. "'Oh pretty baby.'"

He has been on a drunk again, the kind of knackered that lets you remember only a dress, a hand, some woman with her red fingernails curled around a brass headboard in the Salmo Hotel. That shreds your memory until all you have left to take home are scraps of images.

Saw a man with a face so scarred it looked like it was made out of birchbark.

Saw a woman's yellowed and broken teeth.

Saw the trail of saliva my mouth had left on a woman's thigh.

Maybe the Victrola is not really playing but is a memory of last night when the woman stood naked and swayed to the blues thrumming from the bar below and said, "Oh baby" in her low and slurring voice. "Oh baby." This was when and where and how long ago?

Edie's hands have been everywhere on him, but now she is nowhere and Belly, too, is gone. Slim is not fuzzy from drink but edged in frost and when he touches his face crystals flake off like skin, like salt. "'Oh pretty baby,'" someone sings.

Down the stairs and outside tripping. Outside, it's the kind of cold that starves you from the limbs inwards. Men lose toes in the mine all the time for no special reason. If you heat up too quickly the blood comes back wrong and your limbs turn black. The warmth must seep in, must trickle by degrees, and even that hurts worse than having your toe lopped off by a cutter.

He is lucky, though, to have been woken by the Victrola and the memory of the girl whose lipstick was left on his groin like a bruise. The scent of her talc in his pubic hair.

The street is empty but not quiet: the mine's grinding, the mine's perpetual grinding. It's hard to tell where the sidewalk is and the road is and his feet are because they have smeared white into one another. The time might be 3:00 a.m. because lights are coming on as he walks. The windows are blackened with road salt and soot as if the glass had been burned and the crust glows with light, the shadows of men sliding across them. They cannot see him staggering across the snow. Though the war finished without him, the mine hangs blackout curtains on every window.

There are millions of Slims in a million small towns, he thinks. I am named by what I do not have. William Fucking Slim MacDonald. Participant on the On to Ottawa Trek. Chair of the goddamned refreshments committee. The fucking head counter at rallies. Must be I need this coat of ice to wrap myself in, since my flesh can't do the job.

He should be trudging to work right now in all the padding Edie laid out for him on the radiator—if your clothes fall you are bound to fall as well—so he would wake up to the house smelling of lanolin and sweat and later of coffee, eggs, cinnamon. Instead, he staggers past the crusted windows, the lights flickering off. Any minute, they should leave their houses, bracing themselves against the cold, he thinks. Any minute now, they will they take silently to the street and find me dressed in ice, shining along all the places my wife has touched me. But Edie suspects she is wrong to imagine this. Who is to say he didn't wake, close the window, light the stove and stumble back to sleep? Who is she to say whether he lived or died or left or stayed or what he did after?

═╪═╪═╪═╪═

Another version, then. Slim will do what he will do. Edie will do what she will do. Edie's mother will open the door she has always opened. Her mother will say — what? She will look at them and sigh. She will say, "This must be sweet William," her eyes narrow but her voice as if she'd been expecting them, which she had, which she will.

Her mother will let them in. Edie will say that Slim died in the war; her mother will express surprise they accepted a Communist with ruined lungs; she will say he signed up under an assumed name. So you're in a bad way then? her mother will say. They will sit at the same old table and eat icebox cookies. Belly will have clean gauze around his face, his blood fresh from the wonder drug. He will not be able to stop telling everyone how the doctor had a needle and it was this big and he put it in my bum — say buttocks, William — and he put it in my *buttocks* and I was sick but then I was better and the nurse had a little hat that was too small for her head. Anne will be teenaged but will move like a forty-year-old waitress in her boredom and efficiency, topping up coffee cups, bringing cookies, saying, "Uh huh, uh huh, really," at Belly's prattling.

"Just for the night," Edie will say, and she and Belly will sleep together in her childhood bed, and he will hug her around the waist and snore against her stomach. When he is asleep, she will untangle herself from him. His fingers will reach for nothing and he will clench his fists. Her body will be cold in the imprint his sweat has left on her. She will not touch his brow for fear of waking him up. She has not yet decided about whether to leave a note.

She will step only on the floorboards she has learned will be silent. She will unlock the door and open it and walk through it and keep walking. She will press herself into the city's smallest spaces to see how tightly she can fit.

ACKNOWLEDGEMENTS

Thank you to the numerous students and faculty members at the University of Illinois who gave early feedback on this manuscript, especially my thesis advisers, David Wright and Brigit Pegeen Kelly. Thank you to Lorna Jackson for setting this novel back on track. Thank you to Kris Rothstein and everyone at the Carolyn Swayze Agency, to Bethany Gibson for her acuity and patience during this process and to Heather Sangster for her keen eye. Thank you to everyone at Goose Lane Editions and to the Canada Council for the Arts for the generous financial support.

As always, I remain grateful for the support of my family and friends, no matter where in the world they may be.

Though the On to Ottawa Trek storyline is populated by real-life people and events, I have also taken numerous liberties for the sake of fiction. I have, however, tried for historical accuracy wherever possible, and I hope that my version remains true to the spirit of the Trek. Though the On to Ottawa Trek remains an understudied area of Canadian history, the following autobiographies and scholarly works were valuable to my research:

We Were the Salt of the Earth!: The On-To-Ottawa Trek and Regina Riot by Victor Howard

Recollections of the On to Ottawa Trek by Ronald Liversedge

Work and Wages! by Ben Swankey and Jean Evans Sheils

All Hell Can't Stop Us Now: The On to Ottawa Trek and Regina Riot by Bill Waiser

Pubs, Pulpits, & Prairie Fires by Elroy Deimert

And, finally, this book would not exist if it had not been for the raunchy memoir written by my grandmother Elsie McNeney, which chronicled her time in mining camps in the 1930s and 1940s. Though *The Time We All Went Marching* is not based on her life — she has already told her own story better than I could — her energy and her refusal to pretty up the truth were major inspirations in this work.

Kelsey Bowman

Arley McNeney's first novel, *Post*, was shortlisted for the Commonwealth Writer's Prize, Best First Novel, Canada and the Caribbean, and was named one of the Top 10 Sports-in-Canadian-Literature Moments by the journal *Canadian Literature*.

McNeney is a graduate of the University of Victoria and holds an MFA from the University of Illinois at Urbana-Champaign. As a member of the Canadian women's wheelchair basketball team, she received a bronze medal at the 2004 Paralympics and gold at the 2002 and 2006 World Championships. An active blogger (Young and Hip), she now lives in Vancouver where she also works as a communications consultant.